One Night in Paris

Nina George is a multi-award-winning and internationally bestselling author who has been writing novels, non-fiction books, essays, reports, short stories, blogs and columns since 1992. Her novel *The Little Paris Bookshop* was translated into thirty-six languages and topped the bestseller lists, including the *New York Times* chart. With her husband, the writer Jens J. Kramer, Nina also writes children's books and thrillers. Nina George is President of the European Writers' Council, the federation of fifty European writers' associations. She lives in Berlin and Brittany.

One Night in Paris

NINA GEORGE

Translated by Sharon Howe

MICHAEL  JOSEPH

PENGUIN MICHAEL JOSEPH

UK | USA | Canada | Ireland | Australia
India | New Zealand | South Africa

Penguin Michael Joseph is part of the Penguin Random House group of companies
whose addresses can be found at global.penguinrandomhouse.com

Penguin Random House UK,
One Embassy Gardens, 8 Viaduct Gardens, London SW11 7BW

penguin.co.uk

First published 2025
001

Copyright © Nina George, 2025
Translation copyright © Sharon Howe, 2025

The moral right of the author has been asserted

'Ne me quitte pas' Jacques Brel (lyrics) and Gérard Jouannest (composition), 1959
'A l'attaque!' Miossec, 2014
'Feeling Good', lyrics and composition by Anthony Newley and Leslie Bricusse for the musical
The Roar of the Greasepaint – The Smell of the Crowd, 1964
'Our Love is Easy', Melody Gardot and Jesse Harris, 2009
'Feelings', Louis Gaste and Morris Albert, 1974
'Des Touristes', Moissec, 2014
'Je m'en vais', Moissec, 1964
'I Wish I Knew How It Would Feel to be Free', Dick Dallas, 1966

Penguin Random House values and supports copyright.
Copyright fuels creativity, encourages diverse voices, promotes freedom
of expression and supports a vibrant culture. Thank you for purchasing
an authorized edition of this book and for respecting intellectual property
laws by not reproducing, scanning or distributing any part of it by any
means without permission. You are supporting authors and enabling
Penguin Random House to continue to publish books for everyone.
No part of this book may be used or reproduced in any manner for the
purpose of training artificial intelligence technologies or systems. In accordance
with Article 4(3) of the DSM Directive 2019/790, Penguin Random House
expressly reserves this work from the text and data mining exception.

Set in 13.5/16pt Garamond MT Std
Typeset by Jouve (UK), Milton Keynes
Printed and bound in Great Britain by Clays Ltd, Elcograf S.p.A.

The authorized representative in the EEA is Penguin Random House Ireland,
Morrison Chambers, 32 Nassau Street, Dublin D02 YH68

A CIP catalogue record for this book is available from the British Library

HARDBACK ISBN: 978–0–241–43660–8
TRADE PAPERBACK ISBN: 978–0–241–43659–2

Penguin Random House is committed to a sustainable future
for our business, our readers and our planet. This book is made from
Forest Stewardship Council® certified paper.

Tell me: what do you really want out of life?

For women's freedom

I

It happened to people, this longing, emerging from an unknown void, grabbing the soul with a firm hand, the urge to simply let go and sink to the depths of the ocean. Deeper and deeper, without resistance, throwing away yourself and your life, as if you had come from the gorges of the sea and were destined to return there one day.

Vertigo marée, the old Breton fishermen called it, that desire that came from nowhere – to erase the self, to be free, free from everything. It usually came on the most beautiful of nights, that was why fishermen avoided looking into the deep, and hung thick curtains at their sea-facing windows when on dry land.

The thought of this occupied Claire as she dressed, and the stranger asked: 'Will I see you again?' He lay naked on the bed; the brass ceiling fan turned sluggishly, tracing a revolving star of shadowy stripes on his bare skin. The man stretched out an arm as Claire zipped up her pencil skirt at the back. He reached for her hand.

She knew he was asking whether they would do it again. Share a secret hour behind closed doors. Whether this would start to mean something, or end here and now, in Room 32 of the Hotel Langlois, Paris.

Claire looked into his eyes. Dark-blue eyes. It would have been easy to sink into their depths.

In every gaze, we seek the ocean. And in every ocean, that one gaze.

His eyes were the ocean at Sanary-sur-Mer on a hot summer's day, when the Mistral shakes the overripe figs from the trees and the dazzling white pavements are speckled with their purple juice and windswept blossoms. Eyes he had kept open the whole time, looking at Claire, holding her gaze as he moved inside her. The unfamiliar ocean of his eyes was one reason she had sought him out on the terrace of Galeries Lafayette. That, and the fact that he wore a wedding ring on his finger.

Just like her.

'No,' Claire said.

She had known that it would only happen once. No surnames. No exchange of telephone numbers. None of the intimacies of an all too banal conversation about their children, or shopping at the Marché d'Aligre, steak frites at Poulette, movies, travel plans and why they were doing this to each other. Why they had left their lives for an hour to press themselves against a stranger's skin, trace unfamiliar body contours, enclose unfamiliar lips, before slipping back into the regular outline of their lives.

Claire knew her own reasons.

His were none of her business.

Their hands separated simultaneously. Slipped apart. The last touch and perhaps the tenderest. He didn't ask why, he expressed no regret. He let Claire go just as she did him, a piece of flotsam on the tide of the day.

Claire picked up her open handbag, which had fallen from the cherrywood coffee table by the garret window earlier, when the man had pressed her gently against one of the pillars and lifted the hem of her dress, feeling the silk edge of her hold-ups and smiling as he kissed her.

Claire had planned to seek out someone like him among the thousands of faces in Paris. The sudden vision of one's own body pressing against the other. The same vision, mirrored in the other's gaze.

After her last lecture before the two-month summer break, she had put the stockings on in her office at the university for that sole reason. And quietly slipped away from the obligatory end-of-term staff party after half a glass of ice-cold champagne. The other professors were used to Claire withdrawing discreetly from festivities. 'Madame le Professeur always leaves before the moment normal people switch to first names,' Claire had once heard a lecturer say to a new research assistant in the ladies' room. Neither of them knew that Claire was in one of the cubicles. She had waited until the women were gone. Up till then, she hadn't noticed that she wasn't on first-name terms with any of her colleagues.

Some were afraid of her knowledge: as a behavioural biologist, she knew the anatomy of human emotions and actions. They feared her insights into volition and choice in the same way that many people fear psychologists, hoping the experts will see right through them to the very backbone of their being and understand what has made them what they are, with all their transgressions, compulsions and guiltless wounds, yet dreading what such a tomograph of the soul might uncover beneath the layers of good manners and secrets.

She wouldn't put the stockings on again, but dump them straight in the black and gold waste bin in the small ensuite with its art deco tiles on her way out.

Claire gathered together her keys, mobile, leather notebook and university ID card, without which no one could get past the armed guards outside the Sorbonne and its associated institutes, and put them all back into the silk interior of her bag. She fastened it and twisted her darkblonde hair into a neat chignon at the nape of her neck.

'You're beautiful in the light from the window,' the man said. 'Stay like that for a minute. That's how I'll carry you around with me. Until we forget about each other.'

She obliged. He wanted to make it easy for them. He had tasted of milk and sugar, of coffee and desire.

The attic room, with the dark wood Provence dresser, the round white table, the dove-grey Versailles chairs, the bed with the summer linen, was now quite still, and the melody of Paris city life was stirring outside. The hum of air conditioners, fans, engines. As if she was emerging from a faraway sea after floating in a liquefied existence broken only by her own breath, and materialising into the old Claire, in the overheated intensity of a Parisian day.

She looked out over the roofs of Montmartre. At the rows of clay chimneys along their narrow ridges. It was after five in the afternoon, the June sun burning a cavity in time, making the roofs shimmer in the silvery grey that resembled the moment of awakening. When the dream ends and reality fades in, still blurred. The moment Spinoza once described as the 'place of the one true freedom'.

Roofs like one of Erik Satie's Gymnopédies.

That's what Gilles would say. His observations on the world were always musical. He preferred hearing to seeing.

Opposite the hotel was a balcony terrace. A man was

laying the table with blue plates; a small boy clung to one of his legs, chuckling with delight as he rode on his papa's foot.

Like Nicolas, Claire thought.

Her son, her child, back in the days when he was so small that her arms reached all the way round him, that little parcel of trust and curiosity, smelling of pancakes and untapped hope. Nowadays her arms barely reached to Nico's broad shoulders.

What was she doing here?

Standing by the window of a run-down, mid-range hotel, her back to a strange man who still had her taste on his lips, thinking about her son, full of helpless, tender love, thinking of her husband, who used to sing when she entered the room until one day he stopped, thinking of his familiar face that she knew so well, in every variant. The lover's face, the liar's face.

Opposite, a woman in cut-off jeans and a strappy vest came out of the kitchen onto the terrace. She wrapped her arms around the child's father from behind. He smiled and bent to kiss her hand.

Claire turned away from the window, stepped into her open-toe leather pumps, hung her bag over her shoulder, inhaled and straightened up, looking the man on the bed in the eye.

'It's a privilege,' he said slowly, 'to know you're losing someone. That way you can remember the moment. Often, we lose someone without warning.'

A wordless minute passed, then she left Room 32.

She pressed the button for the old lift and deep below her it shuddered into life in its wrought-iron shaft. Too slowly. She didn't want to wait, just a few metres from the bed, from the man, from that moment of freedom.

Vertigo marée: it existed on land too; if she had looked into the depths of his eyes for too long, she would have let herself fall. First, they would have talked about their favourite markets and travel plans, and soon they would have begun to ask each other the dangerous questions: what do you dream about, what are you afraid of, haven't you always wanted to . . .? They would have got to know each other. And they would have begun to hide from each other.

Claire walked briskly down the narrowly winding staircase of the Langlois with its worn red carpet, distancing herself from the room.

On the second floor, she heard the voice.

'*Ne me quitte pas,*' it whispered.

It was coming from Number 22.

Ne me quitte pas. Don't leave me.

2

'*Ne me quitte pas*,' the voice sang pleadingly, carried away with the emotion of an inaudible soundtrack. It sang in a whisper, stopping Claire in her tracks; she had to lean against the wall.

Words could lie.

But the voice, the body, never did, and the sound raining down on Claire from behind the closed door was the baring of a soul. Veiled in a breath that was like the moment before falling silent. Fear, and underneath: no fear at all.

She listened to this singing, *Ne me quitte pas*: the voice was raw, with a dark, warm clarity, and it was . . .

Like a woman dancing in the dark as if no one were watching. So much trapped within the voice. So much turmoil under the breath. And yet beneath the fear, that fearlessness.

How strange. How beautiful.

When the door of Room 22 opened and the singing stopped, it struck Claire that the voice is merely an acoustic outline of a person's inner state: their outward appearance can be surprisingly different.

Emerging from the room was a young woman in her early twenties. She was carrying a caddy with cleaning utensils in one hand, while the thumb of her other hand turned the dial on an MP3 player she was listening to through earphones. She had obviously been singing along to the music.

The singer wore black jeans and a ribbed black vest; her hair was pinned up sloppily and she had a pierced eyebrow. One of her shoulders and part of her left arm were tattooed with tribal motifs.

Her features reminded Claire of the fine lines of a vixen and the bold pen-and-ink drawings of Japanese artists. A delicate nose, strong eyebrows, a full, defiant mouth in a fair face, a resolute chin, and the faint suggestion of dimples at the corners of her mouth. Everything she would one day become was merely sketched out, yet at the same time already there.

But what took Claire by surprise was her gaze.

An old, dark gaze, out of young eyes.

It fell on Claire's left hand, holding the strap of her classic red handbag. Alighted on her wedding ring. Flitted upwards, subconsciously yet unerringly, to Room 32, directly above 22. Then returned to her face.

'*Bonjour*, Madame,' the singer said. Her voice was different now, *disguised*, Claire thought: it was higher, softer, a cloak of modesty. The muted tone said: I am unimportant, ignore me.

But there was defiance in it, too.

'*Bonjour*,' Claire replied. 'You have a lovely singing voice.'

'I wasn't singing—' She paused '—Madame.'

The Madame an afterthought, presumably as she remembered her manners.

'*Pardon*, Mademoiselle,' Claire said pointedly. 'I just assumed. My mistake.'

Two women's secrets exposed, thought Claire, as they stood face to face, each suppressing their mutual discomfort.

There are lies that only betray the liar, Mademoiselle.

She suddenly felt like saying this aloud, but what was the point?

They looked at each other, from two opposite edges of a droplet of time, in a hotel corridor, in the midst of the world, two out of 7 billion people, two out of 3.69 billion women.

'Is there anything I can do for you?' asked the young woman. 'Would you like anything brought to your room?'

Again, that impatience behind the voice, like a penknife wrapped in a silk handkerchief.

'No,' said Claire. 'Nothing else needed.'

The woman stood motionless, looking steadfastly at Claire. 'Because?' her look demanded.

This strange impulse to answer the question. To blurt out all that was left unspoken, directly into this intriguing, unfinished face.

This urge to explain why, in her own case, things weren't what they seemed. It wasn't about sex. Not primarily, at least. It was about the exquisitely painful surrender to a union in which everything is dissolved: all that you represent to others who know you well (or think they do); who define you and cast your personality in stone, as a mother, as the dependable hub of a family and all its organisational needs, as a career woman known for her intelligence, knowledge, prudence and restraint, a rational woman conveniently immune from emotional outbursts, a woman of good reputation.

Reputation! What good was such a reputation, for God's sake? Did it console her, make her breathe easier, protect her from the dreams she awoke from in tears or with a nagging, pale-blue melancholy? Did it mean anything, did it have anything to do with the person she really was?

When a stranger embraced her and knew nothing, expected nothing, and the absence of the Claire that others saw in her didn't even bother him, then everything dissolved. Then she was just a body, an ego without a past in a body that yearned. Until the lips burned, until the muscles ached from the offering, the opening, until the tears flowed as all the shackles broke, once and for all.

Freedom.

Finding herself again, underneath it all, underneath everything.

And because he looked at me: do you understand? Because he looked at me the whole time and didn't close his eyes. Not when I undressed, not when I came to him, not when I left. He never left me alone as we lay naked.

He wanted to see the real me.

The real me, do you hear, you strange Mademoiselle? Because if you hide it, how will anyone ever find it? If you always keep your feet on the ground, your head down, your eyes down, how can you truly live?

They continued to study each other, far too long and far too silently for a chance encounter.

Claire felt a pricking in her eyes.

It couldn't be tears. She never cried.

Or hadn't in a very long time.

The young woman was first to look away.

'*Bonne soirée*,' she said.

'The same to you.'

Their curious moment of intimacy, in the half-light

between the stairhead and the windowless corridor, was over.

Claire carried on down the stairs, crossed the foyer and pushed open the heavy wrought-iron door.

Out in the sun, she wiped the bead of moisture from the edge of her eyelid, tasting the salt.

Claire decided against taking a taxi. She needed to walk, to move, to erase his movements inside her. She walked in the direction of the Marais, the district where she had lived over twenty years ago. Small, precise steps, green knee-length viscose skirt, white silk blouse, red belt, red handbag, the tarmac under her heels, her shadow shrinking and shortening, lengthening and stretching beneath her. She concentrated on maintaining her pace.

Heat lurked in the narrow streets. People stumbled out of the bright light into the shade of the building façades. Walls, everywhere, harshness – this was real life, and here she was in the midst of it, alive and free. In control. She kept walking.

It took her half an hour to reach the Rue de Beauce, where evening was inching its way into Paris, turning the Satie grey to blue-grey.

She still had time, at least another hour, to reset, before carefully rolling up the memory and locking it away so that it was no longer stored in her face, her gestures, or her voice.

It wasn't until she was sitting under a blast of cool air in Le Sancerre, searching in her bag for her purse to pay for her glass of pepper-scented white wine, realising she'd forgotten to throw away the stockings and wondering why she was still thinking about the singer's voice and face, that she noticed.

Something was missing.

She felt for the hard lump in the inside pocket of the lining. Felt again. Nothing.

She picked up the bag, rummaged in it, emptied the contents onto the table in front of her.

When did she last have it? This morning, definitely. Did she leave it behind when she left the Institute? No . . . it must have fallen out, on the bus, or . . .

The open handbag falling off the table. In Room 32. No. Please. Not there. Anywhere but there.

Claire took a few deep breaths, stood up, pulled back her shoulder blades, lifted her chin and made for the bistro toilets. She bathed her wrists under the tap in the tiny washroom; the water wasn't cold enough.

She looked at her face in the mirror: she found it impossible to read herself the way she always read others. The face she had grown into betrayed nothing. A fateful quirk of nature, or did it just become like that one day, petrified into unreadability?

'*Merde*,' she murmured.

The fact is: it's just a pebble, a random whitish-grey fossil with a rust-red pattern, the remains of a five-legged, star-shaped scutella, a sea urchin, of the kind that's washed up by the million onto beaches the world over, stirred up from unknown depths. Thirteen million years old. From a time when the European mainland was still in its infancy. Of no practical or monetary value whatsoever.

Just a stone with traces of a star-shaped fossil. That she had collected as an eleven-year-old, in her very first summer by the sea, on a beach at the beginning of the world. That was what the Bretons called their proud, rugged coasts that once rose up out of the deep and turned into land. For thirty-three years, Claire had carried the bi-coloured fossil that felt like a smooth, heart-shaped stone from trouser pocket to handbag to briefcase to desk, as if by doing so she could carry the beginning of time around with her for ever. As a child, she had wished on this stone heart that she would never have to go back to the tiny flat in Paris-Belleville; as a teenager, she had pressed all her pain and hunger for life into its surface; as a student, she had clasped it in her left hand while her right scribbled away for all she was worth on her dissertations and doctoral thesis; and as a professor, she placed it in the middle of her desk at the university every morning, next to the business card holder. Right in front of the few words that summed up everything she had strived for and continued to work for: *Dr Claire Stéphenie Cousteau, Professeure de biologie et anthropologie, Institut d'études politiques de Saint-Germain-en-Layes.*

And now it was gone.

So how could she be sure that she herself was still here?

Had she left herself behind, too, in that room?

You're not thinking logically, Claire. You're just feeling. Letting yourself be driven by fear and adrenalin. Think. Hypotheses and emotions are not a good basis for decision-making.

'Of course I'm still here,' she whispered.

She thought back to what she had said this morning, in her last lecture before the summer holidays. *Stored at the edge of every human consciousness are emotions which are generally regarded as illogical: aggression, obsession, desire, fear. Hate.*

Usually, these emotions don't affect you adversely. Unless something happens. A rupture in the familiar fabric of your everyday life and habits. A tiny crack, an element of uncertainty, of instability, a change in the normal routine — that's all it takes to shake a person to their roots and drive them to actions that can affect them in ways they are powerless not only to explain, but also to control.

That was it. Just a rupture.

She stuffed the stockings deep into the waste bin.

A rationally meaningless rupture at the end of a salty, scorching afternoon in which she had been just – just? – a woman and no one else, desired, caressed, devoured, vibrant, alive; pure woman, and therefore whole and complete.

She would carefully heal the crack.

She dried her hands and left the washroom.

She finished her Sancerre, thinking with every sip about all the jobs still to be done and people to be called before she and her family left for their annual summer trip to Brittany. The piano tuner. The gardener. Remember to top up the oil in the Chubster, as they affectionately called their old Mercedes estate. Organising, putting things in order, smoothing over the wrinkles of everyday life like a bed – a marital one, not an illicit one.

Claire was aware that some of her male colleagues called her *le glaçon*. The ice cube. It summed up her ability to pay no attention to emotions, except in her scientific analyses. And it was also an allusion to the advances she had rejected, and the chill that men – and some women – felt in her presence.

How strange that I allowed myself so readily to turn to ice in order to be someone, in a man's world.

She swallowed the thought down resolutely with the last drop of Sancerre and gestured to the red-whiskered barman, who placed the bill in front of her with a nod.

The taxi arrived within three minutes and ferried her through a Paris from which the tourists had been lured away to overpriced restaurants, dull erotic shows and over-crowded sightseeing boats.

Claire asked the driver to stop just once more before taking her home.

3

Four kinds of salt. The salt of the ocean. The salt of tears. The salt of sweat. The salt of the 'origin of the world', as Gustave Courbet called a woman's dark blossom.

Claire reflected on this as the taxi battled its way through the evening rush hour.

This summer was different from the previous years. It was more oppressive, with only the occasional light wind blowing on faces, through hair, clothes and scarves, through three of the four kinds of salt.

Through the taxi window, Claire observed the women in the streets, in cafés and outside boutiques, at bus stops and fountains, and it was as if she were seeing them through two different pairs of eyes. Those of the behavioural biologist who read people's gaits and postures, faces and gestures, noting tension, fear, distraction, and silent longing to be seen or overlooked. And another, new and unfamiliar pair that peered through the crack, the rupture in the fabric of Claire's routine. How many secrets were each of these women harbouring? That one there, with the shopping bags? The sales assistant over there, having a cigarette break outside the shop, checking her silhouette in the window and pulling in her tummy? How many secrets, how many lovers, would-be or actual, how many unshed tears? How many unspoken, unrealised dreams? How many people filled that empty space, people to be cared for: children, mothers, husbands, siblings? What space was left at the end of the day for their own thoughts: for the cyclist hiding her gaze behind sunglasses, the bus driver with her eye on the red light; what ambitions had the elderly lady in yellow fulfilled and what had she sacrificed for someone else, whether they were worth it or not? What kind of rupture would it take to turn these women's lives, or any woman's life for that matter, upside down? A man?

A song from behind a locked door?

A lost stone?

Claire felt close to these strange women, so close: here they were, in the world simultaneously, with all their hidden thoughts and unfulfilled desires behind their well-ordered lives, while the taxi sliced through time.

The thought of the summer ahead, eight weeks in Brittany, weighed on Claire. She would have preferred to stay in Paris – getting up each day, as always well before Gilles and Nicolas, going to the Sciences Po, working, lecturing, teaching, analysing, giving tutorials, then fitting in her thousand metres at the swimming pool. She already regretted throwing things out of kilter in Langlois, but it had been so necessary in order to breathe again.

When the taxi turned into her road, Rue Pierre Nicole, a few streets away from the banks of the Seine and Notre-Dame, and lined with typical five-storey Haussmann buildings, Claire collected herself. The way one collects oneself after a movie, before leaving the cocooning darkness and stepping out into the dazzling light of reality.

As she opened the door to their fifth-floor flat, her senses were enveloped by the strains of 'Mr Bojangles', an aroma of rosemary, freshly sliced honeydew melon and lightly fried aubergines, and an indefinable undertone of simmering deliciousness. She laid her red bag on the console table and glanced in the oval mirror. She looked the same as when she'd set off at half six that morning, while Nico and Gilles were still asleep. Claire had left them coffee in a silver pot, as always.

'Sammy Davis Junior, 1985, Berlin,' Gilles said in lieu of a greeting, filling a wine glass with honey-white Savoie Apremont and handing it to Claire across the gas hob in the middle of the kitchen. On the laptop, positioned on the wide windowsill directly in front of the open casements, Sammy Davis was dancing in white shirt, black trousers and hat across a Berlin stage. Gilles loved this version, Claire knew that. And seeing her husband standing there looking at her like that, relaxed, enthusiastic, in his blue, slightly crumpled linen shirt over faded jeans, she felt a warm pang of emotion.

She took the glass, took a quick sniff of the wine and put it down.

'I thought, as it's a special occasion . . .' She lifted the paper bag with the two bottles of chilled Ruinart champagne onto the big natural wood table; she had bought them from the wine and whisky shop next to the Marché des Enfants Rouges while the taxi waited. She placed the bunch of white roses beside them.

'Champagne and fresh flowers? She'll get a totally wrong impression of us,' said Gilles.

Whistling along with Sammy to the finale of the live recording, he turned to the fridge, took four dark-red pieces of meat out of a yellow porcelain dish and placed them reverently on the chopping board in front of him.

He had bought the board in the Dordogne from a carpenter with only seven fingers left.

Claire sat down at the long table they had had for ever. Gilles had always wanted a big table. Big enough to eat around, with friends or children (he wanted three, Claire none, but . . . well, who was most to blame for the other's sacrifice?), to work at and sit around, arguing, playing games, talking. 'A table for life, that's what I want, Claire, a heart: we need a big, strong heart of living wood.'

When they bought the flat in the Rue Pierre Nicole twenty years ago, shortly after Nicolas was born (they were actually still paying for it out of Claire's regular professor's salary, freelance composers like Gilles being viewed then as now as a credit risk), Gilles had had the wall between the lounge and kitchen knocked down. He had built the kitchen around the table, which he'd found in a former girls' convent school in Picardy, and made it the centre of their home. And he'd insisted on doing it up the way he wanted: it was his territory – that and his soundproof, air-conditioned music studio.

Unframed paintings. Driftwood shelves from Brittany filled with spices, a bunch of dried shallots, cinnamon sticks and nutmegs in chipped crystal glasses. Louis XV chairs decorated with bright linen cushions from the Luberon. The worn, brandy-coloured armchair by the window, salvaged from a British tearoom. Old black-and-white photographs of Parisian markets. A huge sideboard from Normandy, sporting earthenware plates, Moroccan tea glasses, dim-sum baskets Gilles had charmed out of the Vietnamese chef at Galeries Lafayette, half a dozen teapots, hundred-year-old ladles, copper pans, mussel sieves, an A–Z of French cheeses, a Laguiole wine opener from Domme, a basket of salted almonds, a faded portrait of Anaïs Nin in a gold frame, a battery of Ricard, Gitanes and *Le Monde* branded ashtrays (from the days when Gilles and Claire still smoked), a harmonica (F major), another harmonica (A major), and an open copy of *Paris Match* featuring Macron and his wife Brigitte on the cover. The French media were highly exercised by the twenty-four-year age gap between the couple and, as the most famous behavioural biologist in Paris, Claire had been approached by a TV channel for an interview, in the hope that she would come out with some juicy Oedipal story. She had politely declined despite the generous fee: *mon Dieu*, how absurd that an older woman should be reproached for still having a love life!

'Faux filet?' asked Claire.

She sat in her time-honoured place at the head of the table, from where she could watch Gilles cooking, singing or humming melodies which only existed because he gave birth to them. And which would sometimes be broadcast a few years later through the powerful loudspeakers of major cinemas. Though alas, not often enough. There was no existential security in his life: Claire was the financial mainstay of the family.

She tasted the wine.

'*Oui*, Madame. And my original ratatouille, based on a closely guarded recipe from my Provençal grandmother.'

'Oh? She's a new one on me.'

'She was my grandfather's secret lover. They had a kind of ratatouille relationship.'

'That would make a good topic of conversation for this evening. Secret lovers and their favourite recipes.'

Gilles cast a quick glance at Claire. His cheek muscles twitched imperceptibly. 'Indeed,' he replied airily. 'And guaranteed to make Nico disown his parents.'

No, Claire wanted to correct herself, no, I didn't mean it like that!

And it was true. She had never reproached Gilles for any of his affairs. Not even so much as hinted that she knew of at least four, despite the fact that he had never talked about them and had never been indiscreet.

Claire talked over the silence, pretending not to notice he had taken it the wrong way. 'And the meat? From Desnoyer?'

'You must be joking, at those eye-watering prices. Until the contract with Gaumont for the mini-series with Omar Sy is signed and sealed, it's plain home cooking all the way. I've discovered an excellent butcher in the Marais. A tiny shop near Galeries Lafayette.' Her husband concentrated on massaging the meat.

This time she took a large gulp of wine.

Galeries Lafayette was near the Langlois.

Then again, Galeries Lafayette was also near the Gaumont TV studios.

Come to think of it, half of Paris was near Galeries Lafayette.

Gilles was now stirring ingredients in a white porcelain bowl he usually used for his morning café au lait: sweet soy sauce, teriyaki, chopped garlic, sesame, homemade ketchup, honey and a splash of raspberry vinegar from Provence. Then he reached for the Laphroaig whisky Claire had brought back from her last work visit to Oxford (a six-week guest lectureship on 'The Politics of Emotions: Media,

Manipulation and Opinion Leadership'; God, sometimes she was so sick of it all), and threw her a questioning glance.

'Just in the marinade or in a glass? You've got eight weeks off from today. A thumbful?'

He extended his thumb, first horizontally, then vertically. A centimetre of whisky or a whole five?

It was an old routine of theirs, harking back to the first glass they ever drank together. They had learnt it from the bartender at Le Mole, the century-old Breton bar in Lampaul-Plouarzel: a thumb's width of whisky or a thumb's height?

The same gesture for twenty-two years.

'Later. And I'll be taking a few exam scripts and books with me to Trévignon. We've got a new research project starting in the autumn.'

'Suit yourself.' Gilles's shrug signalled resignation. Not because of the whisky. Because of her.

Claire could tell this tiny disappointment was the reason why Gilles didn't ask what kind of research project it was. She could accept the whisky, then he would reciprocate by asking. A quid pro quo.

Little things. It was always just the little things.

Gilles poured a generous glug of the smoky Islay whisky into the marinade.

The playlist on the laptop switched to René Aubry. 'Salento'. Gilles stirred the marinade in time to the steady guitar rhythm.

His steady, knowing hands.

His warm-hearted, affectionate nature, filling the whole kitchen, relaxing her. In spite of everything. Because Gilles was so much more than an unasked question about her work. If Claire's life were a tree, he would be all the growth rings. She knew Gilles's affairs weren't about her. They were about him. To broach the subject, to reveal that she knew about it, would mean bringing it into this kitchen. Into this life, her bed, her head.

A waste of resources. She hated wasting too much energy on emotions that couldn't change the past.

'I assume you know whether our guest is vegetarian, or a Jehovah's Witness?' Claire asked presently.

Gilles's fork clattered against the bowl as he whisked. 'Don't tell me I've got to make a warm tofu salad with an orange marinade and plain strawberries for dessert? Without the Armagnac?'

His pained expression was so exaggerated, Claire couldn't help laughing.

'So, is Nico's . . .?' Hmm, what should she call her: his friend? There had been a dozen occasions since Nico's sixteenth birthday where 'just a friend' had joined them at the long dining table, awkwardly squeezing her tender, hungry heart like a stress ball, but few had come a second time. Now Nicolas was nearly twenty-two and had announced the previous week that he wanted them to meet *someone*. Someone: not '*just a friend*'.

Claire could tell from the way Nico said her name that her son loved to roll its soft, dancing, resonating sound around on his tongue. That it triggered a restless little surge in his heart, made him smile in the middle of the day, just looking out of the window.

Julie.

Claire smiled as she remembered. The spark in Nico's light-brown eyes. His unaccustomed earnestness.

Love turned boys into men.
And heartache forged their personality.

That was something Nico had never yet experienced. He was a stranger to the wounds of love, having always been the one to leave. He knew nothing of the despair when desire subsided and friendship began to take the place of passion. When the other's eyes no longer glowed, but drifted distractedly and eventually looked away. The sense of powerlessness. Followed by the realisation that you would survive this too, only as someone different, more cautious, more defiant, more judgemental. And it was only then, once the *grand amour* was over, once you'd been loved and left — and that could still happen even within an intact marriage, could it not? — that you became an adult.

Their son was named after Saint-Nicolas, one of the islands of Finistère's Glénan archipelago. That was where they had conceived him, in a warm hollow in the sand under the Milky Way as it danced upside down on the black, murmuring water. The name had been Gilles's choice.

Just as he had chosen the teapots, the Luberon tea towels, the corkscrew, Claire reflected; that deep-seated, pure and simple desire for something enduring, a mark on the imaginary map of our ceaselessly flowing existence. As if it somehow allowed the immortality of the moment to be preserved.

And yet, something *was* preserved. Claire still remembered what Gilles had felt like, his mouth inside her. It had tasted of sea salt. She knew that because he had kissed her afterwards, with two kinds of salt on his lips. How intoxicated, how embarrassed she had been. Too inwardly aroused and far too alert to let herself go. She had felt pleasure, but no release. Gilles had kept his eyes closed throughout. He always closed them before and during lovemaking, and eventually Claire stopped undressing in front of him. So as not to see him not looking at her.

And she remembered how numb she had felt when, after that summer, back in Paris and bent over the books of Konrad Lorenz, Edward O. Wilson and Dian Fossey, she suddenly found herself expecting a child. A child – and she herself barely an adult! Just twenty-two, and in the first flower of womanhood. Nevertheless . . .

We had a child, then we got married, and afterwards, over time, we got to know each other.

And that's where we are today.

This 'us' with its invisible gaps, its glassy silence that we knock against and pretend isn't there.

4

'*Bonsoir, tout le monde!*'

Nico. Suddenly standing there in the kitchen, as suddenly as he had appeared inside her, in her life, tearing her youth and her body apart. His sports shirt was soaked with sweat; like half of Paris's under-fifties, he went running every morning and evening by the Seine. Physically, Nicolas took after Claire's father, who she only knew from photos.

He went over to the antique porcelain sink Gilles had collected from a farmhouse on the river Yonne (oh, how he loved *things*! Indeed, Claire sometimes felt like asking her husband: 'Are you as fond of me as you are your ladles, *faux filets* and teapots? Honestly? Will you add me to your collection of beloved old objects and look upon me with affection as I age?'). Taking off his shirt, Nico washed his face and tanned, well-toned arms.

His dripping wet face with its dark five o'clock shadow moved Claire. Half boy, half man.

The Centaurian age.

'Is your visitor a vegetarian? Your mother wants to know,' asked Gilles.

'You've heard of the term "inferential beliefs"?' Without waiting for a nod, Nico continued: 'Exactly. I'm giving away nothing about Julie's background, hobbies, appearance or eating and drinking habits. I'm afraid you'll have to find that out for yourselves.'

'How disconcerting. Can you at least give us a tiny clue?' asked Gilles, passing Nico a hand towel to dry himself.

'She likes meat. And this stuff—' Nico turned the Ruinart bottle round to look at the label '—I guess she likes this too.'

'Well, hallelujah!' said Gilles. 'Anything else?'

'Like what?'

'Well, her age, for example?'

Nico went over to the laptop. He had to bend low to reach the windowsill: when did he get that tall? This morning? Then he opened the web browser and typed something in.

'Not YouTube, please,' said Gilles. 'You know . . .'

'Yeah, I know. That evil Google exploits composers. *Je m'excuse*, Papa, but you're hardly likely to have—' Nico switched to Gilles's music library '—Oh. I take it back.'

The voice of the young Belgian-Rwandan singer Stromae now filled the room, hitting the invisible masses with 'Alors On Danse'. Classical orchestra combined with hip-hop rhythms.

'How old did you say she was?'

'If I said thirty-nine, would you believe me?'

'How nice! And where did you find this charming thirty-nine-year-old Mrs Robinson?'

'If I told you that, you'd have to report us both to the police.'

'And you think it's a good idea to have dinner with an unknown criminal?'

'I hereby inform you, Papa, that I strongly suspect this won't be our last as a foursome.'

'Indeed, my learned friend,' said Claire.

'*Pardon,*' said Nico, turning to her. 'You too, of course, Maman.'

Oh yes, I nearly forgot the old girl's here too.

Gilles started to dance; Nico nodded along with the music.

Claire contemplated the two men in her life, Gilles and Nicolas, Nicolas and Gilles. They complemented each other perfectly, and on many an evening when Claire was sitting at the big table marking exam scripts or preparing lectures, she would pause, her pen hovering above the paper and her hair shrouding her face so that neither would notice, and listen, eyes closed, to the conversation between her husband and son.

Their levity. Their seriousness. Their closeness. Nicolas was a daddy's boy. His choice of career he had discussed with her, but everything else in his life he shared with his father.

Claire hadn't wanted a child.

But Mother Nature was unimpressed.

And she had presented her with an enormous, overwhelming challenge that barged its way into her life and saw to it that she would never again be alone with her own emotions and her own body, never again just a woman, but a mother who was there to protect. Out of two such flawed human beings she had created a third, neither flawless nor easy, and for years most of her worries had centred on Nico, rather than herself, the world, or her marriage.

She had lost herself.

And gained him.

The two things couldn't be offset against each other.

Nicolas and Gilles. They were men. Men would never

know what it's like never to be alone in your own body again. How your sexual organs suddenly change. The body put to external use, the soul torn in two, so that part of it would forever belong to the child and go with them wherever they went.

Perhaps that's what drives women to have secrets and lovers: someone who, when he looks at you, doesn't think 'mother' but 'woman'.

'Dance with us!' cried Gilles, holding out his hand to Claire.

She stood up, muttering: 'Not now, I need to . . .' and headed for the bathroom, leaving the two men to enjoy the moment, the music, and their empathy with Stromae – an anagram of 'maestro' – in the colourful chaos of the kitchen.

Gilles's expression changed only minimally before he collected himself. Back to resignation. Claire knew she must be a disappointment to him in many ways. None of them dramatic, but overall – who knew? She was always working. Even during holidays. She never drank whisky before seven and stopped after the first or second glass of wine during the week. She never danced to music in the kitchen. She preferred structure to spontaneity. She analysed emotions instead of having them.

'I'm not always like this, you know,' she said to him.

Or rather, she said it in her head, again and again, but not aloud.

She closed the door carefully and turned the tap on just enough to run a thin, noiseless stream of water into the state-of-the-art sink. The bathroom was small, clean and white. Structured. With flush cabinets. The only decoration

Claire had allowed was a small wooden tortoise she had bought in Sanary-sur-Mer, in a crammed jewellery shop in one of the shady narrow streets of the old town. It was the time when Gilles had just been through a creative abyss – not the first, and not the last – and they had holidayed in the south instead of going to Brittany as usual. He had longed for warmth, for the summer ocean, to make the music inside him flow again.

Claire washed her face, eyes closed. She dipped first her wrists, then both arms in the cold water. Drank thirstily, tasting iron. Drank some more. There was still time to shower and change.

For Mademoiselle Someone. Not too formal: Nicolas would want to make an impression, but it mustn't be too contrived or pretentious. He wanted his parents to play ball, be gentle, intelligent but not blasé, humorous but not embarrassing, warm but not over-familiar. In short, not to make idiots of themselves.

'Promise,' she murmured.

She wished him the miracle of love.

But did he have any idea how long a life as husband and wife could endure? The way a name burned irresistibly on the lips? How wonderful it was, in the beginning, to whisper it over and over, in different degrees of intensity. Until it became a mantra, a foundation, a home.

Or perhaps she and Gilles were invented simply for Julie to find her Nicolas. It was meant to be: they didn't have to do anything. She smiled through closed eyes. Impossible. But wonderful and comforting all the same.

Meanwhile, there were the weeks in Brittany. It would be their last summer as a family.

Father, mother, son.

After the summer holidays, Nicolas would come back to the Rue Pierre Nicole only to pack his things.

Then Gilles and Claire would be alone again, for the first time in twenty-two years.

Son-less.

Just man and woman.

If they really had only been invented for Nicolas's sake, what would become of them when their purpose in life was gone?

She showered and changed. She had to go through Gilles's room to get to her wardrobe; it had once been their marital bedroom, but nowadays she slept on the sofa bed in her study. She got up earlier than Gilles and spent her evenings reading research papers: a young German scholar had written a book on ants that she was keen on. Weren't all these practical considerations good reasons for sleeping apart? When she returned, the table was already laid, the white roses were in a blue vase, the candles were lit, and Gilles was pouring himself a whisky. The music had moved on to Christophe Miossec, the rock-poet from Brest. Claire's favourite musician. 'À l'attaque!'

Claire gave Gilles the horizontal thumb sign. He nodded, smiling.

'And this research project?' he asked. 'Are you leading it, or that bastard, Renaud?' He handed her a glass.

'It depends on the concept. It's going to be about communication and the effectiveness of collective intelligence. And what ants have over Homo Google in that respect.'

'And? What do ants have over us? The queen?'

'Queen ants have no authority. When comparing ants

and humans, we use the term intelligence paradox: whereas the individual simplicity of ants results in a collective intelligence that has a social, sustainable and climate-protecting function, the individual intelligence of humans results in collective stupidity. Populism, achievement discrimination, shit storms . . .'

'I see. It's only in the mass that we're really stupid.'

They clinked glasses. It struck Claire that, if their story were a book, it could be told in a thousand ways. A story of lovers. A story of liars. Sometimes they would be loners, sometimes enemies, sometimes friends.

'Where's Nico?' she asked presently.

'He's fetching his attractive stranger from the metro. And he's taken a white rose with him.'

'In that case it must be serious.'

They smiled at each other. The afternoon had been washed away. This was her life. Right here.

Wasn't it?

Miossec sang: *'You're in my skin. You're in my soul.'*

'And Gaumont? Are they using your music for the series?'

'I don't know why they're taking so long to reach a decision. The more it drags on the harder it gets to maintain that inner tension. You know what I mean . . .?'

She nodded. Gilles needed to feel like a taut string on which he could play out his musical talent. He had to be on fire. If he wasn't on fire, then . . . *perhaps he rekindled the flame from someone else's body.*

When she was in Oxford. Or at the Institute. When she was undressing alone in her room. She felt a vague anxiety inside, and at the same time such defiance: *Do you know that every rejection makes it easier for me to do what I did today, Gilles?*, followed by such a wave of tenderness towards her husband, a fervent wish for him not to lose that fire, because he loved it, and she ought to tell him that more often: *I'm especially proud of you when you lose yourself in your music, when you create something that didn't exist before. When you're truly you and you don't need me.*

'Should I wear my hair down?' she asked instead.

'Why not?'

'Is up a bit too severe?'

'You're not scared, are you?'

'Are *you*?'

'What of? A woman who loves our son? Certainly not. Otherwise I'd have to be scared of you too.'

Miossec whispered more than sang: '*There's a life before you. Is there one after?*'

It's not about fear, Claire wanted to say. *It's about falling. If Nico leaves. If Julie stays. What comes next. What's left. Whether anything will be left, of you and me. Of the old Us. What we'll have – and want – then. Apart from thumbs of whisky and silence.*

'. . . *Même en vrac.*'

Or whether the Us will break up into its constituent parts.

But the answer to that question would have led on to other things they had so far avoided. Barbed exchanges, recriminations, reproaches, hurt, desire, fear, a sudden rekindling of affection just when the other was ready to go their own way: genies in a bottle.

And anyway, this wasn't just half a life, but a shared one, a long-standing, easy familiarity. That outweighed the sealed bottle, didn't it?

Didn't it?

Claire unpinned her hair.

'Ready?' she asked Gilles.

'Ready when you are.'

Two smiles that linked like hands. They had watched *The Silence of the Lambs* on their first video night together and, just like the whisky thumb, that phrase had seeped into their daily life. Ready to keep the baby? Ready for the oral exam? Ready to go out? Ready to part with their son, in a double sense: the parting would have a name and a face as well as a place.

Ready when you are.

They clinked glasses again. A bright, clear sound.

'I love you,' Gilles said suddenly, looking straight into Claire's eyes.

She drank, then put her glass down and started to say: 'I—'

At that moment, the doorbell rang and a key turned in the lock.

Nico's voice called '*Salut!*' and two heartbeats later the pair of them appeared in the doorway. Nicolas and her.

Whatever Claire had been going to say – she didn't know whether it was 'I love you too' or 'I need to tell you something' or 'I'm not sure if you do: why don't we sleep with each other any more?' or 'Why have we turned into the people we are and not the people we could have been? Are we more than friends, soulmates, parents?' – it was completely erased.

This time the vixen-like face wore subtle make-up and was framed by straight, tidy hair. She wore a dress that transformed her, a camouflaging blue dress with a white collar and red ballet flats. The piercing was gone, the tattoo chastely covered. She had metamorphosed, *folded*, it seemed to Claire, into an interchangeable twenty-something young woman. Only her gaze was the same, that old gaze out of young eyes.

    The singer who lied.
    From the Hotel Langlois.
    So that was her.
    So that was Julie.

5

It seemed the height of injustice: that the only thing capable of bringing a woman's life crashing down around her ears should simply walk through her very own front door.

Sitting at the table three or four minutes later, Claire replayed the moment in slow motion in her head.

There had been no sign of recognition on Julie's face when she saw Claire appear behind Gilles in the hallway. Her only visible reaction had been a slight dilation of the pupils; after that, she had instinctively turned her eyes away from Claire and fixed them on Gilles, smiling at him as any young woman would on being introduced to the parents of a steady boyfriend, and hoping the encounter would prove less excruciating than in her worst nightmares.

Gilles had given Julie the obligatory double *bise* on the cheek, followed by a 'Please call me Gilles' and 'Just sit next to Claire and don't lift a finger, the roles are reversed here: the men do the work, the women sit back and enjoy.'

Once again, Julie directed her smile at him, a conciliatory gesture, a sign of submission: Claire registered it loud and clear, mentally clinging to the solid ground of the scientist, as if she were merely an external observer.

'No one'll believe me back home when I tell them that,' Julie replied. Gilles glanced delightedly in Claire's direction, his raised eyebrows signalling: isn't she quick? Do you like her? I do!

From her bag – a colourful shoulder bag in woven fabric with corded straps – Julie produced a small package wrapped in glossy white gift paper and offered it to Claire. '*Merci, Madame le Professeur*, for the invitation. I must confess to being a bit nervous.'

'Tell me about it!' exclaimed Gilles. 'We were all for hiring two actors to rehearse the whole thing with us.'

Nico added, his voice somewhat louder than usual: 'I warned you they're a bit strange, but they're harmless.'

All these niceties had given Claire time to breathe, check the mirror, the oval one: no, she wasn't white as an aspirin, her face was still inscrutable, in fact she was even smiling.

Gilles and Nicolas were watching Claire expectantly; written on both their faces was the unspoken plea: Don't hurt her. Please try to like her!

Claire hadn't taken the present from Julie's hands straight away; they were both still holding it. Only now did she and Julie finally look directly at each other.

Still the same old-school beauty, she thought as she looked into Julie's face. And, in the same moment: *It's all over*.

They had both leaned forward at once for the *bises*, their cheeks touching ever so slightly.

'Oh, come now,' Claire said, feeling her smile tug at the corners of her mouth, 'it's a pleasure to have you.'

Julie's expressions, her gestures, were all impeccably correct. They behaved no differently to any other little family. Both women kept exactly to the script.

And that told Claire everything she needed to know: Julie had recognised her, but decided for some reason known only to her to act as scrupulously as possible as if she hadn't.

We're too good at lying, thought Claire.
We women.

Now Julie was sitting in the corner next to her, looking across at Nicolas, who was opening the champagne, and Gilles, who was busy preparing the aperitif, searching for something on the laptop – 'Do you like Zaz?' – placing some blue and white glazed bowls of salted pistachios, pink melon and black olives in front of them, and generally doing what he did best: spreading a warm feeling around the room.

Claire caught his eye, his unspoken question: *Well, what do you think? Good impression?* Claire nodded and raised her whisky glass to Gilles.

'I'm afraid we're terribly curious,' she began. 'We got no more out of Nico than your name . . .'

'. . . and that you have no objection to this sort of thing,' added Gilles, holding up the marinated faux filet in the earthenware pot.

'*Alors*,' said Julie, spreading her hands, 'here I am. Ask away.'

'And you promise not to cheat?' asked Gilles genially, coming over and sitting down opposite Julie. His knee touched Claire's, and she flinched, before moving it back again. He glanced at her, took her hand in his and picked up one of the champagne glasses Nico had filled in the other.

Claire noticed Julie's sidelong glance at Gilles, and their clasped hands.

'Well, not too much,' replied Julie.

'*Santé!*' said Claire, and they clinked glasses, looking each other briefly in the eye: green eyes and brown eyes. Julie looked away first, then they all clinked with each other.

'Careful, no crossing!' cried Gilles.

'Otherwise it's seven years' bad sex,' added Claire.

'I thought that was just broken mirrors,' Julie piped up.

Nico was half beguiled, half horrified, but he was beginning to relax nevertheless: Claire could tell that from her son's shoulders, which were no longer up by his ears.

He really likes her, she thought. *And he wants us to as well.*

But why did it have to be her?

Or, come to that, why me?

Nicolas couldn't help touching Julie: a passing caress of her shoulder, her bare forearm.

Bodies were rarely discreet. The small gestures, the mutual inclination of the shoulders, the lowering of the chin. Nico's involuntary genital presentation as he sat next to Julie, elbow on the table and one leg resting on the chair next to him. Julie gave Nicolas a private look reserved for him alone, straightened a little, turned her body a few millimetres and tossed her head slightly, making her hair swing back. Her fingertips slid up and down the glass. LFT: longing for touch.

This man and this woman had reached the key negotiation phases in which words were unnecessary; if she were to film them, Claire thought, she could use it to explain to her first years everything they needed to know about non-verbal communication.

Desire. The engine of Creation.

Over starters, Julie talked about her parents: how they loved their little house in the suburb of Saint-Denis which they'd be paying off for another twenty years. The conservatory from the DIY store. Place-mats from Spanish holidays. A modest Peugeot, 'and my mother loved the film *If Not You, Then Who?*, especially your soundtrack, Monsieur Baleira, she was always playing it,' Julie said in Gilles's direction. He raised his glass – they had switched to a Sauvignon from Gascogny that smelled of orchards and stones drying in the sun – and replied: 'Your mother has excellent taste in music. Tell her I'll happily add your account number to my will.'

Julie's laugh had something sensual about it. A huskiness.

Flower constancy, Claire mused. Julie reminded her of flowers – uniquely skilful survival strategists to which insects are only attracted because of the anticipated reward: a constant supply of pollen. The sweetness of Julie's laugh was an endless source of pollen.

Claire sat back in her chair.

Gilles was explaining how he had invented a different musical leitmotif for each character in *If Not You, Then Who?* – 'Remember *Once Upon a Time in the West*? Morricone used the same technique' – and how the tone colours of the music had changed from dark blue to bright orange. He sounded confident and amiable.

Claire remembered how Gilles had struggled over that composition. How he had paced around the flat for weeks, script in hand, refusing to go out in case the muse should strike while he was away from his keyboard, guitar or computer. He had started drinking more, in the hope that alcohol would rekindle his imagination. Claire had kept out of his way, mindful of the quarrels that inevitably resulted from the incendiary combination of alcohol, frustration and tension.

Then there was the time afterwards, during the orchestra recording sessions, when he had spent a few intimate moments with the woman who played the double bass.

Claire had noticed it at the film premiere. Bodies that were familiar with each other had a different language, even when fully clothed. They didn't start when the other approached them from behind. They sensed the other's contours, warmth and presence. Perceptual filtering. It was a capacity common to both humans and animals.

Desire.

Perhaps it was inevitable, Claire pondered. The need to see oneself reflected, as an artist and as a man, in someone new and different, the need to be desired. It had nothing to do with her. It was human nature. No affair in the world had anything to do with the beating heart left behind for the sake of those stolen moments: it was all about the one doing the leaving.

Wasn't it?

Claire had known Gilles long enough. Professional frustration made him doubt everything he was: he struggled with himself as a man, as a lover, as the husband of a woman whose despair was never (in his mind) as black and all-consuming as his own, a woman who relied on knowledge rather than intuition and art. He struggled with the idea of being held in contempt for that. And not without reason: this society couldn't cope with a Brigitte Macron, or any upset of the oh-so-divine order. Eve the hunter and Adam the cook? – *mon Dieu!*

In the end, the long-awaited inspiration had come to the rescue and, combined with sheer hard work, had restored Gilles to an even keel: after those months of crisis he was back to his old generous, vivacious self and busy attempting to make up for the dark clouds he had spread around him.

He was a good person. But even good people sometimes found themselves in trouble and resorted to lies.

Encouraged by Gilles, Julie had started talking about films she liked. *La La Land, Breakfast at Tiffany's, Hidden Figures.*

'And are you musical at all? Do you sing?' Gilles asked.

Julie shook her head emphatically. 'No.'

'What a shame,' Claire murmured.

Julie took a hasty sip of wine.

Gilles began to talk about the resistance he had had to overcome from his parents and friends in order to pursue his passion for music and find his true vocation. 'In my mother's eyes, having an artist in the family was one of the worst disasters that could befall it: the lack of money, the temperamental disposition . . .'

Claire studied the two men. Nico had eyes for no one but Julie; Gilles had let go of Claire's hand.

Gilles and Nicolas reminded Claire of . . .

Of sea-lily fossils.

Sea lilies were related to sea stars and once lived in the deep ocean. Their crowns were drawn to luminous objects. When deprived of light, they shed their stalk ends and crept sideways along the ocean floor to get close to it again.

Nico and Gilles were two sea lilies drawn to the ray of light that this young woman had brought into their kitchen in the Rue Pierre Nicole. With her husky laugh. Her eloquent face. The warmth and vitality that flowed from her. Julie was a wild, wide river, full of emotions: sensuality, defiance, anger, despair, uncertainty – all were there in abundance.

Julie had a generous way of listening that involved her whole face: her eyebrows, her smile, her nostrils. She didn't just listen with her ears and eyes, but with her whole body, with an organ unknown to medical science that lit up with empathy and encouragement. Gilles and Nico saw themselves and their words reflected in Julie's face, that unfashionably beautiful face that invited men to go on talking about themselves because it was all important and interesting.

It was easy to be intoxicated by Julie's capacity for active listening, Claire thought. She wondered whether Julie would shine her light on her too, were she to talk about collective intelligence among insects and the confusion of human individuals when in a group.

Julie. What kind of prehistoric creature would she be? A *marrella*, Claire decided. *Marrella* were arthropods that could absorb more oxygen than other species at times when it was in shorter supply. *Julie, the girl-going-on-woman, guarding the breath of the world.*

'You're very quiet. What are you thinking about?' Gilles asked Claire suddenly.

'About arthropods.'

'Well, there's a surprise.'

Julie cast a glance at Claire. What did it mean?

Was it: I heard that exchange of words? And I know how it feels to be mocked by someone who's otherwise so close, so familiar? If so, it would be mortifying, in some small way. *Tant pis.* Unwelcome solidarity.

Over the main course, Julie and Nico took it in turns,

with much laughter and frequent interjections – 'No, it wasn't like that!' 'Yes it was, believe me, I was there!' – to relate how they'd met. It featured a party, a night at the Gare du Nord, a piano and a pair of lost shoes.

Their first official rendezvous after that was at a Pussyhat march where feminists, among others, had demonstrated against Trump. Their attempts to run away from the police had led them ever closer to each other.

'And now *I* have a question,' Julie said finally. She had drunk her wine too quickly: her pupils were enlarged and her cheeks flushed pink. With her elbows resting on the table and the wine glass clasped in both hands, she pointed with her index finger to the wall behind them, at the end of the former lounge. 'Tell me please, what's *that*?'

'That?' replied Gilles. He had opened a bottle of red to accompany the faux filet; Claire had declined. 'That's Claire's pet. Don't you think it looks a bit like the mad squirrel out of *Ice Age*?'

Nico burst out laughing, and so did Gilles.

Julie didn't.

How hard she's trying not to hurt my feelings by responding too overtly, too gratifyingly to my husband's practised, flippant charm, and to show an interest instead, Claire thought. In my 390-million-year-old ichthyosaur, hanging on the back wall in its stone prison.

'Poor guy, cut off in his prime,' Julie said.

'What makes you say that?' Claire replied.

Her tone lowered the temperature in the room.

No reason to be angry, Claire thought.

But she was. Angry with this girl who was trying to be on her best behaviour. An unnecessary contortion in the presence of a behavioural biologist with a professorship at the Sciences Po.

And she was angry with herself, too. She had lost her stone. The stone that had been her companion for longer than Gilles. It was as if she'd dropped her own self out of carelessness. And now this situation she'd got herself into.

It's your own fault, Claire.

'So what do you know about fossils, Julie?'

'Generally or specifically?' Gilles interjected.

Nico looked at his mother, jaw tensed. Don't, the twitch of his muscles said. It's all going well. Please don't spoil it.

More coolly than she had intended, Claire said: 'It's an ichthyosaur. Ichthyosaurs were the dolphins of their day. They populated the oceans for 157 million years. Then they disappeared, long before all the dinosaurs went extinct. The theory is that the oceans lost their oxygen content and the ichthyosaurs suffocated.'

'That's so sad,' said Julie.

'No. It's evolution. Humans, too, are a never-ending biological building site. Our evolution is based on genetic defects. We either adapt or we die out.'

Silence around the table.

'More wine?' Claire asked Julie.

Julie nodded, holding out her glass.

'Are you sure?'

Julie's eyes were shining. She withdrew the empty glass.

'Well, I'll have some,' said Gilles, 'and I've got a great idea!' He waited a moment – he was a master of the dramatic pause – before continuing: 'Julie, you haven't told us yet whether you're going to be working in Strasbourg like Nicolas . . .?'

'I don't know. I'm in a bit of a . . . transitional phase at the moment. I'm working at a hotel.'

'Very wise. You see many different sides of life in hotels. But, if you'll pardon my poeticism, I imagine eight weeks apart must be torture to a budding young love. How about coming with us to Brittany? Till the end of August! Are you free?'

'I . . .'

'Wow,' said Nico.

'I don't know . . .' said Julie. 'I probably could be, but I wouldn't want to impose, we—'

'Nonsense! You're as good as family now, or is that too presumptuous of me?'

'I . . . well . . .'

'Gilles,' said Claire, 'don't put her under pressure. Julie, please don't feel obliged to say yes. You said you're working at a hotel? Would they let you go in high season? You must have plans for after the summer?'

A hesitation, a glance up at Claire. 'Of course.'

Liar, thought Claire.

'OK, I'll get the desserts now.' Gilles got up. 'And you can sleep on it till tomorrow, Julie.'

'Is there somewhere I can wash my hands?' asked Julie.

'I'll show you,' replied Claire.

The two women got up together.

Claire led Julie through the hallway to the white bathroom.

Julie's footsteps on the parquet sounded uncertain.

As Julie entered the bathroom, Claire hurried in after her and closed the door behind them, leaning her back against it.

'Don't think I'm going to ask you to keep our first meeting to yourself,' she said calmly. 'You don't have to. You're free to tell anyone, any time. My husband, my son. I don't want your relationship to begin with a secret you're not responsible for. It's up to me to bear the consequences of my actions.'

Julie looked at her, a sudden surge of anger flaring in her eyes: such young anger. 'I don't know what you mean, Madame le Professeur. Now can I please . . .?' She pointed to the toilet seat.

'Of course,' said Claire. 'I'm sorry. And I'm sorry for . . . for putting you in this situation.'

As Claire went to open the door, Julie said: 'Wait. Please.' She avoided Claire's eyes. 'There's nothing to apologise for. You didn't put me in this situation. How could you have? I mean, it's not as if it was planned. And I've seen a lot of women at the hotel who . . . I mean, it's just that . . . you of all people.' She lifted her chin and looked Claire resolutely in the eye.

Her girlish face, so open and exposed in that moment. Stripped of everything: the smile, the nonchalance, the ready wit, leaving just the girl and the thousand versions of herself, all the restless turmoil, all the contradictions.

Julie said: 'I don't understand why. When you have everything.'

Claire left the bathroom and closed the door noiselessly behind her.

In the kitchen, Nico and Gilles were still engaged in conversation. Gilles came up to Claire and put his arms around her, and she smelled the familiar blend of Chanel Égoïste and husband. He was so familiar, everything about him, he was everything in one, the good times and the hateful ones.

'Say yes,' he whispered. 'I know you're sceptical, but it's both an ending and a beginning. The last summer as our old family, the first summer as a new one. Nico . . . he wants her. Like we wanted each other. Claire, Fée, please. Let Julie come with us.'

It was ages since Gilles had used her nickname. Fée. From her middle name, Stéphenie.

Fée. That was the person she used to be. In the early days, when life lay spread before her like a great wide river and anything was possible, anything, and all of it was good.

No, Claire wanted to say.

No, she can't, and I don't want to explain why. She just can't.

But because she couldn't speak – and because something inside her that she normally kept so effortlessly under lock and key was curious, so curious, about that strange light that seemed to flicker and glow behind it all – she nodded.

6

This feeling of being a nobody. While everyone around you was a somebody.

Julie drained her glass of wine. The tension remained. And with it this heaviness, this nagging fear beneath her skin, this painfully throbbing pulse in her temples and under her larynx. And this contempt. Contempt for herself.

On stage in the floridly decorated cellar bar of the Très Honoré in the 1st arrondissement – very Cannes, very Balenciaga: why had she come here, of all places? – stood a girl clutching the microphone with both hands. She came in too early with Adele's 'Hello'. The back-up band – pianist, percussionist, bass player, saxophonist, a sound as dense and rich as expensive chocolate – played on regardless. These men inhabited the stage as naturally as their own living room.

That was why she had come. For the sound. Because she had heard from others who, like her, did the rounds of Paris's open-mic sessions, that the Très Honoré had a real 'showbiz vibe'. Every Wednesday, at the Soirée Buzz. Anything was possible for amateurs who wanted to sing their allotted three songs on the open stage. Even for professionals, thanks to the quality of the band. Pop, rock, blues. Burlesque. And jazz.

Open mic: the talent show of the streets. A centuries-old tradition where all-comers were welcome. Anyone with the courage and lungs to hold a note could sing their way to the top, make a name for themselves. Anybody could become a somebody.

Nice one, Beauchamp. You ought to write calendar slogans.

When would she finally dare to get up on stage? She would start with something small, rhythmic, whimsical. By Zaz. Then go on to something big. 'Feeling Good'. The way Nina Simone sang it. The intro free, unaccompanied. *Birds flying high, you know how I feel.* And then the brass section that flung open the curtain to the world and let the light flow in like a great river.

It was uncomfortable to listen to Adele's 'Hello', but even so Julie envied this girl her moment as she stood there in her striped dress, eyes closed, forehead shining, at once withdrawing into herself and coming out of herself.

She was singing to Julie, to the others, to the whole world.

Julie shrank further into the corner of the lavish purple sofa, thankful that the toffee-nosed waitress didn't come to take her empty glass away and pressure her into ordering another overpriced drink.

Something by Nina Simone. 'Summertime'.

Julie practised, in secret and wherever she could. Breathing, tuning, chest voice, head voice, support. There were YouTube tutorials, there were long, lonely paths alongside Paris's railway tracks, there was the silence of the hotel rooms before the new guests' arrival. She had always wanted to sing but never had the courage to attend an audition.

Julie found it unbearable to sing in front of other people. To be watched indulging in her greatest pleasure. When she sang alone, it felt like she was in the thick of life. As if all the longing and yearning had found a home and a calm, glorious sun was shining inside her. This pleasure. This love. This boundless love, for herself, for the world. This freedom. And through her singing she finally felt connected to the world and no longer separated from it; she wasn't just looking at it – she was in it. Truly present in her own life.

Now. Go on, Beauchamp. Get on with it. If you're going to screw up, do it properly.

She imagined herself getting up. Walking past the leather and plush armchairs, the broad-beamed antique sofas, the expensive leather and wood chests that served as tables. All in this red colour: the light, the silk wallpaper, the floor. And then everyone would see what singing did to her.

As if she were masturbating on stage.

She got up and reached for her leather jacket and handbag.

Out of here! Out of this cellar with its too-good sound, its too-good décor, its too-good drinks. She squeezed through the unwilling audience, blinking back the tears. Upstairs in the restaurant, she was dazzled by the brightness of the glasses, the bustling of the waiting staff, the self-assurance of the guests chatting at their tables. Head down, she stumbled through the premises, with its futuristic lighting and art-house chairs, catching a waiter's elbow and knocking a Vuitton handbag off the back of a chair with her hip.

At last: fresh air.

The heat had receded from the streets. The glasshouse of the Place du Marché St Honoré reflected back the lights of the restaurants and brasseries. The awnings, red, green, gold, and the shadows of nighttime revellers on their way to the Hemingway, the Buddha Bar. The Instagrammers' Paris, thought Julie: drinking, eating, photographing reality until it looks grander than it will ever be, then shagging.

What about you people? Is that living? Do you have that sun inside you?

Merde. Did dentists? Teachers?

Did anyone in the world have it?

Julie took a cigarette from the crushed packet.

The last one.

She only ever smoked after her persistent failures to get up on the stage. Fifteen times last month. Three this month.

A *clochard* came up to her asking for change. She could only find a few coppers in the pockets of her jacket, so she gave him the cigarette as well.

'You look even sadder when you smile,' he said.

Julie turned away quickly and carried on walking.

She'd never make the train home now anyway. She might as well wander the streets of Paris until five in the morning, then go straight to the Langlois for her early shift and carry on as usual.

If. If. If.

If she hadn't gone to Apolline's, she wouldn't have met Nico, wouldn't have taken the metro to meet his parents, agonised over what to wear, set foot in the flat in the Rue Pierre Nicole, or known that the world would start to slip out of control, as if she were walking on thin air, and that everything would change.

I should call Nicolas and tell him I'm not coming.

She couldn't accept the offer. Eight weeks. The ocean. Summer.

And besides: if she accepted, she could kiss goodbye to the Langlois job.

Would that be so bad?

But what then? Work at the checkout at Carrefour? Or go to university after all? The prospect didn't appeal to her one bit, and anyway no one could afford to study in Paris unless they had two jobs on the side.

She reached for her phone and dialled Nico's number.

Nico, I love you, but . . .

No. She put the phone away again.

Nico. He always knew what he wanted. And did it. He was so sure of himself! Perhaps it was infectious?

Yes, perhaps Julie could catch his certainty like a cold: a heavy, persistent one.

A group of men came towards her, a bit too invasive, a bit too loud, one wolf-whistling as they passed, another shouting a half-appreciative, half-provocative 'Oh *putain* . . .' It was such a pain, pretending not to notice the cat calls. She raised a hand, and then her middle finger. The men laughed.

She slipped on her jacket, thrusting her hands deep into the pockets, and quickened her pace, heading towards the Louvre.

Nico. I love you, but your mother's cheating on your father. She gave me permission to tell you. So I don't have to lie to you. But I don't want to tell you. I don't want to lie to you, but there are other things I don't want to tell you either. The singing, for instance. Or that I want to try out a thousand things in bed but am afraid you'll be scared of me, and the hunger inside me. Nor do I want to tell you that I'm scared of myself. That I'm scared of my own fear, that it will kill me if I give in to it, if I don't have the courage of my desires, and that it will destroy my light. And that's why I can't come with you.

Julie took her phone out again. She missed Nicolas. His smell, his warmth, his body under his sports shirts. He looked like his mother when he was concentrating.

Claire Cousteau. Madame le Professeur.

Last night, in the bathroom, the woman had been ready to let go of everything. Just like that. That self-controlled, confident woman, who didn't want Julie to have to keep her escapade at the hotel a secret from Nicolas.

For my sake, thought Julie. She didn't want me to have to lie. But Julie had already made her mind up. The moment she saw Claire standing there in the hall with her hair down: for a heartbeat, before the shock kicked in, she had felt something else.

Something bright and luminous.

A kind of joy at seeing the woman again.

A thrilling, fearful, wild, dancing joy.

But she had simply smiled at Gilles, Nicolas's father. She had to look somewhere to cover that bubbling feeling in her breast: a feeling of precariousness, of colourfulness.

She hadn't thought twice. She had reacted. Pretended she was seeing Claire for the first time.

And the strange thing was: it didn't feel like she was deceiving Nicolas.

It had nothing to do with him, nothing at all; Madame le Professeur was the strange woman at the Langlois. The free woman who had listened to no one. Only herself.

Julie would like to have asked Claire when she first knew who she wanted to be.

And how do we know who we're capable of being?

And is it possible to love and at the same time to be so full of hunger for pleasure and foreignness and the thing that lurks in the shadows, in the dark, next to my calm, radiant sun?

And what is it like to cry out in ecstasy, to lose yourself, to have no name and no past?

What is it like to love, how does it feel to be loved, how do you know it's the real thing, and is that happiness, or does it become routine?

And what kind of music do you listen to, and why did you lie for me too?

I want to ask her everything. All the things I've never asked anyone before, I want to let it all out.

She started to feel dizzy.

What was she doing here?

What the hell was she doing here?

Yes, exactly, Beauchamp. What are you doing here? That's the question. Why are you here and not where you want to be? And doing what you really want to do?

She took a deep breath, then another. And dialled Nico's number.

'I want to see you,' she said. She closed her eyes. *Go on. Out with it. Tell him the rest.*

She had never said anything like that aloud. But she wanted to. That and a thousand other things.

She wanted to be able to look someone straight in the eye and say: 'And I want to sleep with you.'

She didn't say it.

They met at the Langlois. There was a discreet agreement between the staff and the night porter. Whenever there were rooms free, they could stay overnight. All the cleaners and hotel staff lived in the *banlieues*, and sometimes it was too far and the night too short to go home.

Julie had never made use of it. Until tonight.

The porter, an amiable, rather chatty elderly Corsican, gave her the key to Number 11 along with a small bottle of Crémant and a couple of glasses. It was a dark room overlooking the rear courtyard.

She waited before switching on the light. She undressed, slowly, and stood naked in the dark. Breathed deeply in and out.

Julie hadn't slept often with boys or men before. A few times on clammy mattresses in noisy, crowded flatshares. In cars. In the boy's bedroom, while his mother turned up the volume on the TV downstairs.

But *faire l'amour*, making love: she'd never done that with anyone. She'd been in love, certainly, and curious, and a few times she'd said yes even though she didn't want to, so as not to cause offence.

During the act itself she had fantasised, dreaming herself far away and combing through images and scenes in her head until she could fix on something to help set her free.

Set her free from the rather clumsier reality where two bodies remained two bodies instead of becoming one, without boundaries, without shame, without the need to escape somewhere in her own head.

Alcohol helped too, but nothing came close to the passion, the pleasure that Julie sought.

Did it even exist?

She switched on the beside lamp, which gave off an intimate, discreet light, and lay naked on the cool, smooth sheets to wait for Nicolas.

She stared into the corner. She could lie on her side with her buttocks towards him.

Or on her back, one knee drawn up, not too provocatively but so that he could see the dark smile between her legs.

Yes.

No.

She sat up. It felt strange, weird, and yet . . .

. . . yes! That was the kind of woman she wanted to be! The kind who leaned back and made love with her whole being, the kind who said: 'Come! Come to me, come inside me, let me envelop you, give yourself to me.' She wanted him to surrender himself completely, and for there to be no taboos, no no-go zones and no awkwardness.

She didn't want to work her way through the *Cosmo* tips. She wanted to play. She wanted to feel. She wanted to taste him, all of him, and she wanted him to taste all of her, she wanted them to do everything two people could do to each other with hands and mouth and teeth and tongue and fingers and bodies.

She wanted him to be inflamed by her.

To caress her face with his penis.

To kiss her, with the taste of her on his lips.

To whisper her name, over and over.

Julie waited. She was starting to feel chilly.

Nicolas knocked instead of coming straight in as she'd asked him to in her WhatsApp. To come in wordlessly, undress, or not, enclose her mouth in his, or . . . But he knocked.

So she got up and opened the door.

He was visibly embarrassed on seeing her naked, and looked furtively around him, down the empty corridor.

'*Bonsoir* . . . aren't you cold?' he said. Then came in, closed the door and stood with his hands in the pockets of his denim jacket, smiling uncertainly.

What did you expect, Beauchamp?

A lot. Everything.

She moved towards him and pulled him to her by the waist of his trousers, then sat on the end of the bed and unbuckled his belt.

'What are you doing?' he asked.

'Seducing you,' she said.

His look was hard to read. Embarrassment. Uncertainty.

Let's do everything, she thought, *please!*

Fulfilment, her mouth full of warmth and soul and trust. Power. Powerlessness.

To have your mouth full of a man was everything at once, and hence inexpressible. There was no word for it, for the courage before, the concentration during, the intimate connection and simultaneous distance.

Nico was always silent and still when she moulded her mouth around his most vulnerable area. Tonight too. As if she had got too close to him, and he was ashamed to let himself go.

And Julie realised, with a bursting feeling in her chest:

I want more.

I always want more than there is.

So she desisted calmly and took Nico's hand. Pulled him onto the bed, at once very strong and very fragile.

Kissing him gently, she lifted his T-shirt and pressed her skin against his, then pulled off his jacket, lay down next to him on the bed, and turned out the light. And so they lay in each other's arms, Julie naked and Nicolas still dressed, listening to the nighttime sounds, and holding each other tight in the darkness.

Her shift began at five. Most of the guests didn't leave their rooms till around seven – except for the illicit couples, who only took day rooms and whose beds were already vacant by half ten in the evening. Julie started on these rooms after making up Number 11. It was remarkable how people behaved away from their own homes. And what they left behind. Phone-charging cables. Underwear. Julie had already found all sorts. A draft marriage contract. Sex toys. Books. She kept the books.

The rule was that you only phoned the guest if they'd left a purse or wallet. Otherwise, Julie's boss maintained a policy of absolute discretion. No phone calls. Many a marriage break-up had been precipitated by a well-meaning concierge sending on a forgotten item. And that wasn't good for the TripAdvisor ratings.

Instead, everything was taken to the lost property store, a room in the bowels of the Langlois dimly lit by a single bare bulb.

Everything except the strange, whitish-grey stone Julie found at around nine in the morning under the radiator of Room 32 while vacuuming.

It had a star-shaped pattern and was completely smooth: quite beautiful.

Julie clutched the stone tightly in her hand: then, and again when she gave in her notice, and again when it hit her, on the train to Saint-Denis, that she was now free.

Free as a bird. She had nothing left in the world. No security, no job, and no plan.

It was scary. It was glorious.

It was like walking towards the stage and shouting out loud, in fear, and in sheer exultation.

7

Two evenings later; Paris by night. The city had shaken off the day, the oppressive embrace of a too-scorching sun: a stressed, living organism, now throbbing with impatience. The night buses were crammed with standing passengers hungry for unforgettable adventures, the café tables were populated with clusters of young women and men, knees pressed against each other under the round marble tables, shoulder to shoulder, bent forward to catch every word. The Eiffel Tower had morphed into a lighthouse on dry land, its body a mass of glittering illuminations. Its light beam stroked the darkness at regular intervals, highlighting parks and roofs and desires and blotting out the stars. In the darkest corners, the homeless slept; in the semi-dark corners, couples exchanged promises they would never keep.

'Ready?' asked Gilles in the passenger seat.

'Of course,' she murmured. She didn't need to turn and look at him to feel his disappointment at her failure to oblige with the habitual 'Ready when you are.'

It had been Gilles's idea to leave Paris after sunset and drive through the night to the end of the world. To wake up the next morning by the ocean. To wake up as if autumn, winter and spring in the big grey city had been just a dream.

Gilles's idea. Twenty-two years ago. They would stay young and giddy, not like the others, promise?

Ever since then, at the beginning of every July, they had set off from the Rue Pierre Nicole just before midnight and driven straight to Trévignon. Claire always at the wheel.

The impulse to be different had become a habit.

Habit (noun): stored process, compressed into command chains of the basal ganglia. Governed by a fixed trigger stimulus and associated with a reward system. This principle underlies addictions such as smoking, for instance, but also individual and social habituation mechanisms such as maternal behaviour, a woman's conduct in public, or the sense of oneself as part of a married couple. See: Biological Relationships in Individual Psychological Cognition, Claire Stéphenie Cousteau, doctoral thesis, 1991.

Claire, dear?

Yes?

Give it a rest.

Sometimes it was easiest to shut herself up.

She twisted her thumb and forefinger and the Chubster sprang into action. She pushed the automatic gear lever firmly to 'D'.

'*Pardon*, Maman,' said Nicolas, 'but I'd like to come too if you don't mind?' He had to tilt his head sideways to fold himself onto the back seat.

This time Nico sat in the back with Julie, instead of at the front next to Claire as he had done for the last four years: it was the only part of the old Mercedes estate that would accommodate his long limbs reasonably comfortably.

Nico was so big and self-contained. So big that Claire would never be able to lift him into the Chubster now. Over the years – hundreds, thousands of times – she had been hoist, fork-loader, monkey swing, lifting her son and carrying him asleep on her back to the car park after the *fest-noz* in Sainte-Marine, Doëlan or Concarneau, or home after picnics in the Jardin du Luxembourg. For years she had enfolded that wide-eyed, radiant creature in the comfort, strength and solicitude of her arms, and now that he had grown through the roof the last thing he wanted was to be reminded in public that he was once little. He didn't need her any more: he was in training to be a man. How did that happen so fast?

So please, dear old Maman, don't be the same as always, be different! You can stop being a mother now, allez hop!

Dear old Maman, that's what I've turned into.

She steered the ageing vehicle out of the underground car park and out of Saint-Germain, weaving skilfully between taxis, Vespas and night buses. Ignoring the satnav instructions to head for the bypass, she took the parallel roads leading to the A6b autoroute and onwards towards Chartres and Le Mans.

When had she finally embraced motherhood? It wasn't when Nico was born. There was a moment, shortly before he started school, when it had hit her. What it really meant. Once she'd started to get over the shock of an unwanted, far too early pregnancy, and the fact that it wasn't just a temporary situation. She had realised that this was her life now, this tiny human, and was overcome with anxiety and fierce courage, determination and love, despair and a strange, weary resignation.

Motherhood was a much longer haul than pregnancy. And seeing her son sitting there made Claire realise that he saw her as a woman without the attributes of womanhood. Just as all other sons do, that was normal, psychologically, socially and biologically, a comfort behaviour to the advantage of all concerned, and yet it was so unfair that Claire felt the urge to box his ears in the name of all mothers. Wherever did these little surges of rage come from? Of exhaustion, anger, impatience?

After all, she wasn't normally like that. She had never been in a temper, in fact in her university days she had been mocked for her trademark composure and refusal to be rattled. Something had happened, it was the rupture that that afternoon at the Langlois had brought about in her.

She glanced in the rear mirror. Julie quickly diverted her gaze outside, to the lights. It was the same face Claire had felt moved to speak to at the Langlois. So familiar, yet so strange.

'I like Paris best after dark,' Julie said. She was sitting behind Claire. 'And when you're just driving past and it can be anything you want it to be.'

Julie's right, thought Claire. Paris is at its most beautiful at the outer edges of the night. When it begins and when it ends, that's when Paris becomes the city of our imaginations.

'That's the secret of its PR,' remarked Gilles. 'Anyone hungry, by the way?'

He was always the same: ravenous after barely twenty metres. For the six-hour journey he had packed survival rations, including a bottle of champagne to celebrate when they arrived at the Breton border on the A81, the Armoricaine, after the Bréal-sous-Vitré exit.

Then Julie spoke. Her words just came tumbling out, almost involuntarily, like tiny, whispered bombshells:

'I've never been to the sea.'

'That's tragic,' said Gilles.

'You've never told me that,' Nicolas observed.

'Why in God's name have you been deprived of the sea?' asked Gilles. He said it so indignantly that Claire couldn't help a chuckle. At the same time, she reflected that some people had indeed never been to the sea and that, when asked why, the explanation was invariably sad. Even if it wasn't the real reason, but a little white lie.

'I don't know,' Julie asserted.

You do know, thought Claire. Why don't you tell the truth? Is it too private? Or are you shying away from your own intensity again?

For a brief moment, Claire felt grateful that she'd had a son. She had witnessed too often what happened to girls. Girls who, having been large as life at the *école maternelle*, full of creativity, intellectual curiosity and contentment with themselves and their own existence, gradually diminished as they reached eleven, fourteen, eighteen. Who folded up instead of unfurling, who held back to avoid upsetting others who weren't remotely in their league.

Sons learned how to please themselves. Daughters learned how to please others.

Claire filtered onto the A6b, which was busy even at this time of night with streams of lorries going south and west.

Gilles talked about his first glimpse of the sea, a trip to Trouville, Normandy, when he was six. How the vast horizon had made him cry, for fear it would come closer and swallow everything up. It was the first time he'd heard a grand piano, played by a man in the hotel lobby, and he'd fallen in love, too, with a female lifeguard from Trouville.

And that combination of things: the open sea, the woman gazing into the distance, the piano, was 'like suddenly noticing that the world consisted of more than just home, school, the way to school, my room. I knew I was just one individual among many, and the world was old and unfathomable.'

'Yeah, and now *you're* old and unfathomable,' remarked Nicolas drily.

A burst of laughter in the car.

Nico couldn't remember his first time: they'd taken him to Brittany as a baby, and – young, green and absurdly conscientious parents that they were – smothered him in suncream, stuck a hat on him and put him under a sunshade away from the light to shield his delicate little eyes from the brightness of the sparkling water . . . and he had simply slept. So deeply. For years after that, whenever Nico couldn't sleep Claire would put on a tape she'd recorded of the sea in Brittany, and he would be enveloped in its mighty breath like a happily dreaming fish.

What he did remember, though, was the first time Claire took him by the hand and told him all about every shell, every stone, every creature buried in the sand.

'My mother couldn't understand why I was more interested in my red plastic bucket and building sandcastles than her open-air lecture on limpets and how their teeth are tougher than spider silk, and how they simply oust competitors like barnacles from the rock. I got an unsolicited free introduction to shore fishing. She lured a razor shell out of its sand bed with a salt shaker by making it think the tide was coming in – a dirty trick that's left me traumatised to this day.'

'Yes, that would explain a lot,' Julie remarked.

'Hey!' cried Nico. 'Can we drop the lady here, please?'

Gilles and Nicolas started to tell Julie about the Brittany coast, in concert, as one man. To explain the big, wide world to her.

'. . . it's never really warm enough to swim . . .'

'But the stones can be as hot as freshly baked sea urchins on toast . . .'

'. . . and denser, yes, the water feels denser and heavier than the Med. Or the Pacific. Both of them are actually quite light and thin, but the Atlantic . . .'

'. . . for yachtsmen, it's about the most dangerous area . . .'

'. . . we should take a trip to the Glénans. Ewan started running motor-boat excursions direct from Trévignon harbour last year, you can be there in twenty minutes . . .'

Nicolas and Gilles talked about the sea like a woman they admired but didn't understand in the least.

Claire glanced discreetly in the rear mirror, at her son and Julie. They hadn't yet reached the stage of the routine gesture, the familiar touch, the knowing, wordless glance between two people attuned to each other.

And there was a pulsing heat that seemed to radiate from Julie's body. An expectation. A restlessness.

A willingness to give. And a reluctantly imposed willingness to wait. This was a woman who wanted to seize life with both hands: her body, her gestures, her looks said it all.

And Nico? The opposite? For his part, he was making her wait. He hadn't the same fire, but was reflective, rarely spontaneous and not given to grand, passionate gestures.

The one who says no calls the shots.
Claire tightened her grip on the wheel.
Positional power in relationships. No joint action, whether in a partnership, family or multi-dimensional social relationship, is possible without the exercise of individual power. Weber, 1976.
Public gestures of togetherness are only appreciated and performed by one in five academics, but one in two blue-collar workers. The higher the level of education, the lower the acceptance of emotional gestures that emphasise community and downplay individuality.

How often had Claire repeated that insight to her students?

And now she was seeing it played out in real life: the reserved academic, the emotionally charged, self-repressing woman, set up like a lab experiment on the back seat of their twenty-five-year-old Mercedes. Could she imagine Julie and Nico as an elderly couple, picking their way hand in hand over the paving stones because one can no longer see and the other no longer walk properly?

'And the sheer openness takes some getting used to,' said Gilles. 'Some days there's no horizon because the sea and the sky are the same colour, and they're no longer separate blocks but merge into each other, it's as if you can swim right into the sky and . . .'

He fell silent. And then? Turn into a smile? A breeze? Disappear altogether?

Silence in the car; four answers in four minds.

Claire overtook a Dutch motorhome.

'And you, Madame? When did you first see the sea?'

'I don't remember,' said Claire.

She did. Of course. But it was no one else's business.

She put her foot down.

8

The first time Claire saw the sea was across a golden-yellow field in the summer of 1984.

It appeared so unexpectedly it made her catch her breath. They had been driving silently through unfamiliar country, in the green light of an overarching canopy of trees that scattered softly dancing shadows and patches of sunlight onto the narrow lanes. Three children on the back seat of a chestnut-coloured Citroën DS Pallas with a white roof, driven by a woman they had never met, and who had never asked to take in these abandoned by-products of a shattered existence.

But she'd done it nevertheless. Because Jeanne Le Du could be more loving than anyone else Claire had ever met before or since. On Claire's right was Anaëlle, pretty, loquacious Anaëlle. Her fifteen-year-old sister had shut her eyes and was already forming her lips into a pout, presumably to let everyone know how she felt about being exiled from Paris to Brittany.

On her left, concentrating on his chewed fingernails, was Ludovic, thirteen and a half, with a wise head on his shoulders and a gentle nature he was wont to disguise by quoting Camus and Hemingway.

Claire knew he felt ashamed, as they all did.

She, the youngest at just under eleven, sat in the middle

of the cognac leather bench seat, knees pressed close together, hands gripping the seat in front.

She couldn't take her eyes off the world outside, as the sea flashed into view and vanished again.

Through the wound-down windows she could see jumbled farms built of granite and pride, ancient fields, acres of sheep pasture, weathered stone crosses beside unmarked roads, welcome signs with enchanted place names: Coat Lan, Kerlijour, Fresq Coz Bihan. And the scent, that scent! Of warm earth, powdery-smelling flowers, hay, and milk. And beneath it, when they drove through the shadows, Claire could smell the coolness of invisible streams and tall, permanently damp grass.

The green tunnel of the road opened into a hamlet, where a tiny black-and-white sign said 'Kerlin'. They passed a farm, an open barn where cows stood in the half-light, their shapes unfamiliar to a city child, and more gardens, richly blooming gardens with low, granite-grey fishermen's cottages in them: a fairy-tale village. At a round boulder as tall as a house, the narrow road veered sharply to the right, snaked past a mighty wind-bent pine towards grassy dunes stretching almost to the sky, then forked left again and, after a narrow, ancient stone bridge, passed a red-and-white welcome sign:

Trévignon/Commune Tregon.

Here the strange land ended and infinity began.

Claire saw the ocean right up close.

The light poured down from the sky and burst into a thousand sparks.

And then something happened that Claire hadn't experienced for many years, not since the first time she went to school on her own because of her mother's fear of people and the overwhelming sky above her. Because it had already begun by then, that descent into her own silent world, which categorically excluded the vast, clamorous reality.

That had been nearly six years ago. Claire felt the faint sting of salt in her heart and, soon after, tears welling in the corner of her eyes.

Look, she wanted to say. Look. The sea.

But she said nothing: how could looking at the sea communicate to her older siblings something you could only feel, something inexpressible, too big for her mouth and her fist-sized, thumping heart?

She drank it in with a thousand eyes.

The summer sun was draining the colours from the world the more Claire looked. The beach was turning white, the waves silver, the clumps of grass on the dunes curry-yellow. The horizon traced a straight line between the sky and the water, broken by a loose chain of islands. Their outlines reminded Claire of a giant recumbent sea dragon with its head half-buried in the seabed and its spiny back populated with white farmhouses, slender lighthouse towers and coves. Only the stones remained intact: they had no colour for the sun to steal.

Jeanne Le Du's and Claire's eyes met inadvertently in the rear-view mirror that was attached to the dashboard in the Pallas.

Two pairs of eyes of such a similar pale green that both were disconcerted for a moment, unsure whether they were looking into each other's or their own.

Apart from an 'everyone in the back, *allez*,' Jeanne

Le Du hadn't spoken to them since the three Cousteaus had tumbled, exhausted and disoriented, out of the early Brittany-bound train, the Montparnasse–Quimper, onto the crumbling platform at Rosporden. The journey had been long, and they had had nothing with them but a bottle of tap water and a baguette each, unbuttered but with a scrap of ham Claire had scrounged from the Chinese family next door back in Belleville. Their neighbourhood was one of the more flatteringly named parts of Paris.

Jeanne Le Du was Claire's paternal grandmother. Anaëlle and Ludovic each had one of their own, having been born to different biological fathers. Brief encounters in their mother's fluid existence.

But none of the other grandmothers, none of the fathers, no one but the writer Jeanne Le Du had felt enough sympathy to outweigh any irritation or indifference and agreed, in response to Claire's long letter, to fetch these three helpless young people, two of whom were not even related to her, from their council flat in Paris-Belleville and offer them protection, food and shelter for a time. Until their mother was discharged from one of the Maisons Blanches, as the psychiatric institutions were known.

The author, who had achieved fame in the early '80s with her novel *The Passer-By*, lived in Finistère. And so it was that the three Cousteaus left their flat one July morning at six, each carrying a suitcase. Claire had briefed her siblings on what to pack, what was necessary and what was to be left behind. Anaëlle and Ludo had made no protest. Claire was the youngest, yet in some ways the eldest. She had understood before her siblings that their mother was regressing into a second childhood, and had stepped in to replace her as the organiser of their day-to-day lives.

Before leaving for Brittany, Claire had paid a last visit to the Gallery of Palaeontology and Comparative Anatomy in the Natural History Museum, next to the Jardins des Plantes with its tropical glasshouses. It was both refuge and hiding place for her, and she was invariably to be found on the top floor, near the fossilised ammonites.

The rocks. The bones. The timelessness. All of this had a steadying influence. The serenity of stone. Immutable. Dependable. That was how Claire wanted to be too. Calm and serene. She wanted to be like an ammonite, a nautilus, coiled around its innermost self.

Claire imagined the skeletons of these prehistoric creatures whispering to each other at night; she imagined that the ammonites were the fossilised dreams of people from long ago, and that the whole museum was really a washed-up kingdom around which Paris had one day begun to coil itself. Once, when she had shown her mother a stone in which the remains of a seahorse tail were immortalised, and asked whether humans could turn to stone too, her mother had said: 'Where do you think all the statues on the buildings come from?' For years afterwards, Claire was convinced there were eyes watching her from façades and fountains.

On the day of their departure, Claire had carefully locked and bolted the door and thrown away the key to the flat without telling Anaëlle and Ludovic. She had dropped it discreetly into a waste bin at Belleville metro station. She was the only one at the time who sensed that her mother was never coming back. She was already too deeply immersed in her own world.

Although she didn't yet have a plan, Claire was determined they shouldn't have to return to this place, to Belleville. She was nearly eleven years old, and had the impeccable logic of a child accustomed to not behaving like one, unless it was more expedient to do so.

Jeanne was first to look away, resolutely switching her gaze to the road ahead. She wore her silver hair pinned up like a young woman, and was dressed in a sand-coloured linen shirt over a ribbed men's vest, jeans and wellies.

Claire stole a glance at the back of Jeanne's neck, which was so different from her mother Leontine's: slender but straight. Tanned and strong.

The soft, delicate nape of their mother's neck had always looked as if her head was too heavy for her body, her body too heavy for her heart, her heart too heavy to breathe.

Jeanne Le Du steered the DS away from the sea and onto the sandy drive of a two-storey, sandstone-coloured house with blue shutters and pale-pink roses clinging to the rough walls. She switched off the engine.

The silence was overwhelming. There was a ping under the hot metal of the bonnet. A gust of wind gently lifted the silver-shimmering foliage of a large olive tree.

But beneath it, absolute silence.

Jeanne sat back, leaning her right elbow on the armrest. She took out a Gauloises from a silver packet in her breast pocket, lit it, and waited.

'Oh. Are we there?' asked Anaëlle sweetly.

Oh.

Yes, thought Claire. She's the perfect actress; now she's playing the sleepy, timid, don't-hurt-me doe. It was a good tactic that had certainly worked for her in Paris. And Claire knew it was something Anaëlle needed to do. She needed to be someone else, to switch roles and faces, voices and gestures, to try out a thousand different lives. She needed it just as Ludo borrowed quotes from dead writers to stop himself from clamming up altogether.

Claire knew all of this: she just didn't know how she knew.

'There? What do you mean "there"?' asked Jeanne, amused. She spoke so fast that her words seemed to swallow each other up, even more so than Claire's biology teacher.

'Well, um . . . at your house, Madame. I mean, we've arrived.'

'Arrived. Ah. Do we ever arrive?'

'*Pardon?*' said Anaëlle, looking helplessly at Claire.

'We arrive when we are dead,' said Ludovic darkly.

'Oh, good heavens! A Bambi and a Sartre. And you, child? Who are you, and do you have a pearl of wisdom to contribute too?'

'No. Not at the moment,' said Claire.

Jeanne kept a straight face. She sat smoking, and none of the children dared get out. Claire heard the chirp of a cricket. Birds began to twitter and chatter in full voice. Claire could hear her own pulse in her ears.

There it was, behind her: the sea.

She didn't dare turn around, but she could see it in the dashboard mirror. And the rocks. Boulders that had bodies and faces: she could see a baby elephant in the mirror. A rabbit with one ear. An armadillo on top of the rabbit.

'There are lots of rooms in this house,' Jeanne began in her smoke-and-coarse-salt voice; as well as speaking quickly, she had an accent that shifted the stress to the penultimate syllable. 'I don't know which ones are good enough for you, but I suggest you get out and find out for yourselves. There are only two doors I keep locked and those are the ones to my rooms. I hope you know the difference between mine and yours. Off you go then.'

Thus released, Anaëlle and Ludovic jumped out of the back of the Citroën on either side, relieved and overexcited.

Claire climbed thoughtfully out of the car, which had smelled so pleasant and strange, of cigarettes, leather and perfume.

She closed the doors her older siblings had left open.

She would find herself a mattress, a sofa or two armchairs to push together. That wasn't important. It wasn't important to her to have a room because everything she needed was out here.

She turned round and moved closer to the dazzling light.

That sparkle on the water.

All that separated her from the sea was the road, a mown wild meadow, a beach car park, and a footpath between tussocks of grass and purple globe thistles.

It was so close.

She could hear it. She could smell it.

So now she was here. In the land of enchanted place names and infinitude, of light and fossilised time.

'Armorica,' she whispered.

These rocks, immobile, powerful, as if anchored in eternity and destined to remain in place for ever, whether the Atlantic waves crashed around them, or firestorms and lava rained down on them one day, driving them to the depths of a submarine valley or, in some distant time at the end of human history, they formed the peaks of a desert massif, its summits littered with fossilised shells.

Claire had read everything there was to read about these rocks. These indestructible, eternal rocks on which Brittany rested. They had once been part of a continent in the South Pacific: Armorica. Armorica had split off from Gondwana half a billion years ago and begun to drift. It drifted northwards past Avalon, collided with Laurussia, then broke up and became submerged, after which a few fragments re-emerged from the sea in various places around the globe and became land again. They formed Greece, the Alps, Hungary, the Channel Islands of Jersey and Guernsey, and Brittany.

Wherever Armorica displaced the primordial ocean and pushed the landmasses down to the ocean floor, slate was formed – the silver-grey slate that now covered the roofs of Paris. Claire was entranced by such miracles – silent testaments to past eras in the here and now.

'Armorica,' she whispered again.

This was ancient land. Older than the Himalayas, older than Europe, older than God.

It was the beginning of the world.

Shortly before three. Gilles was asleep, and in the rearview mirror Claire could see Nico's face leaning against the window; he looked so boyish when he was dreaming. Her menfolk always fell asleep when she was at the wheel, the car a steady ship in her hands. She could see Julie's sleeping face in the mirror too.

Darkness enveloped the car, and the oncoming traffic

petered away to nothing. It was as if they were gliding through an uninhabited land. Two headlights slicing through the dark.

Claire followed the double-stitch seam of lights, her eyes stinging.

She felt the embossed leather of the steering wheel under the heel of her hand. Pea-sized bumps. Their venerable dark-blue Chubster was so familiar, an old friend that was the butt of good-natured jokes at the garage in Paris: so old-fashioned, so indestructible. They'd been driving around in it for a lifetime; under the mats were Breton sand, Dordogne soil and the ash from sly cigarettes. The headlights of the car behind drew closer. Aggressive xenon. It dazzled her, and as she reached to lower the mirror, the reflected square of light fell on Julie's face.

Her abruptly opened eyes were two big dark gleaming nail heads, the kind that are driven deep into the wood of very old doors.

They looked at each other in the mirror, unsmiling. They held each other's gaze until the tyres of the Mercedes drifted over the edge lines and rumbled over the studs.

Neither Nico nor Gilles woke up.

Claire steered the car back into lane.

9

Julie wished they could go on driving like this for ever, open-eyed, through the night. The car nosing its way steadily forward until they arrived at the strange coast. Not getting out of the car but simply waiting until the pale fingers of dawn began to reach through the blackness.

Once the sun had risen, they would open the car doors and walk through the dew-wet grass till they were so close they could hear it.

The ocean that Julie had never heard, seen or tasted.

She didn't know how she would make it through eight weeks by the sea without anyone noticing she wasn't swimming.

The only thing puzzling Julie was that, in her vision, she was sitting in the front next to Claire, right beside her, as the night melted away and the waves surged out of the darkness towards them.

And they were alone.

10

'Shh!' said the man to Claire, closing the door behind him. *Doucement*.

The moonlight conjured a torso out of the night. Hands pulled off a shirt. A mouth smiled.

Gilles lay down naked on Claire's bed.

He looked at her as if her room were an island and the night a river separating them from everything. From the past, the present, everything they had ever said to each other, or kept from each other.

He took Claire in his arms, kissed her, held her body tight, saying over and over: 'I can see you. I can see you.'

Then came the pull of reality.

No, thought Claire.

Not yet. Please. Not yet.

The room disappeared and turned into a different one, Gilles vanished and turned into a pale-blue summer dawn. The warmth of his body, whose hollows and contours she had known half her life, dissipated into a crumpled bed-sheet.

A dream. A goddamn dream.

She closed her eyes again, deliberating whether to shape the dream into a fantasy. When she thought of Gilles, and how long it was since they had felt for each other in the semi-darkness and come together again and again, she felt a pang deep in her breast. She reached for her phone.

The time display said 05.58. The weather forecast said 37.7 degrees for Paris in the afternoon, then the GPS reset the location to Trévignon and corrected it to 29 degrees. Her inbox showed nineteen new emails since 23.30. Five texts from her sister Anaëlle. One from Ludo. A shopping list for the Leclerc in Concarneau.

She kicked off the thin sheet until it landed in a heap at the foot of the narrow, unmade bed. She laid her arm across her face with the phone in her hand and breathed in the smell of her inner elbow. Her own blend of perfume, skin, woman.

Does Gilles still like my smell?

Tonight she would smell of salt.

Smell, she thought. It's always smell that determines erotic attraction. Everything else is secondary – figure, income, compliments. Desire is about smell.

Claire thought of her fellow professor Anne-Claude from the law faculty, how she had sat in Claire's office at the Institute late one afternoon, distraught and surprised by her own readiness to pour her heart out to Claire of all people. The pain that spills out into eloquence, as if the act of shaping it into words allows us to contemplate and fight it; right there among all the ammonites, books and old maps, in the middle of Claire's green sofa. Anne-Claude had always reminded Claire of precious metals and expensive jewels. Golden hair, pearly teeth, emerald eyes, bronze complexion. Constant, precious, hard and shiny.

Claire had poured Anne-Claude a double whisky from her collection of Laphroaigs. Objectively, Anne-Claude had all the physical attributes of a woman who had aligned herself perfectly with the ideal peddled by the Western media. Figure, skin, hair: a woman who turned men's heads and inspired envy in some members of her own sex (those who believed attractive women have no worries). But Anne-Claude had something else too that was rarely applauded in the media: style, goodness and an intellect that was never arrogant. She had honed her crystalline beauty, presumably in the genuine belief that it would protect her against her persistent, nagging doubts over her worthiness to be loved. The age-old mistake from which no woman is immune, not even a clever one.

Anne-Claude's husband had fallen in love, it seemed, with a woman distinctly below average by the cruel standards of these superficial yet potent evaluation mechanisms. Older, too broad in the hips, too narrow in the shoulders, unstyled hair, nondescript skin type, neither precious metal nor jewel: more like damp wood. And he had committed the careless indiscretion of telling his wife that sex with this woman had enabled him to 'find himself at last'.

Anne-Claude was stunned, hurt, helpless, incensed – for her, the loss of desirability was like 'being thrown out onto the balcony overnight while he barricades the door from inside. And suddenly I'm old, older than everyone else. I'm old and rattly inside, a broken toy, and nothing makes sense any more. It doesn't even make any difference that I accept him the way he is! His tics, his phobia about missing trains – my God, the hours we've spent waiting around at draughty stations! His anger with his mother because she didn't give him an expensive education, his insecurity over which fork to use first. I love him, I accept him, I'm not one of those women who are always trying to improve their husbands, however imperfect they are. Does even that count for nothing in the end?'

Claire had tried to explain to Anne-Claude that the brain's limbic system reacted highly individually to pheromones and scent molecules, which had nothing at all to do with external stimuli. In a way, it was a democratic distribution of erotic potential: it wasn't so much what a person looked like that mattered, but whether their specific smell triggered reactions in the other person's emotional centre, and the release of neural substrates such as craving, fear or reward prediction.

The law professor had thanked Claire with a heavy dose of irony: 'Right, I feel a whole lot better now I know there's nothing whatsoever I can do about these substrate things in his head, which this woman seems to spray around like a bargain bottle of Miss Dior. And what's more, I can feel like a true democrat! Thanks a bunch, Professor Cousteau! Is there any more whisky?' She sat for some time, drinking in silence.

'So it's all about pheromones. And what can I do about it?'

'Nothing. There's no arguing with chemistry.'

Anne-Claude stared at Claire. 'Couldn't you lie just a little bit?'

Claire shrugged. 'If you like.'

'No, no. If I want to be lied to, I can go to the lingerie store. But *found* himself? I didn't even know he'd lost himself.'

Something had inflamed and attracted Anne-Claude's husband, something that was invisible and associated with desires within him that had grown over decades. It was the same with most men who had drifted away from the core of their being the more preoccupied they became with their work, only to realise at some point that their name was the only thing left of their identity. Deficit plus opportunity equals emotional knee-jerk reaction.

But Claire refrained from such an observation.

She strained her ears. Nothing was stirring in the house, no radio, no coffee machine. Her husband, her son and Julie were asleep. The sunrise was all hers. She got up and stood naked at the window.

It was one of those exceptionally windless July mornings. The sea was awakened by the light and first turned a pale, almost white shade of blue, until the dawn began to squeeze drops of violet sky into the translucent water.

Claire opened the window quietly. She was exhausted from two hours' fitful sleep, but she loved this hour of privacy before Gilles and Nicolas were awake. It belonged to her. The oxygen-laden, iodine-rich air overwhelmed her – it was so much more satisfying to the lungs than in Paris!

The view was clear: from up here in Jeanne Le Du's old study on the first floor, Claire could see the strip of coast from Fouesnant to Beg Meil to her right, and before her the contours of the Glénan islands, dark-blue silhouettes cut out of the horizon. To her left, she looked towards Trévignon harbour, with its square, chunky green and white lighthouse. The harbour wall rose up out of the low water, pale grey at the top and grey-green at the bottom; an early-morning angler stood at the end of it casting his line. Grey and red rocks and cusps of black stone peeped out of the water: the Soldiers, the Three Siblings, and all the nameless spines, fingers, noses and horns made of granite and fossilised limpets.

Claire listened for signs of life in the house. There was still no sound. She knew every melody of Jeanne Le Du's house, which had been Claire's since Jeanne's death twenty years ago.

But to her, it was still *la maison de Jeanne*. A living thing on the threshold between land and water, so shamefully ignored over winter and spring, an organism that eventually forgot human beings and, abandoning all discretion, gave itself over to various forms of dysfunctionality. Like a cat that is left alone too long and wilfully sets about destroying its surroundings.

A three-hundred-year-old stone creature of the coast, made from coarse rocks from the quarries of the Aven, shot through with the colours of every kind of local sand. With arched window headers, blue wooden shutters, boulders in the back garden as tall as elephants' backs, that had seen the world long before the arrival of humanity and now rested under olive trees, oleanders, pines, yew and a mighty oak.

Claire reached down to her holdall and quietly piled her students' exam scripts onto the desk where Jeanne Le Du had once drafted the plot of *The Passer-By*, about a woman who gradually becomes invisible.

She looked back at the water. The smooth, inviting blue. There wasn't a soul to be seen.

She read the title of the first script that came to hand: 'The primate model: only leaders have the courage of innovation', and put it aside.

No. This wasn't the time for primates and juice carton experiments with Madagascar lemurs.

She took one of Jeanne's white shirts from the wardrobe, crept noiselessly downstairs to the cellar and changed in the dim half-light of the garage between the gardening implements, wine rack, Nicolas's old surfboard and the Vespa scooters mothballed over the winter.

Ever since she had first approached the boundless, breathing, flowing organism out there and entrusted her unsuspecting young body to it for the first time aged eleven, Claire had always worn a skin-tight, seamless black and blue shorty wetsuit that reached to her elbows and mid-thighs. Jeanne had bought her the best one money could buy. And even when she reached her teens, at the watershed between child and woman, she stuck with wetsuits. She didn't want to have to agonise over whether she was attractive enough to go swimming like Anaëlle, who spent hours studying herself in her bikini or swimsuit before venturing out of the house – something that struck Claire as a completely pointless waste of resources.

Besides, she didn't find herself attractive – never in those days and only rarely now. Either in terms of the generally accepted ideal or the way she thought of herself: she never associated beauty with her appearance, but with character traits, or silk, or her sister, or delicate states of happiness and lightness of being.

Her response to her reflection in the mirror was: well concealed. Or: tolerable. Or: not too bad today. And on very rare occasions: I like what I see.

It's as if the beauty that recognises itself only awakens with love, another injustice – or irony, because it's only when a body has been touched all over that it stops doubting whether it's beautiful enough to be touched, and begins to glow.

By the time she reached adulthood, she had grown accustomed on principle not to waste any precious time deliberating over high-cut legs, cross straps, balconettes, half-cups, one- or two-piece designs, colours or stripes. She could never read an article on the perfect bikini figure, as if the beach were a catwalk, without feeling a strong urge to chuck the magazine on the fire.

She left the house through the garage. She could feel the heat of the coming day building beneath the morning breeze.

She walked across the meadow to the beach car park of the Plage de la Baleine without turning round. The meadow had been mown, and the cut grass was dry and sharp underfoot.

And then there it was, right up close: the sea wasn't expecting her, demanded nothing of her, knew nothing about her. And she smiled.

The water lapped cold against her ankles. She registered the sharpness of broken mussel shells that cut the soft heels and balls of her feet. The clumps of tiny hard stones that formed between her toes. The way she sank into the sand, the way it was sucked back into the sea beneath her feet. A tingling sensation, like sparkling Perrier against your skin, she thought.

She waded in further, up to her calves, her knees.

So sparkling, so cold.

She stopped. Exhaled.

The wet neoprene sealed tightly to her skin.

At last, the moment the cool, lapping water reached the sensitive area: the caressing flow of the sea around her loins, the blending of two such similar elements.

Claire stood still, hands resting on her hips.

Just when the frisson had become almost too much to bear, she donned her goggles and launched herself, arms outstretched in front of her, into the cold, pale blue, translucent water.

The Atlantic always tasted saltier than she remembered, and later on she would have a shimmering crust on her skin and the tang of the sea on her lips however much she washed her face.

Sour lemon and white-wine vinegar, bitter sage, ice-cold red wine, bitter yet so strangely satisfying.

The salt you tasted after a night when you were young and danced and sweated and your sweat was kissed from your body, and afterwards you kissed those same soft, feminine lips, and later, soon afterwards on the way home, you lost something. A mouthful of ocean, that's what you are once you have found everything and lost everything.

She hadn't thought about her in a long time.

Chloé.

Claire had never told anyone about her. Not even Jeanne. Like so much that affects sixteen- or seventeen-year-olds so deeply, and that they never talk about because it's too delicate and beautiful to let it be destroyed by a profane comment or an anxious glance.

Chloé had waitressed at the Bar de Quest, now called Le Suroit, a beach bungalow with a wooden terrace, vine-covered roof and colourful lampions located at the top of the small campsite in Kersidan, now a large complex.

No adult ever strayed into the Quest after eight in the evening. Behind the bar were two Breton surfing dudes, slim young men with short dark hair, in jeans and bare feet, and waiting at the tables was a woman, also barefoot, with long dark-blonde dreadlocks and colourful harem pants, in her early to mid-thirties perhaps.

She had rings on her brown toes, and wore red, close-fitting strappy tops. On her shoulder blade was a tattoo, the infinity symbol.

No one knew where Chloé came from, just that she'd always been there, at the Quest, every summer.

In the evenings, the surfers and kitesurfers would lean against the bar with their strong, sinewy bodies and order *panachés* or the local Britt beer from Chloé.

One summer, Claire too paid the obligatory visit to the Bar de Quest. The girls from Paris, Lyon and Orléans sat on one side of the room and the lads from Paris, the Auvergne and Orléans stood on the other, playing darts and table football and drinking too much too fast.

It was a mutual eyeing-up exercise. An expectation that something might – surely! – happen in this brief summer window, at this remote end of the world, where there was nothing but sun, sea and, in the evenings, this solitary bar which they could all just about reach on foot, or on hired bikes, riding double beneath the dark midnight sky. Radio Océan played songs like 'Gold', 'Relax' and 'Enjoy the Silence'. Chloé had brown eyes with flecks of gold in them, and they glowed more intensely the more tanned her face became.

She called Claire *kened*, Breton for 'beauty', and taught her the little signals of recognition between bar-goers the world over.

And she had a special way of looking at Claire.

Like no one had ever looked at her before.

A long, searching, thoughtful look.

As if she sensed another Claire behind the ammonite, the untouched shell of her face.

At that time, Jeanne, the ocean and a fossil handbook dating back to 1897 were Claire's only companions. She had read in her palaeontology book that two people never saw the same thing in one and the same stone, and that our mental barriers often prevent us from seeing the whole truth. Thus, the ichthyosaur found by the twelve-year-old Mary Anning was long thought to be a crocodile because society refused to accept the theory that there was such a thing as extinct creatures.

If that was true, then Chloé would have made an ideal fossil collector: she could see in Claire what remained hidden to others – a being that was once alive before it turned to stone.

And one evening, after everyone had gone, the Parisians, the Lyonnais, the Orléanais, and they'd been dancing . . .

. . . Chloé took the glass from my hand. She cupped my face with her small, strong fingers and kissed my clammy temple, then she kissed me a second time. On the mouth. It was soft and warm and tasted of me and of her, and my lips were slightly parted, in surprise, or perhaps because I wanted her to kiss me without knowing it. Chloé with her dreadlocks and toe rings, her pierced tongue and tattooed shoulder blade. Chloé the free woman.

It was a wonderful, sensual kiss, her piercing just grazing my teeth.

I felt such a sense of release, of calm.

And at the same time a sense of arrival I had never felt before.

It was good to be a woman.

She kissed me. Me. Not some image she had of me, not some

harboured illusion, but me. She recognised me before I even recognised myself, and it was that person — the person I still don't know even today — that she kissed.

I felt so alive. So present in the moment.

It went no further than that one kiss.

The next summer, Chloé had vanished, and the Bar de Quest too. No one knew where she had gone. No one at any of the bars Claire scoured on the scooter, from Cap Coz near Fouesnant to Le Pouldu near Clohars-Carnoët.

Why, she didn't know. She felt diffuse longings to spend an afternoon, an evening, a night with Chloé. Alone. To talk, to listen, to immerse herself in freedom, to explore it. What should she do, what did she need to know in order to become such a free woman? And to be looked at and kissed in that way again, knowing that Chloé wasn't lying when she called her 'beautiful'. Because she recognised something that was more than hair and breasts and ankles. Something Claire would like to have found out more about.

That was the miracle of that encounter: it was as if Chloé already knew the person I could one day become.

Only she never told me in time. And I've been searching for that person ever since.

Claire reached back, drowning the memory, drowning the melancholy, immersing her head in the water as she broke into a crawl. The chill penetrated her body as she wrestled with the push and pull of the waves. Until she found her rhythm.

11

Julie got up quietly, went over to the window and opened the curtains a chink.

The pale green of the dune grasses. The velvety white of the long, curving beach. And the wavy blue expanse, breathing rhythmically between rocks and sky. Silk rippling in the wind, all the way to the horizon, shot through with glinting sunbeams.

It looked beautiful from here.

Beautiful, strange and scary.

A vast, alien, breathing thing.

She had to know how close she could get to it before she would be forced to go down, with Nicolas, beach towels, sunshade and all the other paraphernalia, and confront that thing. At the risk of having a screaming fit along the way. Or wetting herself. Fainting. Crying. Something so freaky it would ruin everything.

Julie crept out noiselessly, leaving Nicolas asleep. She wanted to breathe, she wanted to know what it was like to walk barefoot in the sand, and what her voice sounded like in that vast open space. That was how the first shipbuilders must have felt when they launched themselves into the unknown.

She felt half panicky, half greedy to do it anyway. She had read somewhere that it was female Vikings who were the pioneers. Not men. It was women who wanted more than their lot in life.

As she walked across the meadow, she began to hum quietly to calm herself: a few lines from Nina Simone.

'Feelings, feelings like I've never lost you'

Yes, there were so many adventures to be had. So much to shout about.

I want to live! I want to dance and sing, I want to feel everything there is to feel – ecstasy, pleasure, I want it all and I want it now! I don't want to fit in, to conform, to restrain myself in order to be liked!

Julie took in great mouthfuls of the sea air, gazing out at the ocean before her; it felt like lying on a strange mattress after a night of heavy drinking, with the room spinning around you. This constant, questioning, demanding motion, on and on towards an infinite horizon.

This restlessness. This burning restlessness, as the sea lost itself in a frenzy of movement and power, crashing ceaselessly onto the shore, again and again.

Julie fixed her eyes on the contours of an island with a lighthouse and stood, breathing in and out.

The ocean.

It was so . . .

Like me? Julie pondered.

And just as hard to bear: that ocean inside me, the constant rolling and questioning and wanting. Always wanting.

How was it possible to live so close to the sea, almost as if you were in it: to live with this never-ending motion, with nothing for the eye to latch on to? There would be no more protection from all the wanting and the longing. And the fear. That it would never happen.

There had been a time when she never wasted a thought

on whether she was a girl, a boy or a peacock butterfly – she just assumed life was waiting for her and she would be able to grasp it with both hands. She would experience everything it had to offer, true love, true friendship, true adventure and true peace, when she finally became a singer.

She wasn't afraid of anything.

But at eighteen I became afraid of myself.

Turning eighteen meant adulthood, and the knowledge that from now on I would bear sole responsibility for my actions.

It also meant learning not to do what she wanted. And that was what Julie was afraid of. Of finding no outlet for her true self. Of not daring. Not even to sing, or to find true love, true passion, true despair. Until she succumbed to her own faintheartedness and led a safe, mundane life like . . .

Like my mother.

Like most women she knew.

She felt a restless longing for someone or something on whom to unleash the fire inside her. She longed for blood, for adrenalin, for joie de vivre, she longed to push boundaries so that she could finally see the way ahead, she wanted colour and truth and intensity, to truly live, to be sated at last, more than sated!

But how?

Suddenly, she caught sight of the swimmer.

Ploughing through the waves with a steady crawl, pitting herself against the hungry, searching, tireless sea.

She let the water carry her, she subdued it – or rather, she simply felt no fear of it.

To feel no fear.

No fear amid all the wanting and needing.

Julie concentrated on the moving, floating dot with its pale spot of a face, the dark shoulders, the pale calves.

The swimmer gave structure to the infinite space.

Then Julie knew for certain:

It was Claire.

I only need to look at Claire to know, to almost know, who I am and who I could be.

I must learn to swim in my own ocean, thought Julie.

Instead of sinking and drowning.

Otherwise, she would never truly live, never find out what she wanted, or indeed what she was capable of; would never be someone's whole world, never feel the desire she was so desperate to experience – that mysterious, distant, promethean fire.

12

Claire kept swimming towards Fort Cigogne, the cuboid stone fort in the middle of the sea, with its distinctive lighthouse. Somewhere beyond it was the *Titanic*, and beyond that New York – albeit somewhat further to the right.

Claire swam until the waves grew calmer, smoother.

Treading water, she turned and pulled her goggles down around her neck. The Plage de la Baleine – named after the whale-shaped rock formation in the little bay – and the row of white houses that marked the village formed a perfect diorama.

This was the landscape in which every version of Claire's self was stored. To come back here was to remember. Whether she wanted to or not.

Eleven.

The beginning of a new era. Experiencing everything for the first time. Seeing the Milky Way. Spotting glowworms and hearing cicadas. Eating galettes. Swimming in the sea. Prising open mussels. Going to a *fest-noz*. Having a room of your own. Having someone cook for you. Someone who didn't just stick ten burning matches in a sugar sandwich for your birthday like Claire's mother, but baked a cake, a Breton *tarte tatin*, just for her, with caramelised apples. A summer that stretched everything out. Her thoughts. The feeling of endlessness unfurling before her: endless time, endless possibilities.

The beginning of the world.

It was that summer, too, that Claire found the fossil stone. She had been walking with Jeanne along the beaches and under the cliffs at low tide. Then the sea would deposit large pebbles on the land in wavy lines, and sometimes you could find treasures among them. Jeanne showed her how to sense the rise and fall of the tide and dig around in the sand for their supper.

And it was there, on one of the loveliest days of the summer, that she dug it up: her stone with the star pattern.

Only to lose it one day, after pursuing a long path that she was no longer sure was hers.

Fifteen.

The beginning of the years of doubt, of restlessness. Riding a motorbike in secret. Without a helmet. *Chloé.* And the summer reading list. 'A woman's freedom begins with knowledge,' Jeanne said, 'and a driving licence.' Summer at fifteen was reading, going out on the motorbike at night, talking on the phone to Anaëlle, who was living with a friend of Jeanne's in Montparnasse and preparing for a round of auditions with Parisian drama schools, and to Ludo, who planned to study journalism and was temping in a *bar-tabac* during his internship; it was quiet, cosy nights in with Jeanne, just the two of them, without her siblings, who were already making their way in the world with Jeanne's tacit financial assistance; it was reading and writing, writing and reading.

– *What do you want to do when you grow up, child?*

– Why don't you ask: what do you want to be when you grow up, Jeanne?

– You already are. It's not work that makes us what we are. Most people want to become something or 'someone'. That can be a dangerous thing. It often leads to success but not to inner peace. You need passion. Then success becomes something that's defined by you, not others. Do you see?

– I'm interested in too many things. Rocks. Geology. The ocean. Did you know that we have more detailed maps of Mars than we do of the ocean floor, Jeanne? Or ants. They live in social structures! We share the world with so many unknown creatures that we overlook but which are superior to us in many ways. Why did you become a writer?

– In order to understand my thoughts. In order to find peace. I don't know, ma poule; I've been searching for the reason for a very long time. Sometimes I think the longer we live, the closer we get to our innermost core. But we don't approach it in a straight line, it's more . . . as if we circle in on ourselves. Perhaps that's it: everyone needs a quest in life. Find something that sets you alight. Something you want to explore over and over again. For me, perhaps it was the question: why am I here? What do you find most intriguing? The ocean? The history of the world?

– Human beings. I'd like to study human beings. And why they don't explore the ocean, or why they despise animals, even the ones that are smarter than them.

– Hmm. Human beings. I fear you'll be heading for disappointment. It'll certainly while away the evenings though.

Seventeen.

What was it Jeanne said? 'The first time should be fun, it shouldn't break your heart, and it definitely shouldn't be a shamefaced gymnastic exercise. Find yourself an experienced man that you like and who will soon move on.' Claire wanted to know how someone of her inexperience could be expected to tell whether a man was experienced. And what did 'soon move on' mean – should she wait for the travelling circus? They pitched camp in a different field in Finistère every week! How could she judge the man's potential as a lover until it was too late? After some reflection, Jeanne had said: 'These are good signs: if he eats slowly. If he laughs readily and uninhibitedly. If he's at home in his own body. If his hands know how to handle flowers and animals. If he's not one of those stoics who hate to wallow in grief or joy, or who find it embarrassing to have stronger than average emotions. It's no bad thing if he's a bit rougher around the edges in that respect: an artist, an activist, a sportsman ... And it's handy if he's older. Then at least he'll have had plenty of practice.'

Nineteen.
Claire had gained her one-year scholarship to Oxford. Her tutor had taken one look at her CV and said: 'You'll have an uphill start compared with all those who have lived and breathed money, education and class since birth. You're a woman, which in academic circles is enough in itself to make you an outsider – men tend not to credit women with clear thinking. And finally you've chosen a reason-led discipline in which even smiling is regarded as a genetic defect. Are you sure you want to go through with this?'

'There's no either-or, sir. This is the only path for me. And by the way, friendliness *is* a genetic defect, at least in domesticated dogs. Hypersocial human love is classified as a behavioural disorder, caused by damage to the chromosomes GTF21 and GTF21RD1.'

How confident she had sounded back then.

And she had duly followed that path. She was brilliant, untouchable in her field. A model of self-mastery. And she did it by denying her own womanhood.

She had never had any relationships, not at university. And no friendships either. Only a lover for a few months: a gardener who worked on film sets and ate slowly. Who spent ten months out of twelve designing sets somewhere in the world with his dextrous hands. He was divorced, in his mid-thirties, and they never switched to *tu*. To sleep with a man she addressed as *vous* – even in the dim light of her room, when he was inside her and they were exchanging whispered intimacies (tender but harmless, non-committal ones) – a man who would never suggest living together: the whole thing had been a scientific experiment for Claire. She wanted to know whether physical intimacy, affection and familiarity could impair her powers of reasoning.

She didn't have to choose a life with him. Not a whole life, not even half a life. She didn't have to choose at all!

Not having to choose was the ultimate freedom.

Twenty-one – ah, twenty-one.

That was when she met Gilles. Two drops in the ocean of humanity that happened to meet and merge. After she and Gilles had moved at the end of that summer to Saint-Nicolas, the largest of the Glénan islands, settling together on the body of that stone dragon on the horizon; after she had slept with him: that was when she lost her freedom not to choose.

Here, at the beginning of the world, she had been a rescued child. Girl, pupil, free woman, student, woman, lover. Mother. Wife. Mother. Doctor. Mother. Professor.
And which was the real Claire? Which?
Claire pulled on her goggles, flipped onto her back and spread her arms, opening her hands and laying her head back in the water. She floated and drifted, imagining that the sea was washing her clean of everything.
Lecture halls, data projectors, microphones, TV appearances, Le Pen, Fillon, Macron, the world of wars, never-ending mobile notifications, reminders and calendar alerts. And that moment at the traffic lights in Saint-Germain on her way to the Sciences Po when she'd suddenly felt an overwhelming urge to get away. To climb into a car with someone who would simply nod when you told them: take me anywhere. The superhuman effort of not doing so.
Gradually, beneath her navel and deep in the core of her chilled, drifting body, a blossom of warmth unfurled. If there was such a thing as a soul, then it was pulsing there, and she could only feel it out here, in the cool sea.
She took a deep breath and dived.
Two metres down, the water changed to dark blue.
Three metres down, it was colder and blue-green.
Then she dived into the third layer, where the silence began.
The trapped air chafed in her lungs.
Claire Cousteau vanished into the ocean, that great, slow, ancient power devoid of all things human.

Until she couldn't stay down any longer.

She propelled herself upwards, pierced the barrier between water and air and emerged gasping, sucking in oxygen. The sky was so white: white sea, white land.

She had wrested something from the flow of time that went on emptying endlessly into nothingness. Something for which the rational human had no words, perhaps.

She had felt truly alive.

Now she was ready for a shower and a cup of strong coffee. She swam back serenely, clambered over mussel-covered slabs of granite and picked up the towel she'd left on a rock.

And then she saw her.

Julie.

She was wearing a shirt, cut-off jeans and white trainers, and sat with her arms tightly folded.

The nineteen-year-old's face was coloured with pain. A pain that was much older than her, born of an anguish that was so ancient and yet to her so new, and which was desperately trying to hold steady in the face of an endless horizon.

In the second before Julie noticed her, Claire looked down at her bare feet and pretended not to have seen the young woman.

The myriad gestures of everyday lying, Claire reflected: hide and seek for adults.

She didn't even know why she'd looked away. So as not to embarrass Julie? Or . . . to avoid meeting her eye.

There was something in Julie's face that reminded Claire of someone.

But who?

When Claire looked up, Julie had reverted to that bland expression and acted as if she had only just registered her presence.

'*Bonjour*, Madame,' Julie called to her politely.

You fraud, thought Claire. You fraud.

And walked past her without a word.

13

When Claire came wading out of the water, Julie's world slipped a little further out of joint.

It was the close-fitting wetsuit that blithely covered the parts of Claire's body other women put on display.

Claire in her black and blue wetsuit.

Her wet, bare face. Her strength. Her movements.

She was so . . .

Absolute.

Nothing about her was intended to please a stranger's eyes.

She lives against the tide, thought Julie.

But how, she wondered, how can a woman be so free?

14

In the sea, all you had to do was be present. No one noticed when people lay bobbing on the waves, moving their arms or legs occasionally or simply doing nothing.

On land, doing nothing was never enough. You had to rush from A to B, talk to people, answer them, have an opinion, be for or against something. And it was never Now, but always 'in a minute', 'later', 'at the earliest', 'once, yesterday, tomorrow, when I'm old, when I have time, when the children are off our hands'.

Claire had barely taken a few steps on land, and already she felt as if she were slipping back into her old skin. Her movements purposeful, her thoughts ordered.

Routine. Her refuge and foundation.

It took her less than ten minutes to diagnose the current mood of the house.

Leaving damp footprints, she switched the boiler on in the cellar and checked the oil level. There was something wrong with the gas cylinder, which was connected to the stove via obscurely routed pipes. She lifted the cylinder: it was still half full, but the igniters in the kitchen upstairs just went on clicking away stoically without the spark weaving its wreath of blue flames. Meanwhile, snails had managed to attach themselves to the front door in brown-grey family groupings, the strip of lawn on the drive leading to the basement garage was overgrown with poppies and wild oats, and the sea-facing windowpanes were sticky with salt and sand. The ants, her current personal heroes on the basis of their efficient, decentralised cooperation, had set up major supply routes through loose window joints and gaps in the frames.

Needless to say, a random remnant from last summer's provisions had been left to fester in the spare fridge in the cellar – what Gilles would call a 'long-term biological experiment': a half-eaten Normandy apple tart, now sporting an intriguing layer of fur, and a half-empty bottle of raw milk that had quietly turned to cheese.

In a moment, Claire would check the back garden to see whether Mother Nature had meant it when she'd waved them goodbye last August with a promise to outlive them all.

It was just after half-past seven. Too early. At a more respectable hour, she'd ring Padrig and ask him (or rather entreat him in girlish tones: a high-pitched voice activated the same area of the brain that prompted paternal behaviour in men) to come and help them do battle with the garden, hedge, gas and jungle. She wouldn't mention the fact that he was supposed to have seen to it long ago. Or at the latest last week, following her repeated phone calls. Claire had inherited Padrig with the house and, like the house, the former Newfoundland fisherman had a number of quirks, among them a habit of breakfasting late on brioche and red wine, preferably at the tiny bar attached to the *boulangerie* in Saint-Philibert, and scheduling outstanding chores according to a timeline known only to him. His priorities followed impenetrable rules. Important things included gazing out to sea, digging in the sand at low tide for snails, sea spiders and clams, and serving as linesman at various football matches of the local third-league teams of Rosporden, Riec-sur-Belon or Melgven. Unimportant things included taking care of houses, answering calls and using deodorant.

Lately he'd begun to send his youngest son, Ewan, instead, a grumpy man of few words.

Ewan and Nicolas were the same age, but had never become friends and retained a mutual mistrust. A Breton and a *parigot*: it was like the toxic duel between fire ants and raspberry crazy ants.

Claire went upstairs. The sea-facing window was still open. She reached for her phone to read Anaëlle's texts. A sixth had arrived in the meantime. *What do you think? I promise you'll hardly see us.*

Anaëlle wanted to come for a few days around 14 July, the national holiday, and had explained in detail in a series of texts. Not alone. But with N. Whoever N was. Claire's older sister always reduced the companions of her private life to their initials. At last count, it was a C, before that an M, and another M before that; soon she would have worked her way through the alphabet. She was a live wire, loud, direct, feisty, about to turn fifty and hating it; deep conversations made her nervous, and she could impersonate every French president. Fans, claqueurs, critics and admirers were a matter of remarkable indifference to her – another reason why Claire liked her older sister, even though she'd never been sure if the feeling was mutual. One of Anaëlle's favourite occupations was trying to enrage her younger sister, who she regarded as an icy paragon of reason. Claire had never obliged her by showing her anger or bursting into tears.

Anaëlle wasn't interested in applause – an unlikely characteristic for one of France's most famous film actresses. She couldn't give a damn about popularity: she didn't need to be loved. To her, it was more important to love, something she went about in what one of her critics once described as a 'highly eccentric fashion'. Why that was the case, he had simply no idea.

Claire felt a bright, aching drop of love roll down the inside of her chest when she thought of her older sister, but she answered with a simple: *Do come*. They ought to be able to survive a couple of days in each other's company, if not entirely unscathed.

The next text didn't come as a great surprise. Ludovic. Her brother.

Carla has filed for divorce. Will join your party.

The chances of survival were rapidly diminishing.

Ludo, now an arts journalist at *Le Monde*, and Anaëlle were, like Nicolas and Gilles, a seasoned duo – albeit a dysfunctional one. The alliance between the half-siblings could best be described as a love–hate relationship.

Claire yanked impatiently at the cord of the Venetian blind, which had jammed in its frame. Eventually, it slid down with a metallic clack, sending specks of dust dancing through the room and spilling stripes of light onto the floor.

She looked at the exam scripts. The deep, floating contentment she had felt in the sea evaporated.

She still didn't feel like working, and immersing herself again so soon in the purely abstract thoughts of the country's future behavioural biologists, political advisors on petty warfare, or indeed presidents. The ambition of most of her students at the Sciences Po was to 'cross the lawn' at the end of their degree to the ENA, France's political elite school and breeding ground of presidents and prime ministers. And thence to become part, after a grounding in philosophy, biology and law, of the intellectual arsenal of those whose decisions were fired at the *grande nation*.

Only to end up dreaming – once they had the right address, the right title on their business cards, a suitable partner and an indecent amount of political power – of being free?

Claire looked back at the scripts. She could do something else. Busy herself with chores so as to drown out all the other things that were nagging at her. Buy oysters in Kerdruc, perhaps: they would be milky or *laiteuse* now the spawning period had begun. The mussels weren't yet ripe. Unlike the lawn: that was ripe for action, ditto the shopping, the chimney sweep, the piano tuner, the hedge . . .

A thousand things to take care of, eh, Jeanne? A thousand things, and none of them important.

Exactly, child. We do a thousand things just to avoid the ones that really matter. And what are you doing in my room anyway?

Claire stood there contemplating the stripe of light, the even, regular stripe of light from the blind . . .

. . . and the dent in that even, regular pattern.

And what are you doing in my room anyway?

Two of the slats were bent.

As if someone who wasn't very tall had carefully spread them apart. In order to peep through.

Claire leaned forward and widened the gap a little more with her thumb and forefinger.

Thirty-three years, Claire. The first time you stood here was thirty-three years ago . . .

... right here, in Jeanne Le Du's study. It was against the rules, but this was the only place she could do it from.

Through the gap Claire could see the hidden part of the Plage de Trévignon. A narrow *aber*, a Breton fjord, carved out by the winter storms that sent water surging along the beach ridges from November to April, creating a deep channel.

It was only in high summer that the constantly ebbing and flowing water dried out, exposing an island in time.

The island of youth, Claire mused.

Are they there yet? Like always. Like in the old days. Like yesterday?

Warm and sheltered from the wind, in the lee of an environmentally protected sand dune covered in marram grass and purple globe thistles.

The faces changed from year to year, decade to decade.

And yet they were the same. Girls and boys on the cusp of woman- and manhood.

Adults, families and children avoided the place, this temporary peninsula in the *aber*. As if they sensed that they were too old or too young to be there.

The Beach.

That's what they called it, Claire recalled.

Right there, in that Atlantis that only emerges from the sea from June to September, is the beating heart of the summer. If you haven't been there, you haven't lived. You're missing out. Let's go to the Beach.

The girls hung out together in little groups under the dunes, the boys further towards the sea. Never too close to each other, not in the daytime, heaven forbid, that could spoil everything. There were rules on this beach, of an unspoken, tantalising kind.

The eleven-year-old Claire had studied the goings-on at this special lido from a distance. In this very spot, from this forbidden window.

One day Jeanne Le Du caught her at it.

'Do you know what they call an uninvited observer?' her grandmother demanded sternly.

Claire nodded and replied: 'Yes, a researcher. A man of science.'

Jeanne Le Du corrected her: 'Or in this case a woman of science. Be precise in your language, my child, otherwise you'll negate your own existence.'

Claire didn't understand that bit, but nodded again.

Then Jeanne came and stood next to Claire and asked softly: 'What can you see?'

'A stage without sound,' Claire whispered after a while. 'You can't hear the actors, but their bodies speak.'

'And what are they saying, child?'

'I don't know. They're waiting. But for what?'

'You'll know one day. And then another day will come when you'll forget it again.'

Jeanne Le Du had been right on the first count.

But not on the second.

It wasn't until Claire was in her teens that she was able to decipher this strange, wordless language of gestures and limbs that had appeared such a complicated yet fascinating waste of time to her as an eleven-year-old. Again and again, during her first summer, her second, third and fourth, she had made this stage turn black and white by screwing her eyes up tight until the sun made black dots dance before her eyelids, then opening them again and watching the colours gradually bleed back in.

The girls usually just lay there as if unconscious. Either face down, or on their backs, propped up on their elbows, looking out from behind sunglasses, knees drawn up, legs pressed close together. They didn't go swimming. They didn't climb on the rocks. They didn't go bodyboarding in the sea, whose glare was too dazzling in the afternoon, when the sun hung vertically over the water, to look at it directly.

Yet despite this, their bodies glowed. There was a tension in them: ropes stretched taut like the ones that moored the boats to the harbour, Claire could see that from a hundred yards away. Human ships poised and ready to cast off, but something held them fast. Who would cut them free? Who would be the wind in their sails?

As for the boys, they never stood still. In and out of the sea, on and off the rocks, back into the sea, with huge inflatable rings, on boards, or plunging in again feet first. Raucous, exuberant, restless. The young men threw frisbees, balls, sand and swearwords at each other, clowning and fooling around and creating a continuous buzz.

They were a directionless wind.

The girls looked on without stirring, from behind their dark lenses.

The boys looked too. To see whether the girls were looking.

Their eyes never met head-on.

One day, Claire had felt a sudden urge to go there herself. Things would happen. That was where life began, that was . . .

 . . . *the beginning of the world?*

The same sweet, age-old game, Claire thought to herself

now as she peered through the slats at the still-deserted patch of beach under the dunes.

Would the campfires be blazing there in the evening? Or the heady, sweet smell of joints come wafting up to the house? The laughter from the thicket of darkness, the music that always seemed to be from the '80s? And later, would it all fall quite silent, as the stardust of the Milky Way spread across the night sky and the shadows merged into each other?

'Claire? I'm going for a shower, is there any hot water yet?' asked Gilles behind her.

The blades sprang back into place as she let go and turned to face him. She suddenly felt ugly in her swimming gear, with her uneven patches of brown and wet, salt-matted hair.

Why was it that she felt increasingly unattractive, repellent almost, in the presence of her own husband?

Because he no longer made any attempt to seduce her. Or even touch her. Because a silence had entered their bodies: beneath all the words, they stood helplessly before each other. Like now. It hurt, with a searing pain, and sometimes she hated her husband for being the one who could trigger this desolation, this wretchedness in her. Had they simply grown too familiar?

Gilles stood in the doorway to her room without entering. A small thing she wouldn't even have noticed if he hadn't started doing it more frequently in the last few years: pausing on the threshold of whichever room she was in. Eventually she had begun to do the same. Their conversations had become fragmented exchanges from a distance.

'What are you doing?' he asked.

'The blinds need repairing.'

'What, now? Is there anything in the house to eat, or shall we go to the Mervent for lunch today?' he asked.

'Pistachios, anchovy-stuffed olives and Muscadet.'

'Could be worse. I'll nip over to Saint-Philibert after and fetch a baguette. Do you want a croissant? Milk, jam and . . . eggs? I can swing by the Mervent too and reserve a table for lunchtime. Or evening. On the bike.'

Oh, Gilles, thought Claire.

Dear Gilles, dearest, distant Gilles.

Of course he would swing by the Mervent on the bike. And of course he would talk to Pierre, the *maître*, tell him they were back after a year's absence, reserve a table for four, around twelve-fifteen, outside if it wasn't windy, on the terrace overlooking the harbour and the rocks that looked like faces in profile – an ideal spot for watching what were probably the most spectacular sunsets in Brittany.

And of course he would cycle over to Saint-Philibert to the *boulangerie* next to the chapel with its profusion of hydrangeas, via the scenic route, along the coast road towards the Plage de Kersidan. And call in on the way back on the woman he'd begun to sleep with occasionally a few years ago. He'd never told Claire, so presumably still hoped she didn't know.

The woman was no younger, slimmer or prettier than Claire. Probably a couple of years older, in fact. She worked at the oyster farm at the *moulin à marée*, the old tidal flour mill in Hénan, between Kerdruc and Pont-Aven. Her name was Juna.

Gilles wouldn't follow the oyster woman into her

darkened bedroom on their very first day (she was the type, Claire decided, who found it easier to let herself go when she wasn't too clearly visible).

He wasn't a hasty lover. He started slowly and solemnly and gradually built up to a crescendo. As a composer, he knew the rules of dramatic composition.

Not today. Perhaps tomorrow. Or at some point over the next eight weeks. Did you know I'd tried to get even by the way, Gilles – for the oyster woman, for the double-bass player, for the wife of the man who hired you for the comic film adaptation, and for the others whose names I don't know but who I could see you were carrying on with? Once it was one of those Parisian women, the one with the house on the other side of the peninsula and the husband who was never there – what was her name? Marie-Sophie-Delphine?

I saw them. In you: the way they changed your gestures for a few hours, the way you looked at yourself, your inward gaze, and the way you looked at me. The way you silently listed the things you like about me and why you could never stay for more than a few hours with Juna, Delphine, or Georgette-Lilu-Marie: did you know that?

I tried. To compensate. To restore the balance. So as not to tip over. Not every time, but now and again. Yes. Even with one of my lecturers. Remember him? Alexis. You couldn't bear him. We did it standing up. An absurd affair, wet panties, guilty conscience, no pleasure; I felt ashamed, not better, on the contrary, I humiliated myself. Until I found another way. And then it was no longer to get back at you for your lovers. But something else. To stop losing myself altogether.

The last time was the day I met Julie, at the hotel. I felt attractive. Do you want to know that? Right now?

'Yes,' Claire replied. 'Just after twelve? Or this evening, around half-past eight. The sun'll be going down at approximately ten-fourteen, in time for dessert.' Then, seeing the look on Gilles's face, 'What?'

'*Approximately* ten-fourteen? Nothing is ever approximate with you, Claire. You only say "approximately" to make the fact that you know the exact time slightly less scary to the rest of us. To relativise your perfection.'

'Perfection can be extremely tiresome.'

Gilles smiled from the doorway. 'No. I never find yours tiresome.'

From that point on, it would have been easy. To let go of the office chair. To cross the room, take Gilles's face in her hands, that face so familiar to her, in all its guises.

The overworked one. The happy one. The self-castigating one when he was working on a composition, or the frustrated one when no commissions came in. The loving one.

To kiss him, on his lying face, and simply overlook his lying, because that too was part of life: there were reasons for lying, it wasn't necessarily deceit or malice, it could be hunger, hunger for life, fear of life, in which case you would eventually stop lying once your hunger was satisfied and there was no more fear.

To close the door. To say to him: 'You can ring Pierre and reserve the table . . . for tomorrow,' and pull him down onto the bed with her. Onto the bare mattress, right there amid the stripes of light and shadow.

She tried to let go of the chair.

She couldn't do it.

She looked at her fingers. Her hands were fossilised razor-shells, fused to the wood. What had happened to her body? This stony face, these hands?

She wanted to say: 'Shut the door and come here,' but instead her mouth formed the words: 'Anaëlle and Ludo are coming sometime around the fourteenth.'

'*Bon*, fine. I'm going for a shower,' said Gilles. Then he turned right, down the passageway, and by the time Claire had finally reached the threshold of her room and crossed it in his wake, the bathroom door was already closing behind him.

Knock, Claire. Just a small gesture, that's all it takes to pull down an entire world. Or rebuild it. Simply reaching for his hand, nodding. Knocking, for God's sake.

But what if he's just unzipping his flies and already thinking as he does so of the hour to come?

With that woman. Who can only make love in the dark.

He's already thinking ahead to that moment. Showering, a subtle splash of aftershave, not too obvious, not his best shirt. Getting on his bike, cycling the three minutes to the Mervent, then onwards, through a front garden with blue hydrangeas, past a weathered Breton stone bench with a grotesque sculpture on it, an idiotic blue frog or a chirping bronze bird – yes, this other woman likes grotesque sculptures from Leclerc.

Claire looked at the closed bathroom door.

From the main bedroom next to her came a small, half-suppressed sigh.

'Don't,' a voice whispered, 'they're . . . *next door!*'

Then the charged silence of two people trying to sleep with each other without making a noise.

Claire heard the shower start up, the swish of the shower curtain along the rail, the sound of the water, changing pitch as it ran over Gilles's body.

His body. His familiar, distant body. Such a vibrant,

intelligent man. He didn't lie out of meanness. He lied to avoid hurting her with the truth. He lied because he didn't want it to end over a woman with frog statues in the garden.

She knew that. Knowledge was the basis for survival.
What's your special skill?
Understanding others.
Oh dear, poor you.
Claire fixed her eyes on the exam scripts.
Listened.
Nico's breathing.
Julie's inaudibility.
She had to get out of here.
She would take the scripts downstairs with her. Fish the old coffee beans out of the Italian machine and replenish it. Switch on France Culture and turn it up loud.

Disappear into her own mind.

And later fix the blind – no, best buy a new one from Mr Bricolage in Concarneau, a solid one. A fabric one. In black. Right away.

15

Nico knelt between Julie's legs.

'Don't . . . they're next door!'

Or rather, right outside.

Or rather just her. Claire.

She despises me, thought Julie. This woman with her green eyes. Her careful, neat appearance, her self-control. Cool water, that's what she was, yes, an intellectual, a rock of a woman, and that gaze that could reach right inside Julie and see everything. The all-knowing *professeure*: there was probably nothing that could surprise such a woman.

How close Julie had felt to Claire, back at the hotel. How familiar. As if she knew what Claire was looking for.

Claire's face in the hotel, and as she came out of the sea – it was the same face. It was so beautiful.

And now: how strange and unfamiliar. Julie couldn't work it out.

She wanted to disappear in Nico's embrace. To hide, rest, escape: into fantasy, into soft, gliding warmth. His warmth.

But she couldn't. Not like this. It was OK when they'd been smoking pot. Or drinking, something too strong out of tiny glasses, and too fast. Then it didn't matter what she looked like, whether she was sexy enough. Then, sex was the perfect escape.

But come on, Beauchamp: where are you going to get marijuana in a place like this?

Footsteps passed their room and, soon after, hurried down the stairs.

'Can you turn over?' whispered Nico.

Why don't you say: turn over. Don't ask. When you ask . . . there's no passion.

God, am I stupid.

Julie obliged. She spread her arms and raised her buttocks slightly. Closed her eyes.

Let Nicolas get on with it. He slid his hand under her pelvis, stroking it with a circular motion. Then stopped, to concentrate on his own movements. She tried to extract some pleasure from the moment, but it was no good, her thoughts drifted off, seeking other images, searching and returning.

And yet.

And yet.

Where was it, that melting, all-engulfing feeling of self-annihilation, of wholeness?

Faire l'amour.

Being one with another body. A man who knows the darkness that makes the light all the brighter.

The darkness in me, the fire he longs to burn up in, lose himself in, where we spare each other nothing . . . and I am no longer distant from myself. Distant from you.

Her thoughts veered off again, then reconverged. She was no longer here with Nicolas. She was searching, picking out images.

Nicolas's father's laugh, the back of his neck, the look in his eyes.

Claire, in the hotel. Her face, wet from the water, so absolute.

Claire's steady gaze inside the dark car, in those few seconds when the two of them were alone in the world.

If Claire could see her now.

Something contracted inside her, and she felt a sense of shame. The shame was warm and liquid, and she came in slow, steady waves, fighting back the tears and biting her hand.

Shortly afterwards, she stood at the window. Nicolas lay on his front, asleep.

She watched Claire get into the Mercedes.

She was wearing jeans and a white shirt.

Clear, deliberate movements.

She didn't look up.

Why should she?

Julie clasped the fossil she had placed on the windowsill. She'd found it a while back at the Langlois; it looked like a heart-shaped pebble.

She pulled on her shirt and shorts and left the room.

It was often like this: this urge to be alone after Nico had been inside her.

How strange that the magic she felt in his presence faded when they made love.

But it was as if the two of them didn't share the same hunger. Or not for the same thing.

Julie wandered barefoot through the house; it was full of light and warmth. She crossed the high-ceilinged, open-plan ground floor room and opened the door leading to the garden.

In front of the kitchen was a stone terrace surrounded

by a natural stone parapet along which candle jars had been placed. The large table was an old blue door panel and the benches on either side were made from two halves of a tree trunk. As if people had been eating here for a hundred years, with the morning sun on their faces.

The stones were warm under Julie's feet.

The air smelled of roses, grass and salt. The light danced on the ground and in the tall, wind-bent trees. Between the trees lay large, round, velvety gold boulders, straight out of a fairy tale. Hydrangeas, wisteria, oleander. A cocoon. Julie breathed in the scent and the silence.

She lifted her hands and undid her shirt, one button at a time.

Closed her eyes. Exposed her bare breast to the sun.

There was nothing about this gentle, caressing warmth that disconnected her from herself or made her feel ugly. The sun caressed her and made her feel beautiful. Like in the old days, when she was a child. And free. When life awaited her in all its vastness.

She had gone topless all through the summer. She hadn't worried about not being beautiful: beauty wasn't something you could see but something you felt, and the sun on her skin felt beautiful. Other beautiful things were running until she worked up a sweat and had to pause for breath, or singing to her little brother Franck until he eventually dropped off to sleep.

The warmth penetrated her skin, her muscles, right down to her blood, and dark-red dots pulsed behind her eyelids. This was a peace that listened.

Julie sang. Soundlessly, inwardly: Nina Simone's voice and her own dancing a duet in her head.

I wish I knew how it would feel to be free

There were so many things she should say. But couldn't. To Nicolas. To herself. To the whole world. And to Claire. How did it feel to achieve freedom, really and truly? And weren't the heaviest shackles the ones she placed on herself – out of cowardice, ignorance, shame? She burst into tears, a short, sharp outburst that had been her relief valve since her schooldays, when she would slip off to the toilets at break-times to release the pressure inside her, the pressure of everything and nothing, the pressure of fear – of herself, of acting and not acting.

As she wiped her eyes with her shirt tail and turned to go back to the kitchen door over the warm dry smooth stones that gently kissed her feet, she found herself suddenly face to face with him.

Gilles. His dark, wet hair. 'What's up, why are you crying?' he asked. His hands left off from buttoning up his shirt, leaving the top one undone, and spread into the open-arm gesture fathers automatically extended towards a sobbing child, his face full of concern; he took a step towards Julie, and was suddenly very close.

He smelled freshly showered, and radiated heat, patience and an aura of unshakeable calm.

His proximity was liberating.

Yes. As if the desolation within her was shifting and receding the closer he came.

She took a deep breath.

And dived.

'I'd like to tell you, because I like you, you make it easy, even though I don't know you, or perhaps precisely because I don't, and for other reasons I can't tell you, and look: I've already started, and I don't even know what I'm going to say next, and how much of it is and isn't true, and perhaps I'll be lying to you, or I won't be able to stop.'

His arms dropped to his sides and he stood perfectly still. As if unfazed by her tears, her words, or this far too intimate moment.

He simply waited it out.

Julie looked him in the eye.

I want to live. I want my body to ache with arousal and pleasure. I want to feel myself, Gilles, do you understand? I want to feel myself in order to know who I am. I dream of a thousand heartaches I want to experience. But there's only me, and I'm not enough to fill my own shoes. Do you understand?

He nodded.

Two comrades, she thought.

The moment wore on.

The boundary came closer.

Eventually Gilles raised his hands and slowly fastened the buttons of her shirt, without touching her skin, and without taking his eyes off her.

16

'Let's go for a spin,' he said, after fastening the last button.
'Where to?'

Gilles smiled. 'Nowhere in particular. That's the whole point.'

In the cellar, he plucked the cobwebs from the blue Vespa's mirrors, swept the ants off the seat, handed Julie a helmet with a visor and wheeled the scooter out onto the drive, where the tall grass was peppered with flower spikes and alive with dark butterflies.

Gilles had to kick-start the Piaggio, but the engine finally sprang into life and he climbed on, shuffled forwards and looked expectantly at Julie.

'Or would *you* rather drive?'

'I can't.'

'Not yet. But you will by the end of the week.'

He pulled on his black helmet.

She climbed on behind.

Was all this wrong?

Was it absolutely the right thing?

After a moment's hesitation, she gripped Gilles's powerful shoulders as he steered the Italian machine down the drive, braking at the bottom. The narrow road was clear; a man was running bare-chested along the coast path, and in the distance white sailing boats balanced on the straight line of the horizon.

'Left or right? You give the signals. Quick.'
She pointed to the left.
He put his foot down.

At the T-junction he slowed down. Julie raised her right hand.

They took the route towards the harbour. The first stretch was like a rollercoaster: uphill, downhill, round a sharp right bend and uphill again. They passed thatched houses – '*Chaumières!*' Gilles called over his shoulder – whitewashed cottages with blue shutters, and tiny coves framed by granite rocks resembling giant animals and faces.

At the first roundabout, Gilles stopped the Vespa by the roadside.

'*Voilà*: downtown Trévignon.' He pointed to a *crêperie* in a plain white corner house with three or four outside tables, a bar opposite consisting of a food truck complete with Langnese sunshade and plastic chairs, a slightly larger café in a pink building with a twenty-metre-long window front, a second bar, no bigger than a living room, and a restaurant in a yellow building with a terrace.

And all the houses looked out across the ocean through a thousand open eyes.

'You wouldn't believe it, but there's not a parking space to be had here from mid-July onwards.'

'I guess all the Parisians are here and bring their parking problems with them?'

'Exactly.'

They looked down over Trévignon harbour, where two men in long blue plastic aprons were carrying blue and white plastic vats from a boat to a roofed shelter. White boats with helm stations bobbed about in the harbour basin; a green and white lighthouse clung fast to massive round boulders.

'We can buy some fish later. Or mussels,' said Gilles. 'Do you like mussels?'

'No idea!' she called back to him.

The road veered to the left, away from the harbour. Half a kilometre ahead lay a peninsula. A hand reaching into the sea, made up of land and rocks with a castle on top. No trees or shrubs around it, just tussocks of grass. Scottish, thought Julie, a fort out of *Game of Thrones*, with a tower, stone walls and a high, locked gate, exposed on three sides to the wind and waves.

She pointed straight ahead.

Gilles accelerated, and Julie felt her head jerk back. She held on tighter to Gilles as they hugged the gently curving coast, speeding past stones, beaches, gorse, dunes and waves.

The energy of the wind, her legs pressed against the powerful, throbbing machine, the warm sun and the cool airstream – it felt good, so good.

The sea came into view intermittently, a paler blue on this side of the coast, along with islands and long, sweeping beaches whose names she didn't yet know.

The Corniche took them out of Trévignon, past properties with tall, wind-battered fir, yew and pine trees; the houses grew sparser as the village petered out into the dense greenery. They rode between sand-dunes and field margins covered in brambles.

Julie looked out at the endless expanse of the ocean: it felt as if, were she to follow the lines of the horizon, she would be able to detect the natural curvature of the earth.

After Kersidan beach, they passed through a long, strung-out village where a pack of racing cyclists clad in bright Lycra came towards them, chattering as they went. Gilles raised his hand and the men returned the greeting. The scooter climbed a hill, then the road fell away rapidly, opening up another thrilling view of the sea as it rolled in long waves onto a beach.

After Raguénez, Gilles followed Julie's signals, turning left and right, plunging into the hinterland, veering off at sharp forks in the road and weathered stone crosses, passing low-built, centuries-old chapels overgrown with purple and sky-blue hydrangeas. Granite houses, *cabanes*, *maisons de maître*, old farms converted into holiday *gîtes*, interspersed with the odd neo-Breton house, and even smaller roads whose tiny signs bore place names that invariably began with 'Ker': Kerdavid, Kerambail, Kerascoët.

It felt like riding through a landscape that had always been twenty or thirty years behind the times and had one day decided to simply stand still. The villages, cliffs and roads appeared to Julie like something out of an old film or a quaintly penned poem: this landscape was a ballad of salty stones, wild trees, blueness and wind.

When she signalled left again, towards Hénan, after a zigzag tour past the Anse de Rospico fjord that cut deep into the land, through fields and paddocks, past fruit farms and dilapidated manor houses, Gilles stopped by the roadside.

'We could go to Kerdruc instead, to buy some mussels at the Cabane aux Coquillages!' he called over his shoulder.

'Or to Hénan first, and then on to Kerdruc and the Cabane?' suggested Julie.

Gilles hesitated. Then he nodded and turned left onto an even narrower road that wove its way dreamily between grass embankments, beneath arched treetops and past natural stone houses that dozed quietly behind old, moss-covered boulders, before delving into a dense, silent forest.

It smelled different here. Still of the sea, but coupled with the scent of warm earth, sun-warmed leaves, moss and cool shade. The daylight was dimmed by the leafy canopy: like being immersed in a cool, watery-green dream, Julie pondered.

The dark, mysterious forest opened onto a dam bridge between a lake and the Aven riverbed that looked to Julie as if it was from a forgotten century. At the end of it was a long, low wooden hut, and just as Julie and Gilles were riding across, over the bumpy cobbles, a woman came out and erected a white A-board.

She looked up; Julie could see half of her face over Gilles's shoulder.

The woman raised her hand in surprise and pleasure. '*Demat!*' she called, and Gilles slowed down, turned the Vespa round and rode back, right up close to the dark wooden cabin. Behind the building, a gutted wooden boat lay wearily on its side on the riverbed.

Gilles greeted the woman without switching off the engine or removing his helmet. '*Salut*, Juna.'

'So you're back,' she said. 'Since when?'

'Only just – we arrived about four or five hours ago.'

'And . . .?' Juna looked at Julie.

Julie felt Gilles's body stiffen under her hands. He turned off the ignition switch and Julie dismounted somewhat shakily. He rested the scooter on its stand and took off his helmet.

'*Salut,*' he said again and bent forward to give Juna two *bises* on the cheeks. Juna placed her hand on his bare forearm as he did so.

'Juna, this is Julie. Nicolas's girlfriend.'

They exchanged *bises*, Juna's eyes still fixed on Gilles.

'Do you want some oysters? You've come at the right time, most of them are no longer milky, perhaps one in ten, and the mussels are the perfect size.'

Julie followed Gilles and Juna at a distance into the rustic oyster bar. In a pool of bubbling freshwater were crates of oysters and shellfish Julie had never seen before – *palourdes,* razor clams – while lobsters and edible crabs floated in a tall tank, their arms, legs and claws gently waving.

'There are four of you . . . six kilos?'

Gilles nodded, and Juna scooped gleaming black mussels out of the water and into bags, placing them on the old-fashioned hanging scales. The mussels clacked against each other like brittle pebbles.

'And oysters, three dozen? Take the *creuses,* the small ones, size three or four, the *plates* aren't ready yet.' Juna picked up two oysters at a time and tapped them briefly against each other before putting them in another bag.

Gilles paid a ludicrously low price. How much was it – 45 cents per oyster? How come they cost five or six euros each in Paris?

Julie observed Gilles. He was . . . different, somehow. More inhibited.

He and Juna said goodbye and, spotting a small knife, Gilles asked: 'Can I borrow that?'

Juna nodded. 'See you soon?' It was more a question than a statement.

'Definitely,' Gilles answered. Brightly. With conviction.

Not, Julie silently added. *Definitely not, by the sound of it.*

Gilles stowed the shellfish under the folding seat of the scooter.

They took the same route back, Gilles pointing to the left or right every now and again and explaining something Julie only half caught: 'The castle's up for sale . . . she has three children, but none of them want to run it . . . night festivals soon . . . and in the *pardon* chapel, when everyone awaits the returnee . . . only no one knows who it's meant to be . . . canoeing off the cliffs at Port Manec'h . . .'

This time Julie didn't hold on to him, but gripped the brackets on either side of the back seat instead. He was talking a lot, and she realised why.

That was why Gilles didn't want to go to Hénan. Because of Juna. He didn't want to buy the shellfish from her, but in Kerdruc.

Shortly before Trémorvézen, they overtook a line of children on brown and white ponies, their holiday faces frowning with concentration as the ponies' hoofs clattered rhythmically on the tarmac.

'Can we stop for a moment?' Julie asked, leaning forward.

Gilles steered towards the chapel; it was surrounded by a low wall with rampant hydrangea bushes on all sides.

It was warmer and less windy than on the coast, Julie noticed as she sat on the low, weathered stone wall feeling the sun on her face.

There was a hum in her ears, and it was a while before she realised that it was the silence. The place was so still.

The stillness sat deep in the walls of the chapel, it was in the earth, the oak trees, the fields and the prairie willows.

Julie had never heard such an eerie nothingness all around her.

Gilles took a handful of oysters from the blue bag and sat down next to her with Juna's knife.

Slowly and carefully, he prised open the first shell, severed the muscle with the knife and handed it to Julie.

She looked inside. Water, a whitish-grey consistency, a shiny, mother-of-pearl lining.

'There are chewers and slurpers,' he said.

Julie raised the narrow end of the oyster to her lips. She had seen people eat oysters before, but her parents had had neither the money nor the inclination to try them. Oysters, lobsters, crabs piled high – that kind of thing wasn't for the likes of them. It was for others with the time and easy circumstances to eat for pleasure, not just to fill their bellies.

Did it make her feel decadent?

No. Just intoxicated by the sheer mass of new experiences compressed into just a few minutes.

First, she tasted the water. It was pure, and incredibly fresh. Then the oyster flesh slid into her mouth, and it was . . .

Silky. Firm. Like a kissing tongue, or . . .

She began to chew tentatively, and an unfamiliar taste spread around her mouth.

It was a subtle, fizzy, slightly iodine taste, fresher than the freshest sushi, which she'd eaten twice at Galeries Lafayette.

'Holy moly shit!' The words slipped out spontaneously.

Gilles laughed, freely and heartily. She joined in. And there they sat, on a wall in front of an old village church nestled in the deep grass, at the end of the world, laughing.

Everything dissolved in the laughter. The anxiety, the unreal night in the car, her uptightness about Nicolas, about everything.

'Better?' Gilles asked after a while.

Julie nodded.

'Thank you,' she said softly.

'Never say thank you to me.'

'Shame. I could get used to it.'

They looked at each other and smiled.

It's so easy with him, thought Julie. And yet . . . Juna.

She wasn't angry. Nor was she sad. It was a third feeling, something to do with Claire and Gilles, but what?

Gilles interrupted her silent, fleeting thoughts: 'I could take this opportunity to say: Julie, if you don't know what to do next, the best thing is to just set off and see where your journey takes you. That goes for most things in life.'

'But fortunately you won't.'

'No. It'd come across as a terrible bit of mansplaining.'

He slipped into the familiar *tu*, implicitly inviting her to follow suit, naturally and easily, without making a ceremony of it.

'Did you do that with Claire too?' Julie asked suddenly.

'What?'

'Take her on a mystery tour. Just sweeping her up from her desk and . . . into the sunset.'

He picked up the next oyster, delicately inserted the knife at the side and rotated the shell; Julie could see his upper arm muscles tightening under his shirt. Then he split the shell open carefully and placed both halves on the wall, before reaching for another and opening it.

'Claire isn't one for mystery tours. She always has to have a goal. Always knows what's necessary and what isn't. That goes for everything from child-rearing to work, and it . . . doesn't leave much room for spontaneity.'

He rubbed his face. Perhaps tiredness had made him speak unguardedly.

'From the moment I first saw her I knew she was someone I'd never measure up to. She's still the most interesting woman I've ever known. And I sometimes wonder whether she finds me half as interesting.'

And is that why you spend time with Juna? Julie wanted to ask.

What is it, the thing with Juna? How old is she: late forties? Yes, she's not unappealing, blue eyes, freckles, tanned, a woman who doesn't instantly dissect you with a glance; she fancies you, but you don't feel the same about her, or not any more, right? Hey, Gilles, I'm talking to you! But you can't hear me, of course.

What are you doing, you and Claire? What are you doing in Paris, and why do you bring it with you here, huh?

You give me this proud tour of the landscape, as if it was yours. OK, it is yours. And do you know what mine is? Mine is Saint-Denis. It's the metro just before midnight, the dealers just before the last night trains, the Langlois, every room from top to bottom, loving couples, stressed couples, gay couples, lesbian couples, lonely people, people who just want to catch up on their sleep. It's a Paris far removed from your world: the underbelly of Paris, with the cleaners and the waiters and all the people who don't know what to do with their lives either. Meanwhile you're at the top of the pile, and what are you doing? And Juna? And what about Claire? What is she doing? What makes her so hard: is it you? And why, what reason do you have? Gilles, listen to me, what reason do you have? You're a father, you're a lover, you're Claire's husband, but you're not really like that, you're not a cheat, it's just a cry for help, that's why you're looking at me like that, and there I was thinking you knew everything. You don't know any more than me, do you?

Nowhere in particular, is that your trick?

'It's worth a try,' she said. 'Going for a spin. With her.'

He was silent.

There were a hundred things they could talk about, thought Julie. Brittany, the chapel, the summer, oysters and mussels and films and music.

But she couldn't: all she could think of was how the air between Gilles and Juna had gradually become statically charged.

She imagined telling Claire. *Your husband's sleeping with the woman from the oyster shack.* Then dismissed it immediately.

And yet.

Claire.

She looked at Gilles through Claire's sea-wet face; she remembered Juna and saw Claire's shoulders; she looked down at her hands and saw Gilles and Claire holding hands. She looked at Gilles and saw Nicolas in him. If she married Nicolas, she would see Gilles and Claire all the time.

The thought of Claire finding her ridiculous made her sick to her stomach.

Beauchamp. What are you playing at?
What are you playing at, for God's sake?
You have a special talent for doing nothing.
Why not simply go on developing it?

'*Tiens.* Is there a baker here too?' Julie asked hoarsely.

'And I think I could do with a bit more sleep . . . it was such a short night.'

'In Saint-Philibert. The best *baguette de campagne*. Nothing beats going back to bed after a good breakfast when it's sunny outside and you know there's no rush to do anything. *On y va?*'

17

Her fourth night descended as slowly over Trévignon as the previous ones. This evening the sky wasn't suffused with gold, but began with a pale pink flush, lending a hint of cherry to the sea and blending the greys into dozens of shades of red at its outer edges. At the front, seaward side of the house, a last remnant of daylight clung to the horizon. Four or five youngsters were sitting on the rocks gazing quietly and reverently out to sea. The beaches were empty now, at the end of a blisteringly hot summer's day.

At the back, where the garden was overshadowed by the tall house and dense treetops, it was already dark. Crickets were chirping, and the flickering candles on the stone wall by the kitchen were burning low. The shadows between the trees, bushes and stones were lengthening and deepening.

The table on the terrace hadn't yet been cleared; they had dined on *moules à la crème* and oysters washed down with wine – a bottle of Bourgogne Aligoté with the oysters, followed by a bottle of Quincy.

In the mornings, Gilles fetched the breakfast baguette and pains au chocolat and shopped for ingredients at one of the markets. In the evenings, he cooked; the menu would soon repeat. Mussels in white-wine sauce and cream. Palourdes au gratin or with capellini and spicy arrabiata. Warm *chèvre* with figs, pears and rosemary on a bed of salad. Watermelon with mint and sheep's cheese.

Entrecôte cooked on the Weber grill and served with slices of fluffy white bread rubbed with oil and garlic and toasted alongside, together with soft goat's cheese and peppery sweet tomatoes. Fresh sea bream or perch from the harbour, with oil and lemon and rocket from the wild garden behind the house. And then it would go round again. No one felt like eating very much.

Claire watched her son and Julie sharing a piece of young Tomme cheese.

The sun had given their skin a gentle glow, warmed their bodies, softened and rounded their gestures, kindled a new light in their eyes.

Nicolas and Julie had been spending a few hours on *that* beach every day. Whenever Claire looked up from her term papers and books on collective intelligence to glance out of the window, Julie would be lying on the hot sand while Nicolas swam in the cool water.

Every time.

Morning or afternoon.

Sometimes Julie would be reading. Sometimes she appeared to be asleep, under the sunshade. Sometimes she would be chatting to some other young women, and once she was in conversation with someone squatting in front of her in the sand – Ewan, Padrig's eternally grumpy son. A brown, muscular young man. Julie was sitting up straight and her gestures were larger. She was laughing; Ewan too. He must save his bad humour for special occasions.

Nicolas had emerged remarkably quickly from the waves – which Ewan had taken as his cue to depart, though not too hurriedly, of course – and had spent the rest of their time on the beach next to Julie, stoical as an empty crab shell.

Are you trifling with my son, Julie? Or just with your life?

Anticipation. Jealousy. Seduction. The crossing of boundaries. An open-air cage. The same biotope, the same stage, the same dialogues between bodies, Claire reflected. Just different actors each time. They are waiting. Waiting for life to begin.

She was a partial observer.

She was on Nicolas's side. As a mother.

And on Julie's. As a woman.

The wine was working its way around Claire's body.

She thought of the two plastic bags at the bottom of the yellow sack with the paper and recycling waste she had carried to the municipal skip today. The bags were right at the bottom, otherwise she wouldn't have noticed them. They were from the Huîterie Hénan. Gilles had been to see Juna. She looked at her husband. He treated Julie with slightly more than perfect courtesy, topping up her glass, following her with his eyes – often with a serious expression, as if searching for something in her, pondering something.

Was he lusting after her?

The two of them got on very easily, and Julie had tempered her active way of listening to him. She was more relaxed, less constrained. Gilles had given her the confidence to stop trying to please him all the time, and to simply be herself.

We were in that place once too, where Julie and Nico are now.

Remember, Gilles? At that point where life holds so many possibilities. At nineteen or twenty.

Claire wished she could tell Julie to go away. Leave this house, she wanted to say, leave this place, spend the next ten or twenty years finding out what you want, but don't get stuck with the first man who knows how to kiss you properly.

Sometimes I wish Gilles would perish in a train accident, and other days I wish I could dig myself out of my own fossilised existence. But love ... or what we believe to be love, is so much more potent when you're young. You know nothing of what you will go on to do to each other in the name of love: how you'll impede each other; how you'll inspire each other. Or how you'll suffer, and the suffering will give you wings.

'Coming for a swim?' Nicolas asked Julie this time.

Julie shook her head. Just like yesterday, and the day before, and the first evening. She was either tired, or wanted to clear the things away, or chat to her mother on WhatsApp.

Nicolas's disappointment left a vertical crease on his forehead which Claire had never seen before.

Gilles emerged from the cellar carrying four Grimbergen beers. 'Let's go!'

'You can follow us down,' said Nico in a low voice.

Gilles and Nicolas walked barefoot across the meadow and down to the water's edge at Baleine beach. It was a regular evening ritual: they would take a Breton or Belgian beer (or two) with them, paddle in the sea up to their calves and watch the light gradually drown in the water. Breathing more slowly. Father and son. *Thinking men's thoughts, who knows?*

Julie had disappeared inside the house.

Claire stepped out into the darkness.

The Silent Centre of the World. That's what Jeanne used to call the stone at the end of the big garden. Behind the still, old yew trees, the slender birches, the stout oak, the rustling olive trees. The oldest of all granite stones, worn smooth and round, a proud, recumbent animal with its head and tail buried under the ground and only its back exposed to the present.

There was something special about the Silent Centre of the World: no artificial light fell on the soft grassy hollow behind it. No streetlamps, no light from the surrounding houses, no headlight beams from passing cars, not even the light from Jeanne's house. It was completely dark, a place where the night thickened into black velvet.

Jeanne often used to sit here. Then later with Claire, and later still it was just Claire, always alone.

How many places were there in the world that a person could come back to, that knew them as a child and later on as an adult with a past? The same, unchanging bench, the same, unchanging stone. What else endured so long, remaining unaltered for a whole human lifetime and beyond?

Claire sat down in the soft grass by the Silent Centre of the World; it yielded gently beneath her, a cushion of earth and moss. She leaned back and the great stone felt pleasantly warm on the back of her head.

And there she rested.

While searching in Jeanne's desk for a pen, she had reached right to the back of a drawer and found a Comet lighter and a packet of Gauloises: an old blue one, not one of the new black ones that had been defaced with morbid images. Claire hadn't smoked since her pregnancy.

She lit the tobacco and it crackled faintly. She took a tentative drag. The smoke filled and satisfied her.

God! It was like coming home.

She looked up at the sky and exhaled through her open mouth. This overarching, dark-black canopy. The Milky Way. When city dwellers saw it for the first time, they felt compelled to clean their glasses, or confused the galaxy with thin wisps of cloud. But that milky veil was in fact the spiral nebulae of countless thousands of stars, the home of the universe.

Was Nicolas happy? She hoped so. She wished him happiness, and courage too. That he should feel life unfolding endlessly before him like a mighty river, and carry that feeling of infinite possibility within him as long as possible.

But is that really happiness?

And Julie? Is she happy with my son?

She knew Nicolas. He had developed a view of the world in which things, events, people and emotions were divided into the categories of 'important' and 'unimportant'. He was studying law and wanted to specialise in human rights law – he was interested in the big questions of life, and had little time for the smaller details or for grand passions. And Julie? Would she give up the small things, would she fold back into herself for his sake?

The longer Claire looked, the more stars emerged from the deep black. Diamonds of different brightnesses scattered across velvet, winking away.

Yes, *winking*, that was the word.

What did the pain of a single human matter amid the vastness of the universe?

'May I?' a voice suddenly whispered above her.

Claire felt a tiny tug in her breast, almost too small to

be perceptible. She looked up at Julie, who had pulled on a thin sweater and was holding two glasses of wine.

'Be my guest,' Claire whispered back.

Julie sat down next to her. Close up, Claire could smell Julie's scent. Sun-warmed skin, a faint trace of sun cream: apricot. Washed hair.

Julie rested her head against the stone. Crickets were singing, bats swooping noiselessly under the treetops.

She handed Claire a glass.

'You smoke?' she asked softly.

'No.'

'Me neither.'

They sat in silence. Claire smoked and, after a few drags, passed the cigarette to Julie without looking at her. Julie took it from her fingers. While Julie puffed on the Gauloises, Claire took a sip of Quincy and said, more calmly than she felt, and without taking her eyes off the sky:

'Are you happy?'

Julie released the smoke in a slow stream.

'Yes,' she said eventually. 'Right now I am, yes.'

Claire couldn't see Julie's face. Which Julie was she talking to? The Julie from the Langlois? The gleeful, laughing Julie who had ridden her first few metres on the Vespa under Gilles's supervision, submitting to his instructions, now stubborn, now flirtatious, a summer breeze of playful womanhood? Or the Julie who apologised for existing and disturbing others when she wanted something?

How many women is one woman?

'You just don't like going in the water.'

Julie didn't answer. She handed the cigarette back to Claire.

'Are you afraid?'

There was a rustling nearby; Julie looked up warily. The noise came closer, then the cat, a Siamese with caramel-coloured fur and blue eyes, emerged from the darkness and crept past them through the long grass, ignoring the two women behind the stone.

'That's Tong,' said Claire. 'He belongs to the woman from the land registry office.'

She could feel Julie's tension.

'They'll be a while,' she said softly. 'They've taken four bottles of beer, and both gentlemen are fond of the sea at night.' She took another sip.

'Can you always read people's thoughts, Claire?'

'If I could I wouldn't be a very happy person.'

'Are you happy?'

'As happy as you are.'

'*Touché*,' said Julie presently.

Claire took two cigarettes out of the packet at once, putting them both in her mouth and lighting them together.

Then she passed one to Julie.

'*Touché*... I'm not trying to win a fight against you, Julie,' she said. 'I don't even want to fight you. Although it would be a natural impulse. The mother who's jealous of the new most important woman in the life of her son and apple of her eye, and is convinced that no other woman will ever understand him like she does, or treat him as well. The woman in her mid-forties who feels so old and unattractive next to the young nineteen-year-old and is worried that her husband has noticed it too.'

'Please,' said Julie. 'No – don't think that. Your husband...

not me. That's not how it is, and besides, you're so beautiful, Claire.'

They turned their heads towards each other simultaneously. It was too dark to see Julie's eyes, but Claire knew where they were: there where the darkness condensed into two gleaming doornails, in a face that reminded her of someone, though she still couldn't think who.

'Why are you afraid of the water?' Claire whispered.

'I don't know.' Julie's voice was quieter still.

'Do you feel the same fear when you sing?'

Julie rose to her feet. It was just a movement, but it was abrupt and silenced all the sounds in the garden: the crickets, the whispering of the olive leaves.

Her figure was silhouetted against the sky. The rising and lowering of her chest. Her hand running through her hair, tugging at it angrily.

Warrior, thought Claire. The fearlessness beneath the fear.

'I can't swim, OK? I *can't* swim!'

Julie spoke the words loudly into the night. She inhaled deeply, took a sip of her wine, and turned to face Claire, her face a pale shadow.

'OK,' said Claire.

Julie exhaled audibly and took a few steps into the garden, deeper into the darkness.

Would she come back?

It was some minutes before Claire heard her disembodied voice, now husky with emotion. 'I was eleven,' she began. 'I was eleven. It was at the swimming baths, in the non-swimmers' pool. I wanted to learn to swim, and I had my brother's trunks on and a ridiculous pair of orange water wings. And then these kids came along. Five of them.

They pulled my trunks down to see if I was a boy or a girl. Five of them, three girls and two boys. The boys held my arms by those stupid bloody wings while the girls pulled, and when they saw—' Claire heard a strangled sound from out of the darkness, a sad, angry sob '—they started to call me a "thing". "She hasn't even got any hair!"' Julie imitated a shrill, mocking girl's voice. '"A misfit with too little at the top to be a girl, and too little down below to be a boy. A nothing, with no reason to exist."'

A spot of light appeared as Julie drew on her cigarette, and Claire briefly saw her face, that unfashionably beautiful face, full of outrage and anguish.

'Until that day it was OK to share gear with my brother Franck. Including Adidas swim shorts. It was OK to go to the barber's with Franck and get two short haircuts for the price of one. It was OK to be "one of the gang". It was OK for Franck to clear the table on even days and me on odd days, for fuck's sake! No one had made any distinction between us till then. Girl, boy, it didn't matter. Who invents these distinctions, Claire? What for? Why shouldn't girls wear swimming trunks, why do they have to wear make-up and be beautiful, what's that got to do with who we are?'

Her last words were almost shouted.

There were a thousand answers to her question, and they were all right, yet at the same time all wrong.

Julie sank down exhausted onto the grass next to Claire and leaned back against the stone. She drew her knees up and rested her elbows on them, the smoke from her cigarette rising into the air. Then, dropping her head onto her forearms, she went on: 'Oh yes, I tried. To be a proper girl. How bloody ridiculous! I wore dresses and borrowed make-up pencils. Stuffed my bra out with cotton wool. Everyone complimented me on how pretty I looked. Even my mother. Everyone except Franck, he said I looked stupid. Yeah. Who invents these distinctions? Perhaps it was me! I didn't even have the guts to wear a pair of fucking swimming trunks. And learn to swim. Shit.'

Julie drained her glass and dropped the cigarette end into it; it fizzled out with a damp hiss. She put the glass down on the ground, between her legs.

Where to start? There was so much that Claire could have said in reply. All the things she'd said to Anne-Claude: the limbic system, pheromones, chemistry.

But she said nothing.

Instead, she felt in the darkness for Julie's left hand. Their fingers found each other and interlocked.

Neither woman moved.

Claire could taste her pulse under her tongue. She looked up at the sky and said quietly, so quietly that she could hardly hear herself: 'This is the last night the Belt of Orion, the celestial hunter, will be above us. It's made up of the three stars Mintaka, Alnilam and Alnitak, in a straight line. The names come from medieval Arabic astronomy, and the Pyramids at Giza were built in alignment with them. Marco Polo knew them as the Three Sisters. He'd always known the bottom one pointed to Venice. Legend has it that they were once goddesses who came down from heaven to observe male humans up close. When they returned to heaven they became stars. Tomorrow they will no longer be visible above the horizon.'

Claire could hear Julie breathing next to her. The kind

of breathing that sounded like sobbing, the kind of tears that hovered at the rim of the eye.

Julie held on tighter to Claire's hand.

Another thousand years went by, new worlds were born, and one reality gave way to the next.

Then Julie said steadily: 'I've never seen so many stars before. Never. There are so many "never befores" in my life. So many possibilities I can't see or have never seen.'

It felt as if the two of them had disappeared, in the middle of the night, while time and reality sailed on by.

Claire replied quietly: 'The stars are still there even when we can't see them.'

Their fingers remained interlocked until Gilles called out from the terrace: 'Hello? Where are you?'

The two women returned to the house without looking at each other.

'You smell of smoke,' said Gilles.

'So what?'

'Everything OK with you?'

'Everything OK with *you*, Gilles?'

They looked at each other, and he shrugged. Claire took a couple of glasses and plates to the kitchen, said goodnight and disappeared into her room.

She lay down on the narrow bed in the darkness.

Smiling.

She couldn't say whether she and Julie had sat like that for five minutes or an hour, down there in the Silent Centre of the World.

Amid the beauty of the night.

18

She could break the rules. Or not. The choice was Claire's.

Nicolas had gone off to shower after his run. Gilles had gone to Saint-Philibert to join the other fathers dispatched to the bakery, where they looked on enviously at the old men of the village starting their day with a leisurely glass of Pinard red or a Leffe beer at the counter and exchanging the latest gossip on fishing grounds and local politics.

The two women were alone. Claire looked across at Julie, who was scrolling intently on her smartphone, immersed in her own filter bubble.

Yes, she had the choice. To leave the existing order intact. Not to get involved. Not to lie. To simply look on from her vantage point, to wait and see, and one day to forget.

Or to disrupt the order.

This damned order of things. Order is a tool for survival, order is half the battle – but what about the other half?

And all the time this unfamiliar, burning curiosity to know what lay behind the order. Claire took a deep breath – *yes? No?* What was she getting into: did she really want to know? Yes, temptation beckoned, and yielding to it was mildly intoxicating. It was the fear of falling from a diving board and there being no water in the pool. On her outbreath, she uttered the words:

'Julie, do you fancy a trip to the market in Concarneau? You and me?'

'Now?'

'Yes. Now. Or would you rather go to the beach?'

Julie frowned and shook her head.

'Right then.'

Claire hurried upstairs, two at a time.

Perhaps it was ridiculous.

Perhaps it was overstepping the mark.

But it was necessary, she knew that, and chose to ignore the nagging little question of how she knew.

'Nico?' she called through the closed bathroom door. 'I'm borrowing Julie for the morning, OK? We fancy a wander round Concarneau market.'

'Oh God, count me out!' he called back presently. Claire leaned her head against the door. It was the first time she'd ever lied to her son.

They took the back roads, along the Route des Étangs.

Julie had wound down the window and held her face in the breeze. Her hands were clenched in fists on her lap. Her whole body spoke of flight.

Claire resisted the urge to speak. About Kerlin as they passed through – a favourite hamlet of hers, with its weathered granite houses and blooming gardens, a place with a soft, gentle charm rarely found on the coast. It had magic, sweetness: summers here could go on for years.

She still didn't speak as they took the narrow, winding road under canopies of leaves, passing the field over which she had caught her first glimpse of the sea back in summer 1984. She simply drove, with the light dappling the tarmac and making spots hover momentarily in front of her eyes when they slipped out of the sun into the dimness of a tunnel of trees.

It all mingled into one: the play of summer light, the clear, soft air, the intimate voice of Miossec filling the car, 'Le plaisir, les poisons'; the tension, the smell of Julie's perfume and the warm leather seats, Julie's silence: a loud, questioning silence that gradually changed, grew calmer. Eventually, her clenched hands relaxed and migrated to the armrests, and she turned her head towards Claire.

'What was it about your husband that made you want to stay with him for ever?'

'Wow,' said Claire. 'That's . . . an astonishing question.'

'Is it hard to answer?'

'No, not at all. I knew I wanted to stay with him when I saw him with Nicolas. When he held our son for the first time and looked as if he was holding a tiny miracle in his arms.'

Julie looked out of the window again. 'I thought the way to know was to ask yourself whose face you want to be the last one you see before you die.'

'That's very poetic.'

'You think it's nonsense.'

'I think we tend to over-romanticise death. Very few people have time to say goodbye.'

'I think it's a nice idea. Something meaningful. The image you want to take with you to the grave. The only thing that can comfort you. A face.'

They reached Lambell. Claire took the first road hump faster than usual, causing the Mercedes' front axle to bottom out with a groan.

If only it was that easy, she thought. Those are the kind of ideas you have at the beginning of a relationship. When everything seems clear and simple. A whirlwind marriage (how romantic!), a child (planned? No? Oh well . . .), Paris, a career or maybe none, neglecting yourself for the love of your partner and eventually regretting it all.

'We're not going to the market, by the way,' said Claire, once they had left Lambell and its speed bumps behind and were on their way to Concarneau, crossing the bridge high above the harbour and looking over the *ville close* and the docks, with its grey military ships. 'It's a dreadful tourist trap.'

'OK,' said Julie. 'So where *are* we going?'

Claire didn't answer until they had left the roundabout behind the Leclerc and swung into the car park outside Grolleau water sports.

'We're buying a kayak?' asked Julie, looking at the gear in the window.

'No. We're buying you some swimming trunks. But proper ones,' said Claire. 'Ones that no one can pull down without doing themselves a serious injury. And then we're going to Tahiti.'

'Holy *merde*!' murmured Julie.

The fists again, the eyes turned to the window: flight behaviour.

Then she turned to Claire. 'That's the last time I tell you any of my secrets,' she said quietly, and with a smile that, for a brief moment, outshone even the summer sun.

Grolleau was really a diving specialist, Claire explained to Julie as they perused rows of wetsuits smelling of neoprene and rubber, but it stocked better brands than Decathlon or InterSport, which barely lasted a summer.

Julie picked out two shorty wetsuits, in black and blue and plain black, and disappeared into one of the three changing cubicles.

Claire stood outside, hesitating. Should she buy herself a new swimsuit too? Yes. Why not.

'Oh my God!' she heard Julie exclaim behind the thick grey curtain.

'Everything OK?'

'Are you supposed to use a shoehorn or a lubricant or what?' Julie peeped through a gap in the curtain. 'Claire,' she hissed, 'I can't do this thing up.'

As Claire approached, her eye caught the pile of clothes on the floor: shorts, shirt, red-and-blue striped briefs. Julie's bare toes. Mauve nail varnish.

'Can you come in?' asked Julie.

Claire slipped into the cubicle.

Julie's back was half naked, down to her buttock cleavage, exposing a few lines of her tattoo. She lifted her hair with both hands and bent her head forward.

'There's a cord,' said Claire. 'You use it to pull up the zip.'

Julie reached towards the middle of her back.

'No, at the side first, then from the top,' Claire explained, pressing the cord into her hand. 'Pull,' she whispered.

The thin neoprene closed over Julie's bare back.

Her shoulder blades. Two moles, one directly between them. A faint horizontal white stripe on her sun-tanned skin from her bikini.

Julie surveyed herself critically in the mirror. 'Well?'

'Well, what?'

'Does it look all right?'

'Does it feel all right?'

'I won't have to pull my tummy in any more. It's totally flattened. So's everything else, mind you. My piercing's digging right in.' She rubbed her breast.

'Well then.'

So young, thought Claire. So beautiful. Why do we only realise we were beautiful twenty years too late?

'You don't believe in pulling your tummy in, Claire?'

'No. It's grossly overrated. And it's been proven not to result in a happier life. I'll willingly quote you some scientifically verified statistics if you're in any doubt.'

Their eyes met in the mirror and Julie burst out laughing, then she turned round and, still laughing, gave Claire a big, impetuous hug. Claire felt the vibration of Julie's body against her own, and for a moment she was nineteen too, they were two young women joking about their tummies in a cramped, overlit changing cubicle, it was summer, and they were going swimming – until the sales assistant suddenly said from outside: 'I've got another one-piece in red here, wouldn't that be more suitable for your daughter, Madame?'

Julie slipped out of Claire's embrace and a look of outrage and sympathy flitted across her face – oh, the sympathy, that hurt more than the outrage consoled! Julie went to fling back the curtain but Claire held on to her wrist.

She shook her head gently and laid a finger on her lips. It's all right, her look said. It's all right.

It had hit her. Yes. It was a tiny graze, and she didn't

know why it hurt. She had a son Julie's age, after all, so why was she so upset to be taken for Julie's mother?

She considered the two of them from an outsider's perspective: it was an understandable assumption. Of course, two women, one cubicle, what else could they be but mother and daughter, past and future? Certainly not a shared present: that was another thing entirely, in most people's eyes.

Because I don't want to be her mother.

She took some deep breaths. Our emotions were strictly our own responsibility. 'Thank you, Madame,' she said in a friendly tone, reaching out for the red swimsuit and hanging it on the hook for Julie.

'I don't want the one from that silly cow,' Julie hissed.

'Just try it on first. Red's a good colour in the sea. Use the zip puller,' said Claire. 'I'll wait outside.'

The anger that had sided so readily with Claire was still visible in Julie's bearing. At the same time, it was equally clear that she was pleased with her image in the mirror. Because red best reflected Julie's personality: the light within the silent singer found apt expression in red neoprene and zip fasteners, sturdy seams and proud contours.

The assistant approached.

Julie looked at Claire, an unspoken question in her eyes: is it OK to have this one? Or is that a betrayal?

'If we don't take this one we'll regret it,' said Claire.

And naturally they bought it. Partly because Claire wanted to teach herself a lesson. The red suit would be a reminder to her. Every time she looked at Julie. It would destroy any illusions she might harbour.

She wasn't nineteen any more.

She should stop thinking of her life as entirely her own! It was her job to grin and bear it. To occupy her rightful place as eternal mother, forgotten woman.

But I can still feel, she thought. *I can still feel the girl in me — the girl with the stars and the ocean in her eyes.*

19

Waking up one day and realising you've changed while you weren't looking is something that happens to millions of women daily. People see a middle-aged woman, anything from mid-forties to mid-sixties – but beneath that outer shell is a twenty-four-year-old, an eighteen-year-old, a woman to whom numbers are irrelevant, and whose aspirations are all still young.

Claire was silent as they drove to the Plage de Tahiti, between Raguénez and Trémorvézen. From Trégunc, she took the back roads, the *routes à trois grammes*, so named because locals used them without fear of police checks on the way home from *fêtes* and boozy nights out.

Glancing in the mirror, she was surprised to see how pinched the corners of her mouth were. She looked at Julie, sitting with her elbow on the armrest.

How do the young see me? Someone like Julie? Late thirties, mid-forties, late fifties, it's all old to them.

Old. Clueless, empty, burnt out, dutiful, resigned, compliant, and only very occasionally astonishing, wonderful, fascinating, free, different. 'Different' was a rare epithet: how many youngsters said admiringly of someone they knew and regarded as decidedly old: she or he is so different!

The arrogance of youth, the wisdom of youth.

Am I different? Or am I . . . ?

Grim. Resigned. One of the grey brigade. One of the

many who, after a last summer of freedom a thousand years ago, devoted her life to scurrying back and forth between a cramped, overpriced flat and a small desk, only to find herself stuck in a dead end with no way back and only a vague memory of where she wanted to go in the first place. Just that she wanted to be somewhere else. There, behind those high walls. To have finally arrived.

She drove slowly onto the sand-swept car park above the Plage de Tahiti and parked by a grassy bank under the pines.

Families, teenagers and children were emerging from their cars, the glitter of the sea in their faces.

Does everything repeat itself, generation after generation? We come to these beaches as young girls, teenagers, and after the last summer we begin heading, one by one, into our cages. We look back, like I am today, but all we see are our successors, treading the same well-worn paths.

They got out of the car. They had already put on their new swimsuits at Grolleau, with their clothes over the top. When Claire began to strip down to hers and slip back into her espadrilles, Julie did likewise.

They walked down the steep path to the beach; you could see far beyond the bay, right to the island of Raguénez and, further on, the castle on the Pointe de Trévignon.

Julie stopped. 'Claire?'

She turned round.

'I'm scared.'

'I know.'

They looked at each other; Claire said nothing, determined not to resort to reassuring clichés such as: 'We don't have to do this,' or 'There's no need to be scared.' They did have to do it, and there was every reason to be scared.

The sea wasn't a pool. And nothing, not even a forest in the dead of night, had so much power over the psyche. It was the most powerful element of the world, merciless and implacable.

Julie heaved an audible sigh and carried on. When they reached the water's edge, they took off their shoes and placed them on a rock near the solitary beach shower.

Claire found a place where the incoming water was calm and shallow, and sat down with her legs outstretched.

Julie sat down hesitantly beside her.

The sea came towards them, a curious creature of liquid grey-blue and surf, just touching their feet.

'The first two waves greet you. The third wets you. The sea has a rhythm. Some days every third wave is bigger, and others every fifth.'

Julie sat silently contemplating the seemingly infinite blue.

'You *are* allowed to breathe, by the way.'

Julie released her suspended breath and flinched slightly as the third wave reached beyond her heels and toes, touching her calves and swirling around her knees.

The beach was filling up; you could hear children's cries, sunshades fluttering in the breeze, the thwack of balls on wooden bats.

The coolness of the sea. Its heavy softness. Familiarising yourself with the fear-inducing element.

It was so hard at first.

Who's swimming beside you?

'You,' Claire had replied, 'you, Jeanne!'

Jeanne had shaken her head. Keep practising, she had insisted. 'Don't fight the waves, swim calmly, slowly, they'll take your weight, they're plenty strong enough. Start by diving through the breakers, don't try and swim against them. Breathe in when the wave's behind you. Breathe regularly, exhale fully to make room in your lungs. Always breathe on the same side when you're doing the crawl. If you get scared, lie on your back with your head towards the beach. Fear makes you heavy: let the water carry you, let it take your fear. Leave it to the sea to move *you*. Fear is a wave: it comes and then it goes.

'But most importantly, child: know where you're going! Don't just put your head down and swim sixty strokes like a thing possessed. Look up every now and then. Take time to pause. Otherwise you'll end up swimming in a direction you didn't intend. Dictate your own course. And that means pausing to breathe and look around you.'

Every day of her first summer they had gone down to the Plage de la Baleine, and Jeanne had taught Claire to swim in the sea. She had spat first in the left, then in the right lens of her swimming goggles and encouraged her to do the same.

Jeanne swam alongside her, with a steady breaststroke; she was there to help Claire through the moments of panic, when the water caught her mid-breath and filled her mouth, eyes and stomach with salt water. She was there when Claire's aching muscles gave in and cramped up. She was there when Claire started crying, all of a sudden, as they swam through a patch of water with dark, moving shadows in the depths, and tear salt mixed with sea salt. She was there when Claire swam the crawl against the current, and she smiled when she decided not to fight the undertow, but to find another way back, turning onto her back and using the energy of the waves by way of resistance.

Whenever Claire returned to the shore, panting, proud, or simply empty and serene, Jeanne would go back into the water alone, slip on her flippers and swim briskly and steadily to the harbour and back, and Claire would watch her through the binoculars, counting her strokes: one, two, three, inhale, one, two, three, exhale. Pausing on the crest of the wave after every twenty strokes, looking round, adjusting her course.

Afterwards, they would linger on the beach for an hour or two. Claire would reach into the rockpools and dig around for snails and shellfish. She ran her hands over the fossils and watched the mussels grow bigger week by week. She listened to the sounds and breathed in the air. Once they found washed-up giant jellyfish the size of rucksacks.

They hiked along the GR34, the coast path once used by customs officers and smugglers alike, between lakes and grassland, cliffs and slopes covered in lichen, moss and heather, the rocks glowing copper-red in the morning and evening light. Every day Claire collected something from the sea, and her room filled with the smell of the ocean and the open air, and her heart wrapped itself in a salt crust beneath which she buried the first eleven years of her life. She collected whelk shells, and Jeanne showed her how to make cleaning sponges from the egg cases. And itching powder, in case Anaëlle annoyed her again.

By the end of the summer, Jeanne began to let Claire swim out by herself.

And on her fifth day alone in the waves, Claire sensed who it was that swam beside her. There truly was someone by her side, nodding earnestly to her.

Now Claire had the sea and the stars in her eyes, Jeanne

said, and she had heard the music of her soul. 'Don't forget *yourself*, Claire,' her grandmother had insisted. 'Listen to yourself. Sing. Breathe.'

That was the day Claire found the scutella. Jeanne explained to her that it was the discovery of fossilisation that started the conflicts between religion and science, because fossils were evidence that the world wasn't a recent creation of God. Rather, there had been other worlds before it, with beings and forms, intelligent life, and a great unexplored history in which humans were a mere grain of sand. Jeanne had closed Claire's small fist around the heart-shaped fossil, saying: 'Neither your future nor your past are fixed. You can always recreate yourself, again and again.'

I never learned that lesson well enough. Never took time to pause and draw breath. I just kept on swimming, and now it's as if I'm just drifting on the surface: where the hell have I ended up? Jeanne, it's only now that I understand what you really wanted to teach me, only now, and life is so long, life is so short, and I was so busy fighting the waves that I forgot to look where I was going.

Claire rose to her feet. 'Come on,' she said, wading into the sea until the water lapped around her calves.

'Wait!' cried Julie. 'It's . . . I can't . . .'

Claire held out her hand.

Just to here, her gesture said. Just to here.

And no further: Promise.

Julie waded into the water, eyes wide, alternately staring in panic at the horizon and down at her feet again.

Claire had chosen the spot deliberately: the water was clear and shallow, the sand free of seaweed and stones, and they could wade another twenty metres into the water without it even rising above their knees.

Julie grasped Claire's outstretched hand tightly and concentrated on the horizon as if a wall of grey water might suddenly rise up above them and come crashing down onto the beach, sweeping them and everything else along with it: sand, pebbles, cliffs, car parks, buildings. She breathed quickly and shallowly through her nose.

'Tell me what you feel,' said Claire.

'I'm sinking,' said Julie. 'The ground's dissolving under my feet. And . . . the water feels warmer the longer I'm in it.'

Their fingers interlocked.

'It's loud. It's . . . as if the sea's watering me. Like a flower. Only from the bottom up, and . . . I don't know. It feels like I'm growing more arms. More legs. More hairs even, as if I can feel each one individually. Am I talking rubbish?'

'No.'

No. You're going back into your body, thought Claire. That's all. And yes, that's probably all that matters.

'"The sun, the wind, the salt and the rolling, sparkling sea fuses the strings of broken souls back together." That's what Jeanne, my grandmother, said. And wrote, later on, in her novel *The Light at the End of the Night*. She wrote about people by the sea "who go back into their body and fill it with its own individual music".'

'That's beautiful,' murmured Julie. 'But I feel sick.'

Who knows, thought Claire.

Who knows whether it will take the whole ocean to restore the music to this silent singer?

'And I'm scared,' said Julie. 'Of going in further and suddenly finding there's no more sand and the water's hundreds of metres deep and I'm falling and falling and I can't swim. And I hate myself for it, and suddenly I'm two people: one's scared and the other gets a mean sort of pleasure out of the fact that I'm getting exactly what I deserve. That I'm drowning.'

Oh, don't hate, my love, thought Claire. Don't hate yourself: too many people do, and it's such a tragic waste.

'The sea looks at us with a different eye every hour of the day,' she began, without looking at Julie. 'When the moon's still in the sky, it has a silvery gleam, like molten mercury. At sunrise, the flat, gentle waves have a transparent, lucid shimmer, in a pale, watery lilac, as delicate as if someone has washed a paintbrush in them. Over the day it changes from pale blue to ink blue, turquoise green, grey-blue, violet and back to white again. The whole spectrum of colours. But where do they come from?' Claire knew of course why the eye perceives the sea as multicoloured. Light incidence, dispersion, the nature of the objects reflecting the wavelengths of the sun. 'I like to imagine that the sea is coloured by all the emotions we pour into it. Hope, pain, desire, doubt, impatience, certainty. We are the colours of the sea. We are reflected in it. And it washes away all our colours when we enter it.'

Claire bent to pick up a whelk that was bobbing about in the lazy waves. It was empty, the spiral shell white with a pale brown pattern.

She handed it to Julie.

'And just as sea snails draw calcium from the sea to make their shells, and emotions feed into its colour, perhaps every chamber of a mollusc, every ridge of a whelk shell is a calcified emotion, a sigh, a thought, which we can only hear when we close our eyes and listen.'

Julie studied the grain of the shell, tracing it with her finger.

Then she licked her finger and, after glancing at Claire as if to check whether she was serious or just teasing, raised the shell to her ear.

They took off their swimsuits in the car park, behind the car. They unzipped each other at the back and turned aside to roll down the stiff, tight neoprene.

When Claire turned round again, Julie was concentrating on removing the piercing from her nipple.

This strange impulse to blow soothingly on the self-inflicted wound.

Back in Trévignon, they stole quietly into the house through the cellar and hung up their swimsuits in a corner; Claire knew neither Gilles nor Nicolas would notice whether there were three, four or five different neoprene suits hanging up to dry.

When Gilles heard them coming up the steps and laid his book aside to enquire how they'd enjoyed themselves at Concarneau market, Julie answered: 'Oh, it was OK,' and Claire: 'Well, you know what it's like.' Neither she nor Julie told Gilles or Nicolas where they'd been.

It was an unspoken agreement, and Claire didn't dare think about the reason behind it.

20

It is an illusion to believe the ground under our feet is solid. The world is its own wrecking ball, and year by year continents are shifting imperceptibly. Coordinates are losing their meaning, the plates under the landmasses drifting apart with every heartbeat. One day Paris will be where Berlin is now.

Claire watched Gilles bustling around the lounge between the open-plan kitchen and 'his' room. From tomorrow evening, 14 July, they would have to change their existing sleeping arrangements. Ludo would go in Claire's room, Anaëlle and the ominous N in the attic room. The room where you felt as if you were on a ship high above the sea. As a child, Anaëlle had bagged the attic with the big porthole window with the instinct of a girl from Paris-Belleville who knows she has to run faster than everyone else to have a chance in life.

How long was it since Claire and Gilles had slept together in the same bed? The whole night, side by side? Five years? Seven? How long had they been co-occupying space without really sharing it?

The imperceptible drifting apart of souls.
'Claire, where are my binoculars?'
'In the bag.'
'Which bag?'
'The one you took with you last time.'

'And where's that?'

'My money's on the cellar. Where all the other stuff is.'

This had been going on all morning.

Gilles was searching for binoculars, dip net, fishing bait and six-pack cooler. Nicolas complained he couldn't find his favourite hoodie (it was in Paris: why hadn't she reminded him to bring it? he chided a laughing Julie), hunted around for his swimming goggles (they were hanging on a hook in the bathroom), and noticed that one of his flippers was torn (which had already annoyed him last summer, though clearly not enough to get a new pair).

This morning the men planned to set off for an overnight stay on the Glénans, their first trip in Ewan's black speed-boat; he and some friends ran a business, Glénan Découverte, offering tours of the islands. In a Zodiac straight from Trévignon harbour, it would take them just twenty minutes to reach Saint-Nicolas, as opposed to an hour and a half on the sluggish Vedette tourist ferries from Concarneau or Benodet. 'Nicolas on Nicolas' was a longstanding tradition between father and son.

Claire and Julie would be alone until tomorrow afternoon.

At least, if the gentlemen can manage to pack without supervision, thought Claire.

It brought back one of her first summer academies in the US, on the theme of visual perception in animals and humans. One of the female professors had explained, to the amusement of the female students, why men never noticed clumps of dust in corners and could never find the butter in the fridge: 'Because it doesn't move. If the washing-up danced or the laundry made its own way towards the machine, those objects would rise above the stimulus attention threshold required by the testosterone-saturated brain in order to initiate an action such as hunting or a heightening of vigilance. In a nutshell, *mesdames*: teach the rubbish to shake its booty.'

This was of course crude, populist gender nonsense, but it had at least helped them grasp the concept of visual stimulus threshold patterns. If we registered everything we see on a daily basis with the same degree of attention, we would soon drop dead from all the adrenalin. The ability to ignore things was an important one. Claire remembered how some of the students had continued to debate the subject with the lecturer later on in the park. 'And how can we teach men to stop ignoring women's achievements? Should I wave whenever I have something to say?' The lecturer had replied with a weary smile: 'One of the protective defences of the human brain is the premise. In other words, woman equals "creative and intellectual potential blocked by offspring", not: woman equals "groundbreaking invention". Ideas are no longer examined on an individual basis, but collectively assumed. It's astonishing that, even in these most progressive and enlightened of times, we still commit the blunder of denying the female intelligence potential instead of encouraging it.'

She didn't have an answer to the question.

Claire checked her email. Most Parisian newspaper editors found the state-ordained summer break an unnecessary inconvenience. There was a request for a comment on Melania Trump, and what her videos and photo poses said about her inner thoughts.

'She wants to throw her husband out of her life but doesn't know how,' Claire muttered as she wrote to decline the request.

'Will you miss us?' asked Gilles, draining his half-empty cup of cold coffee.

'Of course,' said Julie.

'Not at all,' Claire replied at the same time.

They looked at each other and laughed.

'Nasty little hobbitesses,' Gilles harrumphed. Then he looked around. 'Where are my trainers, by the way?'

'Bathroom,' said Claire.

'How come?' asked Gilles.

'You took them off there yesterday after your . . . cycle tour. So one would expect them to be there still, unless they've somehow made their way to the wardrobe by themselves.'

Gilles kissed Claire without batting an eyelid at the words 'cycle tour' (she could have dropped in 'your visit to Juna', she reflected, just to see what would happen), and she returned the kiss. Perhaps because she was glad he was going.

He stroked her cheek. 'My clever wife. You are the summer,' he said softly.

'Not Juna or Marie-Claudette?' asked Claire. But again too quietly, so quietly that it was a mere echo in her head.

Nicolas hugged Julie goodbye.

They held each other awkwardly, and it was strange seeing her son kissing, seeing him kiss Julie. The one holding back in the presence of onlookers, and the other trying to overcome the distance he was straining to keep. Claire looked away, only to catch sight of Nico's mouth brushing Julie's in the old mirror above the chest of drawers.

'*Salut*, Maman,' said Nico, and Claire had to stop herself from reminding him to take sun cream, water and a scarf for protection against the wind. Few children knew it, but their mother's exhortations to wrap up warm were simply another way of saying I love you.

Part of her was relieved to see him go. Another part would be relieved once he was back safe and sound.

Then the men were gone, and the house suddenly felt very still and light.

Those twenty-four hours were the ones Claire enjoyed most every summer. Alone, with the entire emotional space to herself. Without coming up against someone else's boundaries and being forced to make herself smaller; without feeling Gilles's inner tension and frustration weighing on her soul. His moods permeated every room like a perfume, wafting out of the kitchen into the lounge, up the stairs and across half the garden.

Sometimes it enraged her that Gilles took up a shared space so uninhibitedly, that the emanations from his inner struggles oppressed her like stinging jellyfish tentacles that could reach her even through closed doors, enveloping her and forcing her to dive deeper and more doggedly into her term papers or texts. Because as soon as she relaxed – whether reading a book or just gazing out to sea – she involuntarily picked up on both Gilles's and Nicolas's mood swings and reacted with concern and vigilance, her whole body a clenched muscle. Despite herself she opted for kindness, bringing Gilles a herbal tea or a smile, luring him to the table and topping up his wine until he was ready to offload it all, the sayable and the unsayable.

The anxious wait for a commission. The wait for inspiration. The unbearable wait for the end of your own life; the fear of having forgotten how to live by then anyway.

Once he had got it all off his chest, Claire's buzzing tension would subside, only to be replaced by a reluctance to leave him alone with his struggles.

How was it that affection and anger could coexist so closely?

The 'Nico radar' that had operated since her son's birth swept the house a few more times: where's the baby? There's the baby. Where's the baby . . .? The baby's away. With his father. He's in charge.

The Nico radar switched off.

Divine emptiness.

Her life was her own at last.

Time crackled away quietly and luxuriously. The sun rose higher, shining on the wood in the lounge until it shimmered like dark acacia honey, catching the bunch of hydrangeas in a milk jug and playing among the leaf shadows.

'Do men remain sons for ever?' asked Julie after a while.

'Some more than others. I guess it depends on the women and mothers in their lives.'

'Whether they're always chasing after them with stuff and clearing up after them?'

'Yes. And yes: guilty as charged! At first it's pure necessity, then later it's quicker if you do it yourself, and eventually it becomes a habit, half out of love, half out of vanity.'

'Vanity?'

'Yes, of course. Doesn't it feel good to be the sole guardian of knowledge when it comes to the whereabouts of dip nets, binoculars and flippers, so that others are practically dependent on you and condemned to eternal gratitude?'

'Not to mention how to load a dishwasher and where to find stuff in the supermarket and in the fridge.'

'And the satisfaction of knowing: what would they be without me?'

'Happy-go-lucky bachelors with disposable underpants?'

They chuckled, enjoying the harmless bit of ranting between women. And the tacit acknowledgement that they would still go on falling into the same trap – whether out of love, vanity, pragmatism or any of the other geometrically unequal justifications that lead women to adopt the role of family dogsbody.

They clinked coffee cups ceremoniously.

And burst into another irresistible fit of giggles. Then Claire grew serious again.

'Let's go swimming.'

This time, Claire chose the Plage de Trévignon. It was still the early part of the morning; the main wave of tourists would surge onto the beach after lunch, populating it with colourful towels, sunshades and plastic buckets.

The waves rippled onto the shore slowly and evenly; the water was clear. Even if they did swim a few metres, which Claire wasn't anticipating, there were no hidden depths, no clumps of seaweed, no underwater rocks to cut your knees on.

'She looks bigger to me today,' said Julie.

She. *Elle. La Mer.*

Side by side, they walked towards Her Blueness.

La mer sees the land through different eyes, Claire mused.

She doesn't deal in morality, but grace and favour. The sea is the supreme arbiter.

Julie's swimsuit was resplendent in its proud, magnificent red. She herself was unaware of its effect, and moved with a wary uncertainty.

The first things to learn were standing and lying, Claire remembered from her lessons with Jeanne. How to breathe, how to stand in the water, how to lie on the water.

Julie and Claire waded in up to their hips, into the gently pricking aqua blue, a few steady steps at a time to get used to the rhythm and power of the swell. Claire splashed water onto her face and arms; the coolness was so clear and immediate.

Julie did likewise, cautiously and with screwed-up eyes. Her arms were downy with gooseflesh. Looking into her face, Claire saw the fear of the deep: a viscous, clammy fear, but at the same time a determination not to be defeated by it.

'Ready?'

'No.'

'Good. We're never ready for life and do it anyway. The most important thing to learn is that you can lie on the water. Without any great effort. I'll hold you. Nothing can harm you, there's solid ground beneath you.'

Julie nodded: a brief, silent, resolute nod.

Claire planted herself alongside Julie.

'Lean back against my arm. I'll keep it under your neck the whole time. Imagine I'm carrying you. Like . . .'

'A bride over the threshold?'

'Exactly.'

'But don't let go.'

'I won't. I've got you.'

'And it's not a trick? You won't let go after all and leave me to my fate?'

They looked at each other, and Claire knew she would never be able to allay Julie's fear herself. Only Julie could do that.

Your decision, she thought. Trust me. Or don't.

'OK. Time for the honeymoon then,' said Julie with forced gaiety, her voice cracking with the tension.

She leaned back into the crook of Claire's right arm, her left hand gripping Claire's back, nails digging into the neoprene. They looked into each other's eyes.

'Now . . .' said Claire, widening her stance. She imagined herself as a rock, rooted up to the ankles in the seabed.

Gently, she tilted Julie's shoulders, then deftly raised her knees and gradually slid her arm upwards to support her tail.

Julie's body was light in the water and she floated easily in Claire's arms. Claire could feel Julie's tensed muscles, her fingers boring into her side; she could feel the roundness of Julie's body, the curve of the shoulder she held and the head that lay on her arm, the perfect roundness of the wide pupils fixed upon her. Two nails in wood, an anchor, devouring Claire's gaze.

'Breathe, Julie. In . . . two, three. Out . . . two, three. Breathe. And now relax your glutes for me and wiggle your toes. Can you wiggle your toes?'

'No!' Julie gasped.

'Do you want to put your feet down again?'

Julie breathed through her mouth, audibly; her expression had changed to that of a frightened little girl.

'Breathe,' Claire repeatedly softly, 'in through the nose – two, three. Out through the mouth, two, three.'

She kept her eyes fixed on Julie. Julie in her arms, in the sea, so light. Julie looking at her. Julie, whose body was slowly, infinitely slowly, beginning to relax.

'Wiggle your toes,' whispered Claire, smiling.

Claire rocked Julie back and forth in her arms, gently pushing and pulling her in the surf until the young woman and the sea had explored each other. Julie opened her clenched legs, and her right arm swept freely and easily through the water.

'*Tout baigne . . . tout baigne . . .*' Claire sang softly; she sang Miossec's words directly to Julie, full of an inexplicable tenderness.

Everything's fine, Julie, everything's fine . . .

After another eternity – how long had they been out here? Half an hour? – Julie closed her eyes. Her cheeks softened.

'*Tout baigne,*' whispered Claire, over and over.

Like the gently flowing water. Everything's fine. Everything's cool. Everything's good.

Everything.

Julie entrusted herself completely to Claire. She let her head sink back gently into the water and her dark hair spread around her, floating and swaying in the current.

She surrendered herself to the sea, to the sea and Claire,

with open arms and legs and a smile on her face, a sea-wet smile, water droplets shimmering on her lips.

Something snapped inside Claire, almost imperceptibly.

'I won't let you go. Ever,' she whispered, too faintly for Julie to hear.

Of that she was sure.

21

It was as if nothing had existed before now. As if time had only begun, only become real, in that moment.

Everything had melted away except Claire's voice, the thread from which she was suspended. Floating in the sea.

So weightless, so free from the burden of herself, suffused with a serenity she had never known before.

Nothing was heavy any more. Her steps, her movements, her head, her heart. All the dead hours washed away.

Inside her head, everything had grown light and transparent, a radio that had at last fallen silent, a still, beautiful room in which every harsh lamp had been extinguished.

The sea had touched her everywhere at once. Between her fingers, behind her neck, between her thighs, hundreds of kisses, bites and caresses. Silk and liquid light.

She had felt the tingling, the gooseflesh, the stroking all over in the same moment, and finally understood the meaning of the words: 'I am my body.'

She had felt so comfortable in her own skin. Like never before.

And the black fear that so often kept her trapped in her room was gone.

Later, Julie had tried to give this sense of self-liberation a name as she sat on the rocks separating the Plage de la Baleine from the Plage de Trévignon watching Claire, who had swum back out to sea. At first, Claire had swum with quick strokes, as if fleeing from something. Then she had settled into a steady crawl. She always breathed on the right side, with a controlled sideways movement of the head. As if everything was a question of concentration. Breathing. Life.

I want to be able to do that too, Julie thought. I want to experience that feeling again. So free, so light. So complete.

She had felt warmth, a growing ball of red heat between her navel and ribcage.

And . . .

Boundlessness.

She had felt herself expanding. Yes. She had felt seamlessly connected to the sea, the air, the sky and the woman holding her. Her body was the ocean and Claire, and underwater she had heard her pulse, her heartbeat, the life inside her, the muted singing of the waves. She had felt Claire's singing. The words *tout baigne*.

Finally, she had felt nothing but Claire – her touch, her sound – and herself inside Claire and Claire inside her and the sea.

The sun dried her skin, her hair. She tasted salt on her lips. It was already beginning: her body was already resolving back into separate, unloved parts, her mind darkening again.

She must learn to swim.

It seemed the logical answer to all her questions. She must learn to swim the ocean of life.

When Claire waded out of the sea, sweeping her hair firmly out of her face and back over her head, she was once again Madame le Professeur, Madame Cousteau.

Indivisible, she was a free woman, and the sea belonged to her alone.

There was so much that Julie had wanted to say to Claire: she should have shouted it out without hesitating:

That was the most beautiful moment of my life. No, it was the true beginning of my life.

I feel like everything's changing.

Everything's changing, and you're the one who did it.

Not a man. Not a career. Not a place or a kiss or an exam – it was you, Claire.

Your mouth. Your hands. The sea.

The ocean inside me, inside you.

You.

But Claire had swum away and returned as Madame Cousteau, and they walked back to the house in silence, in their red and black wetsuits, and the sun beat down on the car park, hotter than on the encrusted rocks of the beach; the mown yellow grass smelled dry, the prickly gorse spicy, and all around them were tiny flower stalks with fluffy white heads, cotton-wool balls nodding in the breeze.

Julie plucked a few grass stems to cover her awkwardness and ran them over her palms. They were soft as cat fur.

'You can have first shower, you're cold,' said Claire.

Julie simply nodded, finding it increasingly hard to speak because there was so much she wanted to say.

Let's go back in the sea, she thought. Now. I want to be me again, and I want you to be you again, my version of you.

What we were to each other just now.

What were we?

Can we go swimming tonight?

Naked. I want to feel it, all over, I want to feel myself. And you.

But the thought drifted off, lost its way, uncertain of where it came from and where it was going, and eventually turned to flotsam, to be sucked back into the ocean.

The powerful jet of hot water from the shower head was Julie's second supersensory experience of the day. The sea seemed to have done something to her nerves. Recalibrated them. Removed their numbness and tautened their strings.

The water hit the nape of her neck, making her nipples contract. It ran down between her buttocks and flowed warm between her thighs. Heat spread over her face and her body sang, and she felt like singing with it.

She closed her eyes and traced the contours, cavities and surfaces of her body with the hollow of her hand. Her hands told her she was beautiful, and she decided never to look in a mirror again, but to trust her fingers instead.

'Leave a drop of hot water for me, will you?' came Claire's voice from outside the door.

Julie hastily turned off the switch.

She emerged wet and steaming from the shower and looked round for her towel, then remembered: she'd left it in the bedroom. At the end of the passageway.

'Finished!' she called. 'But . . .'

Then she took a deep breath in. And out. And before all the voices in her head telling her *please don't* had a chance, she opened the bathroom door as she was.

'I haven't got a towel,' she said, looking Claire straight in the eye. And later, many years later, she would sometimes wake up at night wondering why they both acted as they did. Why.

Claire stood in the doorway of her room with her bath towel draped around her; it was dark green. She came slowly towards Julie and unwrapped it.

'Take this one. I'll fetch another.'

Julie reached out and took the towel slowly from her hand. Her eyes wandered inadvertently from Claire's limpid green eyes down to her breasts, belly and beyond, then back up again the same way. She had no idea whether the whole thing happened quickly or slowly.

Claire kept her back turned to Julie in the shower. She showered as if she were alone, without embarrassment, without posing: every movement was natural, unforced.

As Julie dried herself, Claire said without turning: 'Use the body lotion. The green one, on the top shelf. The sea acts like a magnifying glass – your skin burns quicker.'

She's treating me like a child, thought Julie. It was happening again. As if they were drifting apart – but then, perhaps it was all an illusion anyway. This closeness. That inexplicable connection out there in the sea.

Claire had merely wanted to teach her to swim. That was all. No more than that.

More? What do you mean by 'more', Beauchamp, eh?

She reached for the lotion, which smelled of coconut and pineapple, and rubbed it into her skin, annoyed because Claire was right: her legs were glowing from the line of her wetsuit downwards.

The gush of water stopped, and Julie left the bathroom without looking back at Claire.

In her room, her phone was spinning and vibrating. Two voicemails and a flurry of WhatsApp messages, all from Nicolas. The last one said: *Hello? Are you two still alive?*

He had sent photos from the island. It looked as if they'd landed in the Caribbean. Curving beaches with dazzling white sand, turquoise water and bobbing yachts.

Just over there, on the horizon, a whole sea between them; Nicolas, as if from another life, the old one that had ended an hour ago. Before her hands had told her she was beautiful, before she had sensed that there was a freedom out there just for her. While she was deliberating whether to send Nico a naked photo of herself or a plain *We're fine, just lazing about,* she picked up the curious fossil and rolled it between her fingers. She could ask Claire what the tiny star was in the stone's surface, whether it was an animal or a plant or one of her beloved – what were those things called? – ichthyosaurs.

Claire. The image of Claire in the passageway was burned into her retina. She put on a summer dress, picked up a novel, started reading it, forgot what she had read, and no longer knew what to do with herself.

She heard the bathroom door, the door to Claire's room, footsteps, silence, more footsteps. On the other side of the wall.

She texted Nico back: *Look forward to seeing you.*

Behind those words lay a whole, unwritten universe.

A knock on the doorframe.

'I'm hungry. You too?'

'Starving.'

'Do you want to go somewhere? Galettes with *vue mer*?'

No, Julie wanted to say, I want to stay here alone, with you. I want to talk, I don't want to talk, I don't want anyone else around us, there are always other people!

'If you like.'

'Not really.' Claire smiled.

They made themselves an omelette, garnished it with the wild rocket that grew profusely around the walls of the house, and took it out into the garden with them.

At the front of the house, on the seaward side, the usual commotion had begun. The car park was filling up with cars, children were shouting, parents chiding. Out the back, though, it was like lying in a bed of stillness, green, and dappled light.

'Is it too early for wine?' asked Claire.

'It's always the right time for wine somewhere in the world.'

When Claire came back with a bottle of Muscadet and poured them half a tumblerful each, she said softly: 'It's fun to malinger with you.'

'Are we malingering?'

'I think we can go one better.'

Midday swam gently into afternoon. They fetched loungers from the cellar and chose a spot each in the garden: Claire by the olive tree, Julie by the yew.

They stood together in front of the big, wide bookshelf in the lounge. Claire picked out one volume after another, asking: 'Have you read Delphine de Vigan? Marguerite Yourcenar? Olympe de Gouges? Oh, look, Nathalie Sarraute, *You Don't Love Yourself*, that one's to die for. No? Great women, great champions of women's rights. Oh, I loved this one when I was your . . .' Claire stopped, murmuring:

'*Pardon*, those are words I never wanted to say or hear.' She put the book back.

'"When I was your age," you were going to say.'

'Yes. Forgive me.'

'Why? I assume you were nineteen once.'

'Eighteen, even.'

'So you say!'

Claire retrieved the book from the shelf and tossed it to Julie.

'*A Certain Smile*. Françoise Sagan!'

'It wasn't done to read such things in those days. Too low-brow. A woman who drifts through life and starts an affair with her fiancé's uncle out of sheer boredom and world-weariness. I loved it.'

'Then I must read it.'

Claire turned away quickly.

Had Julie said something stupid? And why did Claire keep intimating with tiny gestures that she didn't take her seriously?

Claire reminded her of the sea swell. Two gentle waves and the third a stinger.

She is like the ocean, she thought: it doesn't lie, and wants me to learn to carry myself.

They retired to their loungers.

They read, sipped their wine, and every now and again Julie caught Claire smiling at her across the lawn, her eyes invisible behind large sunglasses. Claire had engrossed herself in a novel by Laetitia Colombani, *La Tresse*.

It felt good to simply do nothing. It was a benign nothing, guilt-free and undemanding. Julie felt the sun warm her, and when she closed her eyes red dots danced pleasantly behind her lids. A cricket chirped, the wind lifted the leaves of the olive tree, and she felt full and drowsy from the food, wine and swimming.

Peace, she thought.

Peace at last.

And she fell asleep.

22

How many women is a woman?

And how many years ebb away until a woman finds her true self? And will time still have a place by then for the person she truly is, for her plans, her ideas, the wealth of her abilities – or is it already bricked in with all her day-to-day activities and obligations? With little chance of escaping the daily grind, that jailer of the inwardly free but effectively shackled woman who cleans, works, cooks, shops, organises? An eternal Sisiphyna?

Laying aside her book – a novel about three women's lives on three continents – Claire took off her sunglasses and contemplated Julie, who had been asleep for two hours. Her head had fallen to one side, and her face looked relaxed and youthful. So young.

The image of Julie in the passageway flickered before Claire's eyes. The scar on her left nipple where the piercing had been. The memory of how the piercing in Chloé's tongue had felt in Claire's mouth, all those summers ago. The involuntary pain as she imagined her own breast being pierced: for whom, for what? For herself? For the eyes of another? The supposed beauty that you had to suffer for?

Or was it a different kind of adornment? One that said: this body is mine, not yours?

Julie's nakedness. She had worn it like a long, flowing summer dress.

Claire looked at Julie and saw herself. She searched for the young Claire in her hands, with their fine lines and creases, in her legs, with their age spots and sun damage; she looked at her shadow and wondered where all the years had gone.

At nineteen I was closer to my true self. I've been moving away from it ever since.

Wordless: that was what Claire's inner transformation at nineteen had been. She had locked herself in the room of her own mind, engaging only minimally and superficially with the outside world and remaining alone with her own thoughts. It was the year of transition, when she stopped being a teenager but didn't yet count as an adult. The year when she entered the world that was finally opening up a chink to her with the clear, humiliating knowledge that there was no one waiting for her. No one saying: you're just the person we need! I can see you're destined for great things! No one who had any idea what she was capable of and which direction she should go in. Least of all Claire herself. It was the time of self-negation.

And not the first time either. There were already two Claires: the hidden, inner one and the one who acted, made decisions and spoke. The split had occurred on her first morning at school, in September 1979, when her mother Leontine had pleaded with her: 'Promise me you won't cause me a lot of trouble, like the other two? You won't be like that, will you, child? All that trouble . . . I don't know if I can go through it again.'

And her mother had started to cry. Something in Claire, aged six years, forty-one days and a few bitter-sweet hours of sleepless pre-school excitement, something deep down inside the child, opened its eyes.

She could see. Suddenly, she could truly see.

Behind her mother's face she saw an anxious little girl who had simply been on this earth longer than her, but who was at the same time probably even younger than her. Significantly younger, in fact: around four, perhaps. And that anxious, four-year-old Leontine was tired, having never had a decent night's sleep due to endless nightmares in which snakes were always swimming up the toilet bowl and biting her on the backside (a fear Claire partially shared); she had never had a cat to love, and she was afraid of horses, roadster bikes, people, the questions doctors asked her, and the twelve o'clock siren on Sundays that reminded her of war. And the last thing that tired little girl wanted was to accompany her to school. She never wanted to go to school, or grow up, or be a mother: all she wanted was to flee into the arms of her father, who she said was built like a bear: big and warm and gruff. Or like a wardrobe. A bear-shaped wardrobe. She wanted to huddle inside him and be carried through the world.

The only thing Claire was afraid of was snakes in the toilet. Although she already knew from her beloved animal books that the French adders with the zigzag pattern on their heads rarely lived in toilets: they liked the sun, and besides, they smelled with the tip of their tongue, so they wouldn't have been very happy in the sewage pipes of a fourth-floor council flat in Belleville-Paris.

She swung the leather satchel over her shoulder and drew herself up to her full height, making her a centimetre taller than her mother, who had sunk to her knees. She raised her small child's hand and stroked her mother's hair tenderly.

'Of course, Maman. We have an agreement. You don't need to worry about it any more. Now go home and make yourself a hot caramel milk.'

'I don't have to come in with you?' asked her mother in a thin voice, without looking at her.

'Of course not,' said Claire.

It was important to say it airily and with conviction, so as not to worsen the terrible anguish the child saw in her mother's eyes.

She hit the note perfectly.

And with that she kissed her mother on the forehead, turned and entered the school building with her head held high.

How often had she avoided the truth since then?

'And you, Julie?' Claire whispered into the garden.

Will you reveal the real you one day? Will you have a sense of who you are and what you can be, and what decision will you make then? Will you continue to hide yourself away or will you let your true colours shine?

Julie opened her eyes. She looked straight at Claire.

'What are you thinking about, Claire?' she whispered. 'You look so sad.'

'About the things we decide for ourselves, and the things others decide for us,' Claire replied, fighting a lump in her throat.

Because if Claire's mother had ever stopped to wonder why her youngest child spoke and behaved with the assurance of a trusted flight attendant from her very first day at school; if she could ever have brought herself to send her daughter to some kind of intelligence laboratory over the years to find out why she had lucid dreams, could read human gestures like a book, and easily memorised things she had read once only; or if she had entrusted her with the Tunisian handyman's welding torch, along with a few generous tons of love and scrap metal, instead of, increasingly, the task of organising their fatherless family; and if she had realised that her youngest would rather have spent her time, torch in hand, rooting around in books or in the anthills of the rundown local playgrounds than acting as the Cousteau family's conflict mediator, purchase planner and foreign secretary; and if, finally, she had ever noticed that Claire vented her repressed longing for hugs on the warm body of their Chinese neighbour's big shaggy sheepdog – then . . .

(That's a lot of 'ifs', Claire – too many for the universe, with the best will in the world, to manoeuvre into the realm of the possible.)

Then things would have turned out very differently.

Or maybe not.

But it was quite likely. Because the strain of hiding a second, secret, yearning personality behind the external one, of avoiding the truth too often and stifling the urge to scream, cry and laugh, wildly and uncontrollably – such things can't help but leave their mark on a woman.

'In the end, every life is what it is, and you never really know how you ended up where you are and not somewhere else,' Claire said aloud, unable to stop a solitary tear welling out of the corner of her eye and trickling down her cheek.

Julie jumped up and bounded to Claire's side, kneeling next to her in the grass. 'No, no,' she soothed, wrapping her arms around Claire's neck, a gesture that was almost more than Claire could bear. It hurt to be hugged, it hurt to have someone feel sorry for her, it hurt to have someone else hold her because it made her lose her own grip on her soul and she could no longer control herself.

It was as if she were embracing her younger self.

And she held it tight.

She held it tight and embraced herself for the first time.

I can't hold it in any more . . . she thought, her arms simultaneously pushing Julie away and enfolding her.

Julie tightened her grip.

'I never cry,' said Claire, feeling those quick, silvery tears again.

'Me neither,' Julie murmured into her neck, her breath warm and sweet.

The strength of her embrace was nothing like Claire had ever experienced before. No male embrace had been as powerful and at the same time as innocent, no female embrace as vehement and fearless as Julie's enveloping arms.

'Do you know the Irish saying? About reality?' said Julie, her arms still wrapped around Claire, her face nestled in the crook of her neck.

'No . . .'

'Reality is the state of not having drunk enough.'

Claire laughed in spite of herself.

Julie released her tentatively, whispering: 'I'll be right back.'

And she hurried inside on her half-tanned, half-white legs. Claire slumped back into the lounger and closed her eyes.

What was that?

What on earth had just happened?

It was as if they had swum out too far and didn't have enough breath to get back.

As if her only chance now was to either tread water or look for something to cling to. She hadn't managed to seal the rupture, it was widening, and her life was being washed through the crack, all her foundations were being uprooted and she was falling fast.

Menopause. Empty-nest syndrome. Sunstroke. The trained biologist could find dozens of good, rational reasons, but none of them comforted her because none of them were true.

It was Kafka's frozen sea all over again, and the axe – the axe was Julie.

The Julie who now reappeared with a second bottle of wine, a half-guilty, half-impish expression on her delicate, watercolour face. She took a roll-up out of her shirt pocket and lit it.

The distinctive, sweet smell of marijuana soon filled the air. Claire should, ought, must . . . After all, she was the responsible adult – wasn't she? She ought to pull herself together, restore order, refuse, read Julie the riot act, or at least make some gesture in that direction. She ought to for her son's sake, surely? Julie was her son's girlfriend: morally speaking, Claire should be on his side, not hers, they shouldn't have any secrets from each other, that wouldn't be right. And the very last thing she should do was what she did next: she took the joint, puffed on it, held the smoke in her lungs and slowly exhaled.

'You've done this before,' observed Julie.

'Not since the beginning of the carbon age.'
They smoked.
'The girls from Lyon had some on them. On the beach.'
'The Beach. Yes . . . they used to in my day too.'
'Were you different then?'
'What am I like now?'

Julie puffed, released the smoke through her nose and said: 'Cool.'

'The weed's going to your head, my dear.'

'I take it all back. You're not cool.'

Shame, thought Claire.

'You're wonderful,' whispered Julie, looking at the ground as if there was something to see there.

They shared the marijuana in silence, and it soon began to fill Claire's head. Everything was light and warm, and she should have held her tongue, but everything was so strangely out of kilter.

'I've never been wonderful,' she heard herself confess. 'And when I was young, I desperately wanted to be taken seriously. Yes. By a vague officialdom. People I admired. Female scholars, academics, and some nameless judge who would have the last word on whether I was good enough.'

'I think I know the shyster you mean,' muttered Julie, snorting with laughter.

Claire knew the joint was to blame, but she too could no longer hold back the giggles, and they fell about laughing on the dry, warm, scented lawn.

'The grass smells of grass,' Julie slurred, setting Claire off again.

They lay stretched out on their backs, head to head,

gazing up at the early evening sky, where a few timid clouds had begun to appear.

'What about you?' asked Claire. 'Were you different when you were younger?'

'You mean yesterday?'

'The day before yesterday.'

They sniggered again.

'I'm hungry,' said Julie. 'And yes, I was different. I was . . . I liked myself. I wanted to be a singer. Or a boy.'

'There's some frozen pizza left,' said Claire.

'Thank God. We can survive on this island. Would you take me with you to an island?'

'*You*, yes.'

'As opposed to who?'

'That shyster of a judge.'

A husky Julie-giggle.

'D'you know when he came to me, Claire? That shyster, that oh-so-high authority that judges everything? Who you are, what you're capable of, what you look like . . .?'

'The first time you had sex.'

'Shit, Claire! You really do know everything.'

'No, but we did at least agree that I must have been nineteen once.'

'And the same thing happened to you when you had sex?'

'That pizza would be just the thing now, don't you think?'

'You're changing the subject, Claire. The first time I had sex with a man I was sixteen and two months.'

'With a *man*?'

'Well, sort of. He was nineteen.'

They burst out laughing again.

'It took me till I was eighteen,' said Claire. 'Much too

late really, because . . . I was hungry for it before then. Curious. I'd read so much, Anaïs Nin and all that . . .'

'Oh God, me too!'

'. . . and she had a way of describing it, as if . . .' Claire paused, searching for the right words: were there even any that came close to describing what the encounter with another body could feel like? 'It was dissolution, it was surrender, it was self-destruction, to emerge reconfigured, as one's true self. To know who one is. Or something like that.'

'Yes.' Julie gave a slow, heavy sigh. 'But it was never like that,' her soft mouth murmured.

'No,' said Claire. 'Not like that.'

She spread her arms and idly plucked a long grass stem, then reached back until it was tickling Julie's face.

'Pizza?'

'I thought you'd never ask!' cried Julie after a moment, rolling onto her side. She knelt up, hovering just above Claire, her dark eyes very close, while Claire remained lying with her arms extended behind her.

Their eyes, exploring each other.

The strange vision Claire had of simply raising her arms and encircling Julie's shoulders. Pulling her just that little bit closer.

She remained motionless.

They both laughed at once, a half-smile, half-chortle of contentment, before decamping from the garden to the lounge.

Half an hour later, they were ensconced at opposite ends of the big sofa eating steaming hot pizza from odd plates, drinking wine out of chipped glasses and listening to the music of Melody Gardot.

'That woman has a gorgeous voice,' said Julie.

'She had an accident that left her with a permanent limp. She started retraining her voice while she was in rehab.'

'What did you want to be when you were little?'

'Grown up. As soon as possible. And a marine scientist. Or a metal artist.'

'What, a proper one with a welding torch and all that?'

'Yes. A job where I could get my hands dirty, swear, sweat, work with the music turned up as loud as it will go, and feel awkward and out of place at *vernissages*.'

'Why don't you just do it?'

Claire realised she was on the brink of saying something idiotic like 'When the time is right,' or 'You can't always follow your dreams,' and was shocked at herself.

'And you? What about your singing? What if someone asks "Why didn't you?" one day, and you feel sad and at a loss to answer?'

'Are you sad that you didn't get into metalwork?'

'It's an awful moment when you realise you were too cowardly or let yourself be diverted, yes.'

'OK,' said Julie slowly.

They ate and drank in silence while Melody Gardot sang '*Our love is easy, like water rushing over stone*'. The lyrics belied the music, which enveloped Claire in an unbearable blue embrace. She got up and clicked on the next song in her library.

'Do you have any women friends, Claire? I mean real friends?'

'Jeanne was my friend. And yes, I get on pretty well with some of my colleagues and . . . no.'

A friend. She had never managed to venture far enough

out of the room in her head to share with another woman what went on behind the closed doors of her inner self. Not in its true entirety, its unsounded depths. The contradictions: feeling this way today, that way next week, and forever haunted by the same questions: am I good enough? Am I too good: who am I upsetting with my knowledge, my too-quick words? Am I lovable enough to be loved? What difference does it make if I do or don't exist? No, there was no one she could have explained all that to. Even if she'd wanted to. She was the fossilised nautilus she had wanted to be as a child, the ammonite coiled around itself; perhaps that's what all women were: pebbles in a giant hand.

'And you?' Claire picked out an olive from the remains of the pizza.

'That's something I've been pondering for a while. Of course I have besties. I don't know what else I'd call Laura, Christin and Apolline. The girls I always hung out with the last four years at school, drinking, smoking, dancing, bumming around, talking about Anna Gavalda and shaving your pubes and about the dark skin of boys from the *banlieue* and what it smells like, about things you can nick from Galeries Lafayette, about philosophy and Macron's bum and whether Brigitte ever gives him a blow job at the Élysée Palace . . . The in-crowd, in other words. The ones who are in the know.'

'And what do they know?'

'Oh, things like: a woman shouldn't love more than necessary.'

'Very progressive.'

'No, wait. I mean sex, for a start: there shouldn't be any sentimentality about it.'

'I see. More Muscadet?'

'You bet. So all the emotional stuff is just for girls who don't have a clue, Laura says. For dumpy country bumpkins, Apolline says. Girls who haven't figured out how it works, Christin says. How to bring a guy, or two or three, to heel, not the other way round – never the other way round, that's the end of freedom. The Apocalypse. Death of the heart. Paralysis of the soul.'

'And what if they have a point?'

'So what? But what if you can't do that? I just don't get why they think love is so shit! With me there's always love involved, even if it's only enough to make me suffer like crazy afterwards, whether it was just a one-night stand or a long-term thing. I enter into it because my heart's somehow opened up, I can't keep it closed and then . . . never mind. But my friends? They can *love*, all right: "Oh, I just *love* quinoa, caramel ice cream, lingerie in the same colour as my shoes, the latest film with Shia LaBeouf."'

Julie's imitation of over-the-top teen-speak struck Claire as spot-on.

'I mean, they love things, places, sensations, music, food, the evening sky over Paris after a joint, all that they love! Superficial, undemanding stuff that's really no big deal. But they never love a man.' Julie paused. 'Or a woman.' She leaned back into the sofa.

Melody sang a song about the stars, then one about the rain, and time stood still: perhaps it had already stopped hours ago, once again, and Claire and Julie were in some sort of time warp. The night had enveloped them completely by now, but neither got up to switch on a lamp or light a candle.

'Could you love a woman?' asked Julie, when it was so dark that Claire could only make out the silhouette of the young woman sitting just a metre away from her.

Again, that tremor in her heart. A baby bird trembling before taking to the air.

'Yes,' she said.

And once Melody had stopped singing, many tracks later, and the silence had grown deep and old, Claire got up.

'Let's get to bed. And tomorrow morning we'll go swimming.'

'OK,' came a whisper from out of the darkness.

Claire held out her hand. Julie grasped it.

And together they went upstairs.

'Right, then,' said Claire, when they reached the door to Julie's room.

'Right, then,' said Julie.

Claire couldn't see Julie's face in the dark passageway, just the whites of her eyes.

'Thanks for a lovely day,' Julie whispered.

Claire leaned slightly towards her.

Her lips brushed Julie's face, just below the hairline.

Julie held quite still.

Claire gently let go of her hand and said goodnight, then crept to her room and closed the door noiselessly behind her.

Her pulse was racing, so much that it hurt, in her ears, in her teeth.

Wrong! it chided. All this is wrong!

I don't care, thought Claire.

I will tomorrow, but right now, at this moment, I don't care.

As she stood by the window looking out at the bright night sea shimmering in the moonlight, she heard the voice.

'*Ne me quitte pas,*' the voice sang pleadingly, carried away with the emotion of an inaudible soundtrack. Only the singer's voice could be heard, and it stopped Claire in her tracks. She had to lean against the wall.

Words could lie.

Always.

But the voice, the body never did, and the sound raining down so unexpectedly on Claire from behind the closed door was the baring of a soul. Veiled in a breath like the moment before falling silent.

Fear, and underneath: no fear at all.

23

Shortly after sunrise, Claire and Julie made their way down to the sea. The water was suffused with red, the sun still low in the sky, and the red of Julie's swimsuit made it look as if she were wearing the ocean on her skin. The meadows surrounding the ponds of the nature reserve were wreathed in mist, turning the dune landscape into a Caspar David Friedrich painting.

The water, though still cold, felt familiar by now.

Claire waited until the chilled blood from her calves and ankles began to pump around her body, then waded in up to her hips.

Julie followed, her arms covered in downy gooseflesh.

Then Claire looked at Julie.

'On the count of three.'

'Please, not yet. I can't. Not yet. It's so cold!'

Claire contemplated the horizon. It heralded one of those mornings when the faded blue of the sky blurs into that of the sea. Hazy and warm. White sky, white sea.

It was remarkable how most people assumed the world around them to be all countries and cities, when the earth was actually more water than land. More uncertainty than certainty. More depth than height. There are so many things we get wrong, Claire reflected.

'We don't have much to endure,' she said. 'We Westerners. Except for ourselves. On the count of three.'

'*Zut!*' cried Julie. 'You can't do that to me.'

'What?'

'The sermonising. Don't be a baby, there are others worse off than you.'

'OK,' said Claire. 'On the count of three, then.'

As she dived below the surface, eyes closed, and shortly afterwards heard the splash of Julie's body entering the water beside her – Julie, her own pulse in her ears, and above it the muted outside world – it struck her that fear always hides what's most important. The thing we shrink from is the thing that really defines us.

Claire got Julie to lie on her front, arms outstretched holding a small polystyrene float while Claire's hands supported her hips, and taught her how to breathe and kick her legs in rhythm. Chin out of the water, inhale, one, two, three, exhale in the water, one, two. Eyes closed, legs co-ordinated, 'We need to get you some goggles,' head to the right, inhale, two, three, exhale . . .

It was no good.

'What am I doing wrong?'

'Nothing.'

'Yes, I am!'

'No. You're doing fine. Patience is—'

'You're lying so as not to discourage me!'

'Oh, please. That would be a cheap trick – not my style. Listen: learning to swim means getting to know someone properly. Someone we thought we knew well, but once in the water, they're completely different: a whole new set of fears and perceptions are activated. We get closer to our core, and—'

'That's just psycho-*merde*!'

'You think so?'

God, it made her furious! Furious and helpless: the fact that Julie wouldn't believe her, wouldn't trust her! She slapped her hand down on the water. 'Julie,' she said in a quiet, strained voice. 'Do you really think I want to patronise you? That that's the sort of relationship I want with you? Is *that* what you think?'

Julie clung to the float and looked up at her tearfully. There was anger and impotence in her eyes, despair and wretchedness. And rage. Such rage. At herself. And at Claire.

'I don't know,' she replied.

She spat out a mouthful of water.

They hit rock bottom on the scale of wordlessness.

They took it in turns to shower and started getting the rooms ready. Then Julie helped Claire carry her things into Gilles's room, the blue one overlooking the garden, as Ludo would be occupying Claire's room with its single bed.

Julie looked at Gilles's bed while Claire was arranging a second pillow on top and smoothing out the sheet. Gilles liked to sleep on the left. That was Claire's preference too, but over the years she had learnt to put up with the minor inconvenience of lying on the right for his sake.

Another thing she didn't know whether to blame him for, or herself.

'Why are we still using *vous*?' Julie suddenly asked in a reproachful tone.

'Do you want to switch? We can if you like. Right now.'

Julie sat down on the edge of the bed, and Claire beside her.

'No,' she replied slowly. 'Not today. Not like that. And . . . I don't know why, but if we changed, something would be lost somehow.'

The silence wore on. In the garden robins were chirping, and through the open window came a gentle rustle of leaves on a warm breeze; sunbeams danced on the wooden floor. And yet: that feeling of being hidden inside a fold of time had gone. Now the time was racing by and . . .

'I wish the others were never coming back!' Julie suddenly cried impetuously, jumping to her feet and running out of the room.

Claire remained sitting on the bed, shell-shocked. The honeymoon was finally over: yes, that was what it had been, a chance to be themselves and begin tentatively to explore what that really meant. Now her thoughts were already on the nights to come, and the bed that would force her to squash up to Gilles and turn whenever he turned. She looked at her bag in the corner, the exam scripts she had stacked sheepishly behind the door.

I wish the others were never coming back.
What are we playing at?
What do we do now?

As Jeanne lay on her deathbed she had said to Claire: 'Life is the eternal mismatch between ourselves and the universal flow. Whereas time and the world go on for ever, you strive for completion, and usually you don't make it in time. We all drop out of the stream of life unfinished.'

How present was Claire in her own time? A hundred per cent in the last twenty-four hours, she reflected. She had focused on no one but herself. More than on any day in the past decades. Then, her thoughts had never belonged to her alone, but to Gilles and his mercurial moods. To Nico and his journey to adulthood.

Perhaps that was what love was, she pondered: devoting your thoughts to others. Or perhaps it was just the least risky option.

She smoothed the sheet again and hung up Gilles's scattered shirts in the built-in wardrobe.

A whistle outside, the tune of Miles Davis's 'So What'. She knew that whistle all too well. Ludo! Whether he was approaching the house, her office at the Institute or the beach, he would always whistle the bass melody and Claire would respond with the piano chord sequence.

She went to her room, clocking that the door to Julie's was closed (she was already calling it Julie's room rather than Nicolas's: you're forgetting your own son, Claire, do you realise?), then waved to Ludo from the window and whistled the response. Ludovic stood grinning, arms akimbo, then reached out towards his half-sister.

'I'd forgotten how wonderful it is here!' he greeted her.

Claire received his hug, remarking: 'You're too early.' She noted his drunken face, that had grown more and more like his father's, and realised as she did so that she was turning back to stone. Back into the Claire who said things like: 'You're too early, you're too late. According to scientific research, this behaviour is a defensive reaction.'

'I drove through the night. I couldn't stand it any longer on the camp bed in the *buanderie*.'

'You're sleeping in the laundry room?'

'Carla deems any other arrangement inappropriate. So

does her therapist. But I'm allowed to carry on paying the mortgage.'

'Congratulations. Coffee?'

'Any cider?'

Claire pointed mutely to the cellar.

She glanced up at Julie's window. Nothing.

In a pack of animals, according to behavioural biology, each member occupies a different role and chooses whichever one happens to be vacant. With humans, it's not the material hierarchy that counts, but emotional dominance. There is always someone whose states of mind determine the emotional dynamic of the whole pack.

Claire's mother had bagged the role of problem child early on: the person everyone else had to pussyfoot around. Claire's older sister Anaëlle plumped for that of temperamental artist, bringing tension and volatility to the table but also a touch of stardust, organising pyjama parties in the middle of the day, treating Claire and Ludovic to bedtime stories about talking peacocks, stuttering elves and Atlanteans living beneath Paris, or imitating all the presidents of the Republic in a one-woman show. As a foil to his sister, Ludovic assumed the role of cynical, introspective intellectual with a hint of pale blue, casual depression. He applied himself more readily to the meta-themes of life — where does Marx lead us? What is collective guilt? — than to tasks such as making his bed, for example, and was already drinking supermarket cola with Jim Beam by the age of fifteen.

Claire had dealt with this at the time by borrowing the books of Sartre, Camus or Dashiell Hammett from the mobile library and only giving them to him on condition that he make his bed and clear his stockpile of bottles at regular intervals, something she'd seen in the late-night films she wasn't supposed to watch. Their three fathers all played the same role: that of the absentee who is consequently idealised by their misty-eyed offspring.

When Claire – an accident like her siblings before her – was reluctantly brought into the world by her mother Leontine, there was only one vacant position left: that of mediator.

Every family has one of these. One who keeps the channels of negotiation open between the constantly feuding parties, arbitrating, placating, cracking a joke where appropriate to defuse the charged atmosphere of despair and tears. Or who makes a big soup and summons everyone to the table after they've retreated sulking to their rooms, slamming the door and vowing NEVER AGAIN to speak to their antagonist. The mediator sees to it that the routine doesn't break down, that the post is opened, the fridge replenished, the quarrels settled between problem child, diva and cynic. That everyone gets their share of attention.

And in the Cousteau family, that person was Claire.

Why, Claire?

'Because the others' needs are so much greater than mine. That's why.'

Not that anyone ever put such a question to her, or that she could have expressed it in those terms – but that was how she had felt on her first day at school. And that was the basis of everything that piled up on her six-year-old shoulders from then on. Looking back, Claire realised that she of all people, the behavioural biologist, had clung to a premise that was in fact a nonsense.

*

'There's something different about you,' said Ludo, coming out into the front garden with a ceramic mug and the bottle of cider and sitting down on the blue bench facing the sea, next to the white camellia.

'That's probably just your imagination.'

'I guess so. You still come out with the same irritating, know-all comments as always, so it must be you.'

'I know.'

He sipped his cider. 'Low tide,' he observed, then added: 'I'm sorry. I haven't had enough sleep, and then being here without Carla . . . I don't know.' He took another sip, took a packet of crumpled Marlboro Reds out of his shirt pocket and lit one.

'Give me one,' said Claire.

'You're smoking?' Ludo remarked, passing her the soft pack.

'No.'

'Everything OK with you two?'

'Why shouldn't it be?'

He pointed to her cigarette. Looked closely at her face. Brushed away a strand of hair the wind had blown over her eyes with his little finger, breathing smoke into her face. Ludo had an expansive style of smoking: rather than blowing the smoke away, he let it waft everywhere.

'You look younger,' he said, smiling and tapping her on the nose.

He took another sip, and massaged his eyelids with his thumb and forefinger.

'*Bonjour*, Monsieur.' Julie's voice suddenly piped up beside them.

Julie wore a dress Claire hadn't seen her in before. A

pale violet, floor-length halter neck in a fantasy print with flowers and butterflies. The ties hung down her bare back and the smooth material fluttered slightly in the breeze. She wore open-toed sandals with large glass beads that sparkled in the light. She had replaced the piercing, its outline visible through the fabric, and her tattoo shone.

Julie was the southern summer personified: young, feminine, *séduistante*. Ludovic smiled again, though this time not in a brotherly way.

'Mademoiselle.' He jumped to his feet and gave Julie two *bises* on the cheeks.

'Julie Beauchamp, Nicolas's partner,' said Claire automatically. 'My brother, Ludo, from Paris.'

Julie had cast aside all her anger and despair, effortlessly, it seemed, and if not effortlessly, then pointedly; she had pinned her hair up and put on mascara and lip gloss, her eyes two dark, mischievous sweet cherries.

Of course: every human being is a weather vane. According to behavioural psychology research, there are six pronounced and fundamentally different sides to the average personality. Each person a kaleidoscope, a six-sided figure, a weather station with sun, rain, tempests, despair, malice, passion. So easily swung to and fro. Claire knew that. She too was a mistress of disguise, and not out of ill will: more out of self-defence. Habit. Cowardice, perhaps.

But this display of Julie's – Julie, who had morphed so readily from a . . . well, what? Confidante? Friend? What had Claire seen in this woman in the past twenty-four hours? – to a stranger seeking to please the male eye: this made her furious.

Not with Julie. Or not only.

With the whole world, for offering so little escape.

On the other side of the meadow, an estate pulled up in the car park, the door opened, and a little boy could be heard whining loudly and self-pityingly. Meanwhile, a Renault Espace stopped next to the drive and the driver sat looking out to sea with the engine running.

The grizzling child, the maddening noise of the engine, the dinosaur cries of the seagulls, the distant hum of a remote-controlled toy drone, Ludo's careless habit of letting his cigarette smoke waft in her direction. Julie's shiny cherry eyes.

Everything combined to produce a wild, absurd urge in Claire to shake Julie, to see what would burst out of the beautifully groomed shell; she wanted to seize her and shout at her, 'Did all that make no difference at all?' She searched vainly for herself in Julie's eyes: no, she hadn't changed Julie – *did you really think you had? Honestly? Or wished it so? Why, why in heaven's name, Claire? Get a grip!* And just when she felt like screaming, she finally realised who Julie's face reminded her of – that face of a passionate woman who wants it all but shies away from her own appetites and doesn't know where to find the life she seeks. It reminded her of herself.

24

From tomorrow until the end of August, there would be only three windows in the day when one had the beach to oneself, with only the wind and the stocky herring gulls for company. The first was between sunrise and nine in the morning. The second was between twelve-thirty and two, when the beachgoers migrated en masse to the *crêperie*, brasseries and set-menu restaurants, or else to their camping stoves and kitchenettes, their flip-flops and swimming trunks leaving a trail of sand on plastic chairs and aluminium tables as they sat conversation-less and exhausted from gazing at infinity. And the last was after eight in the evening, when even the hard core of youngsters finally abandoned their regular spots and purred home on their Japanese machines, to their holiday flats and villas, their mobile homes and tents, for supper, board games, the obligatory film, or a game of pétanque on the increasingly yellow and threadbare patches of grass.

Gilles and Nicolas returned shortly before lunch, laden with fresh fish, oysters, mussels and prawns from the harbour.

'The Baleiras . . .' murmured Ludo.

Baleira was Gilles's surname. And it was true, he and Nicolas were 'the others'. From Ludo's standpoint at least, there had always been the three Cousteau children on one side of the divide and the rest of the world on the other.

There may not have been much love lost between the three of them, but together they had guarded the secret of a mother adrift from reality. They had stood shoulder to shoulder against the youth and social-welfare office and the prejudices of the majority against children from poorer backgrounds with no father or status. And they had survived. None of them liked to answer questions about 'the old days'.

This time Julie flung her arms around Nicolas, kissing him with her head tossed back. Nicolas hugged her back and exchanged a serious look with Gilles.

Gilles nodded and whispered to Claire in passing: 'Big news. Our boy has plans,' before turning to Ludovic and embracing him with a kiss on both cheeks.

Ludo and Claire's husband had found a small handful of topics of shared interest over the years: mostly wine and politics. Otherwise their temperaments were quite dissimilar. But it was enough to get by, and Gilles now engaged Ludo in a conversation about the latest coverage of Macron in *Le Monde*, where Ludo worked as an editor. 'The man should spend less time in make-up and more time on politics, for God's sake!'

'Plans?' Claire wanted to ask: what plans? But Gilles was already busy directing Nico and Julie to lay the table, while Ludo stood at the kitchen counter prising the cork out of the next bottle of cider.

Julie exchanged only the necessary minimum of words with Claire, and in a consciously breezy tone: 'Can you pass me the glasses? *Merci!*' She had obviously come to some sort of decision.

Just as they had finished laying the table in the garden,

a brand new Peugeot saloon, shiny and black with tinted windows, swung onto the drive with a crunch of gravel.

Anaëlle got out – or rather swept out – in an extremely chic silk one-piece in emerald green, Audrey Hepburn sunglasses shielding a face familiar to half of France, and a designer hat. Beside her was a man: tall, slim, broad-shouldered – and about twenty years her junior.

Even as a girl, Claire's older sister had behaved as if she were moving with every step across an invisible stage. No, that wasn't quite the right image, Claire reflected: it was more a case of the stage moving with her. Whenever Anaëlle entered a place, whether a bedroom, a restaurant, or in this case an increasingly rambling fisherman's cottage on the Breton coast, it was like a curtain going up. Something happened. Anaëlle happened. People felt more alive than before, objects overcame their coyness and lit up. Anaëlle Jaricot – she had taken her biological father's name as a stage name – transformed every room into a backdrop against which life appeared more colourful and significant.

Claire noticed Julie's hand slip out of Nicolas's as she stared in amazement at Anaëlle: she clearly hadn't realised Claire's half-sister was one of the country's best known film actresses.

'*Bonjour, ma frangine!* You should see your face!' cried Anaëlle, giving Claire one of her signature bear hugs. She smelled of La Vie Est Belle and expensive hair lotion.

'I'm quite familiar with it already.'

'Really? So you do it deliberately?'

'Do what?'

'Look at me like *that.*' Anaëlle pushed her sunglasses to the end of her nose, knitted her brows and squinted at Claire, lips pursed. 'As if I were one of your insects, a silverfish or a cricket or a guppy or something.'

'Guppies aren't insects.'

'See what I mean? You're always studying, dissecting and observing, as if one were a laboratory specimen. You looked at me like that from the moment Maman spawned you, and it always makes me think: what have I done now? Anyway, greetings, it's your grasshopper sister here! Happy holiday, everyone... oh, this is Nikita. He's a tango teacher, we met when we were filming *Breakfast at His*. Nikita, this is my incredibly clever sister, just be careful what you say.' Anaëlle turned seamlessly to the young man, her voice rising a fraction of a pitch.

Great conversation so far, thought Claire. Great day all round, in fact.

Nikita had smiling blue eyes and answered with a mischievous grin and a slight Russian accent which gave his words a gently mocking undertone: 'In the car you told me she was the best sister in the world, and that you would never have become an actress without her because she used to test you on your lines, and threw away the key to your flat. I see you weren't lying.'

Claire laughed – Nikita seemed nice. What a pity she probably wouldn't have a chance to get to know him.

Her sister and her new companion exchanged sweet nothings.

Billing and cooing, thought Claire. That's something humans and mosquitoes have in common. Females of the species *Aedes aegypti* signalled their willingness to mate by buzzing at a certain pitch. Male *Aedes aegypti* then followed suit, but only when Monsieur Mosquito hit the right note did Madame Mosquito take a break from a busy day spreading yellow and Dengue fever and consent to an act that would ensure the survival of her species, not to mention that of Dengue fever and a few other creative diseases besides. Twenty-three years of comparative behavioural research couldn't help but colour your view of life.

As they went through to the back garden – where, Claire noted, Ludo had already emptied the next bottle of semi-sweet cider from Fouesnant: that's a bad sign, she thought, a very bad sign – Anaëlle launched straight in: 'You brute! How could you!' she cried, pointing a long, carefully manicured finger accusingly at their half-brother.

'*Bonjour*, dear sister. I see you've brought your adopted son with you?'

Nikita burst out laughing. 'How sweet,' he said in his rolling accent. 'That's the best compliment I've ever had.'

'Er . . .' Gilles tentatively intervened, 'shall we eat . . .?' He looked helplessly at his wife.

Claire shrugged. It was always like this. As soon as Ludo and Anaëlle met, the biting and scratching would start. No one else could wind them up like this: it was as if they needed that friction in order to define themselves. They were a mutual substitute for parents and friends, the conspiratorial duo of the Cousteau family, while Claire was the loner. Claire knew all this and, moreover, she knew that her half-siblings did not.

'How could you let that happen, Ludo?'

'Go on?' replied Ludo nonchalantly, his speech slightly slurred from the alcohol.

'Your people gave me a real panning. Or did you write that piece, huh? I had a good average till then. Not fantastic but pretty good, until *Le Monde* went and did that hatchet job . . .'

'For God's sake, *Le Figaro* showered you with enough praise.'

'As if they had the faintest idea about art!'

'Your words, not mine.'

'Wonderful,' Claire interjected. 'May I introduce you both to Nicolas's partner, Julie Beauchamp, *now*, or shall I wait until she has a thorough impression of our family?'

Ludo and Anaëlle both looked at Claire with a half-guilty, half-angry expression.

It still works, she thought.

Whenever Claire decided to intervene, it was essential to avoid taking sides: the trick was to appeal to Ludo's and Anaëlle's sense of shame. Shame was something to which all three of them were slaves. They felt it whenever it emerged all too clearly that they hadn't enjoyed a middle-class upbringing, and had tried to disguise the fact with self-taught knowledge, bookish cynicism and bold eccentricity respectively. All Claire had to do was rebuke the other two, and they instantly became allies again – against her.

Classic pack behaviour, she reflected.

Anaëlle embraced Julie, Nico and Gilles, hugging left, right and centre with her customary vehemence and disregard for personal space. She was vitality personified, the polar opposite of Claire, whom she had been known to call 'our deadwood plant': ah, that was long ago, thirty years, in other words practically yesterday.

'Champagne, anyone?' asked Gilles, holding up two bottles of Nicolas Feuillatte.

'*Mais oui!*' said Nikita, who was evidently not easily

perturbed. He took one of the bottles from Gilles and uncorked it deftly. Then he filled the glasses and, with a charming glint in his eye, handed them round, beginning with Claire.

Soon after, Anaëlle and Nikita were sitting together at the table on the long bench, their hands intertwined.

Nikita is like Anaëlle, thought Claire. He glows. At the same time, the affable tango dancer left the limelight to her alone. The way an actor's mistress traditionally did, she mused. No question that Anaëlle should have extra champagne. They ate and drank, and midday spilled over into afternoon. Gilles and Nicolas talked about the dolphins they'd watched from the island that morning: a whole school of them. They had counted shooting stars and gone diving.

'What did you mean about Nicolas's plans?' Claire asked Gilles discreetly while Anaëlle was regaling the others with an anecdote about her last film with Gérard Depardieu and Catherine Deneuve, assisted by Nikita, who was forced to play Gégé, the director, and the caterer in turns. Even Ludo laughed, though probably with a little help from yet another bottle of *cidre demi-sec*.

'We spent a long time talking it through, and I told him to go for it. Not everything has to be rationally justified, you know.'

'No, I don't, because you haven't yet told me *what* you talked about.'

'Come on,' said Gilles with a sigh, 'I'll tell you in there.'

He sat down on the piano stool and patted the leather seat beside him.

And suddenly it all came flooding back.

Swimming under the full moon. Naked from top to toe. Gilles's guitar, the sunset, wine, and their first kisses.

Dancing at the *fest-noz*.

Endlessness and infinite possibility.

Sitting beside each other on the stool before the Petrof piano. Where he sat now, taking Claire's hands in his. They had sat close together like this back then too, and Gilles had played for her. Then he had stood up and let Claire take his place. With his arms around her, he had grasped her index fingers and guided them over the keyboard, picking out a tune.

They were twenty years old.

Her body remembered, and she felt a brightness in her chest, a brightness tinged with sadness.

That time when they were sweetheart and lover, woman and man, dazzled by the heady magic that arose between them.

Before they sailed over to the Glénans on their penultimate evening, to spend the night on Saint-Nicolas, and made love there under the Milky Way, in the sand, on that island of gold amid the blue, blissfully unaware that it would be the last free summer of their lives.

Gilles was still clasping Claire's fingers in his.

And then it dawned on her. What Gilles was about to tell her.

A tremor gripped her from the inside out.

A tremor that consisted of just two words.

Please, no.

Gilles misread her reaction. He smiled, squeezed her hands and said in a low voice: 'He's going to ask Julie to marry him. I'm so proud of him. Aren't you?'

'They're so young,' replied Claire, 'they don't have to – or is there another reason?'

Gilles's response was just as she expected: 'The same age as we were – we can hardly blame them for that.'

'Not them,' whispered Claire. 'But ourselves.'

Gilles let go of her hands.

How easily, almost casually, the big upheavals in life occur. Two words, 'but ourselves', and suddenly there it is, the big crisis, the rupture that had started with a fracture here, a couple of hairline cracks there. They had filled it in temporarily with silence, but had Claire ever really tried to heal it? Hadn't she rather sat back and watched the crack widen and lengthen under the filler, waiting until the entire edifice began to topple?

Gilles flinched, suddenly pale with shock. Why now? his look said, what's beneath all this, what is it that's peering out at me from the depths of those words 'but ourselves'?

She saw his guilty conscience and his fear, his anger and his shock. She saw love and something that only distantly resembled it, all passing over Gilles's face in less than three or four seconds.

'It's not because of Juna,' said Claire, and Gilles closed his eyes, raising a hand defensively: please. But Claire went on: 'Not because of the double-bass player.' This time Gilles looked away, suspending his breath. 'Or the Parisian woman the year before last, from Raguénez, or the year before, I don't remember exactly. It doesn't matter, Gilles. Not because of that.'

'My God, Claire,' he said. 'I didn't mean to . . .'

A noise at the kitchen door. Nicolas came in and asked

tentatively, suspiciously: '*Tonton* Ludo is asking if we have another bottle of cider in the fridge?'

Claire answered: 'Tell him that's all we've got, and give him water and a coffee.'

Gilles called out: 'Of course we have!' then got up and hurried out of the room.

Nico looked at his mother. Waited.

'You've had a row. Because of me?'

'Nicolas,' she said. And again: 'Nicolas.'

The person whose fault it was that her life was no longer her own, the person she loved, the person who had absolutely nothing to do with what she had been doing wrong for a thousand years.

Disappointment in his face, that crease again, that new, vertical crease.

'So Papa's told you, then.'

Claire nodded.

'And you're not happy about it.'

'It's not a question of whether I'm happy. I think you should always do what you want to do. I trust you implicitly. Even if . . .'

She sighed. How to say it? And what to say? And was it even true – was it really *him* she was concerned about?

Or was it Julie?

And if it was both of them, what was the real reason?

What did her child – my God, her *child*! – have to do with her life? He had one of his own!

One that he is free to ruin if he chooses. Everyone has the right to their own misfortune.

But no, Claire, you're deceiving yourself.

There's something else here. Something else entirely.

It was so close up that she couldn't see its overall shape.

'But?'

'Getting married means wanting to spend your life together, maybe your whole life.'

'Exactly. And what's wrong with that?'

'You haven't enough experience to know what you're letting yourself in for.'

'Oh? And when does one reach that point, in your opinion? At sixty?'

'Nicolas, you don't even know each other properly yet!'

'Maman, you're just jealous. I can see the way you are with Julie. The way you look at her! Do you know how you look at her?'

'No, I'm not . . .'

'And the fact you're still using *vous*: you couldn't make your dislike any clearer! You're envious of everything she is and you're not. You're the one with the problem. Not me.'

'And *what* is she, Nicolas? Since you know her so intimately?'

'Your irony really pisses me off sometimes, you know that, Maman?'

Bring up the child you've got: don't try and turn them into the child you want. That principle had served her well for twenty years. She took a deep breath.

'You know nothing about her,' she said presently, in a calmer tone. 'Do you know her true character? What she really wants? Do you think you're the only person with whom she can live out all her hopes and dreams?'

'What's that supposed to mean? Are you trying to say I'm not good enough for her?'

Before she could stop herself, Claire said straight to

her son's face, that familiar, cherished young face: 'Please, Nico, don't do this to each other. Live together, but give each other a bit of space first! Love is a true miracle, but it can also be the worst prison: it can be the biggest obstacle to realising your true potential!'

Nicolas held firm. Then he said slowly: 'You're a castrating mother, that's what you are. You can't accept the fact that I don't need you any more. Just get over it.'

Claire couldn't breathe: it was as if she'd been swimming for miles. You're wrong, she wanted to say, yet she didn't know if it was entirely true.

'Your dramatic compartmentalising is affecting your ability to make decisions, Nicolas. You're reacting like a child instead of an equal. You can't accept that I'm a person in my own right talking to you about a momentous decision. You just see a mother, and in doing so you're relegating yourself to the position of a child!'

'Oh, am I? You're twisting everything! That's exactly what I mean. You're always doing it: resorting to your lousy academic jargon! You try to put me down with that stereotyping bullshit so you can carry on being the great, all-knowing mother! But it won't work any more! Forget it, I don't want to discuss it any further.'

'So when things get difficult you just walk away from them?'

Nicolas looked at her wide-eyed. She had grown loud and heated. She had never, ever shouted at her son before.

'Ah, there you are, having a slanging match, I see,' exclaimed Anaëlle, her heels clicking on the old flagstones of the lounge floor. 'Shall we go down to the harbour? I could do with a bit of fun.' She looked from Nicolas to Claire and added: 'Looks like you two could too?'

Nicolas used the opportunity to go out into the garden. He was shaking with rage, and Claire understood him perfectly, absolutely. And yet: just when she was finally realising that she'd yielded far too often to convention, he was about to make the very same mistake.

'What's up?' Anaëlle asked tentatively.

'I don't really know,' Claire replied.

Anaëlle raised her immaculately plucked eyebrows in surprise. 'What do you mean, you don't know? Now I *am* getting worried.'

'Nicolas wants to get married.'

'Oh, to his charming Julie? How lovely!'

'Do you think so?'

'No, of course not, I think marriage is an invention by people who want their right to fidelity to be enshrined in law. But this daft business of exchanging rings always makes people so happy, I've got used to trumpeting "Oh, how lovely!" like a sawn-off calabash.'

'Calabashes are only used as wind instruments in Ethiopia.'

'Thank God, Claire the Know-all is still at home after all,' remarked Anaëlle drily. 'And why are you so . . . I mean, you look like someone's been beating you up. Just be glad someone else can fold up his sweaters in future and give you a break!'

'I don't know,' Claire said again.

But she did know.

She didn't want Julie to marry.

It was that simple. That ludicrous.

'Firstly,' said Anaëlle, 'it's not your decision. Secondly, any woman can always say yes or no, even those who don't know what they're getting into. And thirdly, let's get changed, go down to the harbour and behave like good Bretons.' Anaëlle held out her hand to Claire. 'Come on.'

25

All the things one did for love.

All the things one didn't do, for love.

Claire and Gilles cleared up, such a well-rehearsed team that they didn't need to speak or ask each other anything. She passed the things to him, he sorted them, he washed the glasses, she dried up, as always, a flashback to the smoothness of their past years. Only quieter, as if they were tiptoeing around the bed of a fever patient.

Nicolas and Julie were in their room, Anaëlle and Nikita in theirs. Ludo was busy inspecting the liquid reserves in the cellar.

Claire contemplated Gilles's back. That familiar back.

The faint crackle of the radio, playing Noir Désir's 'Le vent nous portera', the wind will carry us, with its infinitely pale-blue melancholy, led her irresistibly to reach out and place her hand on her husband's back. Between the shoulder blades, where the warmth collects, the 'wind gate', as the Chinese call it, the place where the breath breaks when life tightens the noose, or when we're cold, or at the end of a sleepless night.

Gilles held still, his hands immersed in the washing-up water. He held perfectly still.

Half an hour later, they were ready to set off. Anaëlle had changed into white jeans paired with a red-and-white striped Breton top whose expensive Paris label was clear at a glance.

The roads leading to the harbour were closed: the Hent Feunteun Aodou, the Route de la Pointe, the Corniche. The entire meadow around the car park in front of Jeanne's house had been repurposed as an overflow car park.

Gilles and Ludo led the way along the GR34, Gilles extending an arm every so often to help Ludo over a root or an uneven bit of ground. Behind them were Nico and Julie, followed by Anaëlle and Nikita. Claire had ended up at the rear of the party.

She felt as if she were walking alongside her own shoes.

They made their way along the coast path towards the villa-château on the Pointe de Trévignon. The air smelled of barbecued tuna, sardines and sea bream, and the sound of Celtic bagpipe music floated towards them from an open-air stage.

Spread out across the field above the harbour were hundreds of curious onlookers, in position hours before nightfall with their picnic baskets, tablecloths, champagne and cameras. Others occupied the rocks, dunes and beaches. Children were running around, playing catch or retrieving balls from excitable small dogs.

The *crêperie*, the Mervent and both bars were full to bursting; people were buying Britt beers and Orginas and spilling over onto stone parapets and car bonnets. The firework display organised by Trévignon-Concarneau sea rescue was legendary on the Finistère coast. After a parade of light vessels, huge fireworks would be catapulted into the star-drenched night from the quay next to the lifeboat station.

After a while, Claire stopped. She watched the rest of them walk on another ten metres, then thirty, and finally disappear around a bend.

Then she turned slowly and retraced her footsteps.

It was actually quite easy. To turn round and go in a different direction.

To exchange the pain of not being missed by anyone for the sweetness of freedom. As she walked the hundred metres back to the harbour, Claire imagined what it would be like not to be herself. Not married, not a mother. Not the woman who had lost her lucky stone to a stranger in a hotel, or had felt close to her son's girlfriend in a way that seemed to her unfamiliar and uncontrolled.

No, she was just Claire – aged, let's say, twenty-four? – single, and a swimmer. A metal artist – yes, she created metal artefacts and artworks from things she found along the shore. She didn't live in the city and wasn't a professor, she lived in an ageing stone house, had a studio in the barn, her horse had no name, and the welts on her hands burned when she went to sleep. Perhaps she was about to meet someone, a man or two, or three women, or no one.

She ordered herself a cold, freshly tapped Leffe beer from one of the pavilion stalls and wandered with her plastic cup through the expectant crowd. Finally, she sat on the wall above the harbour and watched the sun slip down the sky. She saw faces in the big stones. And sometimes, she saw faces that had turned to stone.

She accepted a cigarette from a group of young women. Girls still, animated by the fierce desire to grow up as quickly as possible, and meanwhile imitating the poses of their private heroines, gazing enigmatically into the distance, showing off their flat stomachs, and sweeping their hair gracefully out of their eyes.

Claire was surrounded by emotion and sensibility. Womanhood in the making. She smoked and drank beer with her foot on the stone wall and her elbow resting on her knee: it was good to be twenty-four and free.

'There you are!' cried Anaëlle an hour later, embracing Claire from behind. 'Shall we stay here?' she asked the others, who were just walking up. It sounded more like a decision than a question. Anaëlle sat down on Claire's left.

'Excellent!' said Nikita, who was laden with paper plate-fuls of barbecued fish and gripping two bottles of beer between his fingers. He sat down gratefully next to Anaëlle.

Ludo settled himself on Claire's right, after a debate with Gilles: 'Do you want to sit next to your wife?' – 'No, you sit there, I'm sure you've got lots to catch up on' – so that she was framed by her half-siblings. Julie sat furthest away from Claire, eating the galette Nico had passed to her.

The sun was sinking. Lumpy cloud shadows painted light- and dark-blue stripes on the sea, which was varnished with a shimmer of gold.

Remarkable really, Claire pondered. How we fail to see the world as it is. The earth rotates, and we sink into darkness while the sun stays put. We're the ones who go down.

'We need more beer!' said Nikita, nudging Ludo and Nicolas to go with him.

Anaëlle had leaned over to Julie and engaged her in conversation; Julie was laughing. Gilles was looking intently towards Bénodet, where the edge of the earth had begun to swallow the sun.

Then he turned abruptly to Claire.

'We need to talk. But not today. And not while the others are still here. Would you grant us that bit of time?'

She nodded. She felt like reaching out and touching his head, his hair.

What if he'd been waiting all along for her to open the gate for him? If what he was going to say was: 'I don't want to stay'?

She was no longer twenty-four.

Julie laughed again, the attractive, husky laugh of Julie the listener, the laugh that says there's nothing in the world as fascinating as you. You, Anaëlle.

Had she ever laughed like that when talking to Claire?

Just then Anaëlle put her hand to her neck, her mouth forming an 'Oh!' as she fished a chain out of her shirt. She turned to Julie, raised her arms and held up her hair at the back of her neck, signalling to Julie to fasten the chain for her.

Claire observed all this. Julie's fingers closing the catch. Anaëlle's hand briefly touching Julie's hand, her shoulder.

Nikita and Ludo came back with beer and two bottles of wine and poured drinks all round, even for those who said 'Nothing for me', and they all drank as they watched the colours of the day bleed away and the night rise out of the sea towards them.

The streetlamps were extinguished, the lights of the restaurants gradually dimmed, and eventually the rescue boat glided out into the black water. Soon it began to glow with the red mist of flares that swirled around the vessel, transforming it into a flaming torch of blood red as it sailed majestically out of the harbour, around the little bay and back to the quay amid loud clapping and cheering.

'Wow!' cried Nikita, genuinely impressed.

They applauded; the sea was a giant stage.

The pyrotechnicians on the quay began to let off the rockets. Three firecrackers whistled an aria, followed by gushing waterfalls of white sparks, chrysanthemums of light and golden rain, arrows that fizzed across the sky, violet-blue fountains, comets and peonies. The sky over Trévignon exploded in celebration.

Nikita and Anaëlle were holding hands and gazing, heads back and eyes wide, into the glittering, spark-filled night. Gilles had propped himself up on his hands, as if to let the rockets rain down on him. Ludo murmured: 'Amazing, amazing!' He had a smile on his lips and was fifteen again.

The lights coloured people's faces: engrossed faces, ecstatic faces, closed faces. Claire leaned forward and looked over at Julie and Nicolas. Nicolas was staring intently at the sky, and all the colours were reflected on Julie's cheeks. Blue. Red. Gold.

Claire was the only one who noticed Nicolas slip down off the wall and kneel in front of Julie.

She saw his mouth move and Julie look at him.

Blue. Red. Gold. White.

The firecrackers and rockets were too loud for Claire to hear what Nicolas was saying.

He held Julie's hands in his as he spoke.

And then it happened.

Julie turned her head away from him – and looked straight at Claire.

When her mouth finally moved, she could have been saying anything:

Oui.
Non.
Peut-être.
Yes, no, perhaps, give me time?

After a moment, Nicolas got up and hugged Julie, holding her tight till the finale was over and a single white smoke bomb rose into the air. Then the night was darker than before.

I wish you all the luck in the world, my child, thought Claire. From the bottom of my heart, I wish you a place where you feel at home, and peace, and the ability to learn one day who you are and who you can be. And this young woman, the very woman you have just asked to be yours, I wish all those things for her too.

But I don't believe you will find all this together.

I hope I'm wrong.

A wave of applause broke, blending into the sound of the sea; rocks emerged from the darkness and turned back into individual people. The restaurants turned their lights up again. They walked slowly, more slowly than the other holidaymakers around them, back to Jeanne's house.

Claire felt incredibly alone in that moment. It was as if everyone could go their own way quite easily without her, each with someone else. Julie with Nico. Gilles with some other woman. Anaëlle with Nikita. Even Ludo with his wine bottles.

Gilles and Claire lay in his bed, side by side, with the layer of sheets between them.

Claire could tell from Gilles's breathing that he was awake, staring open-eyed into the darkness.

'Claire,' he said eventually.

'Yes?'

'Are you sorry you married me?'

'Sometimes. Yes.'

He swallowed. 'Why do you never lie to me?' he asked gruffly. '*I* did to you.'

His hand reached for hers.

In vain: Claire slipped it under her hip.

'I've always loved you, Claire Stéphenie Cousteau. From the very first night.'

That's not fair, she wanted to say. That's not what it's about. Love. Love! Love can't do everything.

But she did remember. That first night with him.

It was in this room.

This was where it had all begun.

The very first night with Gilles, she hadn't slept. She had watched him as they lay, foreheads touching. Before, they had sunk slowly into one another, kissing again and again, never tiring. Their mouths playing with each other, alternating between tenderness and greedy desire. Their hands and fingers reaching for each other, caressing each other. They had dived down deeper and deeper, until the night and the room had enveloped them like a giant hand and their bodies interacted without shame, without caution.

A mutual immersion.

Over and over again.

Claire had wanted to retain everything, every minute, Gilles's skin, his smell, his breath. She wanted to imprint it all on her memory: the sounds he made, the way he whispered her name, called her name, in different shades of intensity. In case she never saw him again.

In case she wanted to remember it one day.
Every touch, every moan was stored inside her body.
And now she was remembering.
I want to be different, she suddenly thought.
I don't want to fit in. Be compliant.
I don't want to be the fossil in the stone, collected and retained out of habit.
I want to be *present*, for God's sake! In ecstasy, in love, in colour: anything is possible, I'm not dead yet, after all!
And what if she took Gilles with her? Back to that time?
In the approaching full-moon nights, when the disc of soft light shone directly over the sea; during the August meteor showers, when the Perseids whizzed across the night sky. To go down to the beach. Alone. Alone to the *fest-noz*, in Sainte-Marine, in Moëlan-sur-Mer, or further afield in La Baule. To rent a room. With one bed. One quilt.
Candles.
And love.
The bastard.
Do I love him?
Do I even love myself?
To reach out to each other with their bodies instead of words.
Those same bodies that now lay motionless next to each other, not even daring to hold hands.
No. There was no way back. Not now.

26

Julie surveyed the Plage de Kersidan. She lay back propped up on her elbows under a sunshade, right up against the wooden fence at the edge of the dunes. It was hazy, like yesterday, the horizon as white as the abutting water and sky. The heat scorched the yellow-blooming gorse bushes and the clumps of grass on the dunes, shaped by the wind into solid waves. The rocks rose out of the water like black fingertips in the gauzy light.

And above it all, the ceaseless sound of the sea.

Julie was wearing her bikini again. When Claire saw it – did she actually *notice* it? – her face had remained inscrutable. Indeed, Claire was no longer the person the two of them had got to know in the previous twenty-four hours. She had turned back into Madame Cousteau. Her future mother-in-law. Claire had given Nicolas a long hug today, and he looked visibly relieved.

Claire's smiles were now few and far between.

'The stone woman,' Julie murmured to herself. The rock. That you could cut yourself on if you got too close.

Julie flopped back onto the soft, bright beach towel, her arm bent across her face, one knee drawn up. The sun shone between her legs.

Her skin burned. She still felt damp from Nicolas's semen despite having showered.

Nicolas. He too had changed.

His lovemaking was different the night after the fireworks. 'My wife,' he had said, 'I'm kissing my wife,' and worked his way down her body, with his mouth, his fingertips, his chin, its rough five o'clock shadow chafing her skin. It still burned, especially here on the hot beach. After breakfast, Anaëlle had requested a bit of 'girl time', and so she, Julie and Claire had strapped a canoe and a stand-up paddleboard onto the roof-rack of the chunky Mercedes and driven to Kersidan beach, where they had dragged everything onto the sand on a small *chariot*. Anaëlle had tossed the suntan lotion to Claire, who had applied it first to Anaëlle's back and then to Julie's.

Her fingers had slowed down in certain places. Where the marks were, thought Julie. Nicolas's fingers had left bruises, and there were red patches from his whiskers. Claire's fingers had moved gently, like a cooling balsam, over the sore areas.

'Are you happy, Julie?' Claire had asked.

She had said yes. Of course.

How casually Anaëlle had climbed into the canoe afterwards, how confidently Claire stood on the board as the two of them paddled out to sea. Further out, Claire glided over the water, her right leg slightly further forward, upright, steady, while Anaëlle took off her top, leaned back in the canoe and drifted.

Julie envied the two sisters their carefree ease in the water.

She would be able to breathe more freely if she went into the sea.

But alone?

She sat down, crossing her legs restlessly.

She thought back to yesterday evening, to the fireworks,

the proposal, the warm night. It was so intense and yet over so soon she could no longer remember Nico's exact words, only the frothing emotions inside her, and her recollection didn't fall in the right places. While Nicolas was speaking, she had felt touched. Yes. Yes! And proud and surprised and in love (with his love, perhaps? Be honest!) and buzzing with a mixture of energy, embarrassment and amazement that this was really happening to *her*.

Yet she couldn't even remember exactly how it had come about: did he take her hand? What happened after that? Julie had sunk into the solidified froth, and every minute, every hour had simply slipped through her without catching anywhere.

The sea. Just being close to it wasn't enough to make her breathe easily. There was something in her chest she had to breathe past, something that was suffocating her; the air was a wet towel pressed over her face.

Are you happy?

She needed to think about it. But her thoughts kept sliding around restlessly, erratic as the wind.

Nicolas.

As if he were trying on a new mantel, a new skin, larger, more expansive than before, the skin of a husband.

'My husband,' Julie said to herself. 'How do you do. Have you met my husband?'

'My husband.' Mine. 'My wife.' His. 'My boat, my degree, my vinyl collection, my wife.'

Property, territory, clear boundaries, don't overstep the mark, that's my wife you're staring at. That's my wife whose vulva I'm touching with my lips and reshaping with my tongue.

I'll have to ask my husband first, mind.

Julie whispered the phrase: 'Shall we invite Nicolas and Julie?'

Yes. That had a ring to it. Nicolas and Julie.

Not Julie first – shall we invite Julie and Nicolas to Marie-Alexandrine's christening? Let's go to Santorini with Julie and Nicolas! No one would say that. It just didn't sound right. 'Are you and your wife coming with us to Trévignon again next year?'

That's how Gilles would say it.

And Claire?

'Julie, are you coming with us to Trévignon?'

That's what Claire would say.

Gilles and Claire.

Gilles and Claire, yesterday evening after the fireworks. They had sat as far as possible from each other, and it reminded her of one of those B movies she remembered her parents watching on TV when she was small: whenever Gilles looked at Claire, she would be looking into her wine glass or listening intently to Ludo's increasingly rambling speeches. And whenever Claire looked at Gilles, he would be in conversation with Nicolas. Neither knew that the other was looking at them, and things were clearly bleak between them, very bleak. Hadn't the others – Nikita, Nico, Claire's siblings – noticed it? Or perhaps they had, but wanted to drown out the painful silence between the couple with their cheeriness?

Julie had been in too sweet a state of numbness to do anything. They had lingered in the garden, burning lavender oil to deter the mosquitoes: it smelled awful, but it worked. They had had a drink and attempted to locate the constellations in the night sky using an app on Nicolas's phone, and Ludo had talked about how his sole purpose in writing nowadays was to wound and attack: 'I want to target people with words, nothing else touches them these days.' Nikita and Anaëlle had danced the tango in the lounge with the sofas pushed back, and it looked sad and divine and beautiful and unattainable.

They had got out the champagne and toasted 'Nicolas and his wife-to-be'.

No one had mentioned her name. Except Claire: it was Claire who had raised her glass, looked Julie in the eye and said: 'To Julie. To Julie and Nicolas.' Claire had said her name twice, Julie now realised, as if to make up for the omission. She was 'his wife, my wife, your wife', like an Afghan woman or somesuch who is never mentioned by name, but merely as 'my cleaning lady' or 'my home help'.

Now she belonged to him. She belonged to Nicolas.

She counted the waves. Every fifth one was bigger than the others, and the sixth one too.

What if she gave it a try? She could go into the water up to her ankles. Or her knees. Perhaps to her hips. As long as she could feel the ground under her feet she couldn't come to any harm.

That's what other people did, after all. They didn't all swim. Most just stood around in the waves to cool off, or walked along chatting to each other in the shallows.

Every day, Gilles had explained to Julie over a very late *petit déjeuner* – with more champagne to toast the engagement, my God, would they have to talk about it at every meal now and use it as an excuse to drink themselves into oblivion? – every day now the French would be descending on Brittany in ever greater numbers.

Julie squinted. Kites rising into the sky, the colourful sails of kite-surfers, the roar of cheap, souped-up Japanese mopeds as teenage holidaymakers zoomed and wheelied their way to the beaches, and out on the water a line of sailing-school boats with their orange sails, wobbly goslings bobbing on the ocean. The air was spiced with outdoor swimming sounds: shrieking children, crying babies, shouting adolescents, scolding parents. And bodies everywhere. Bare bodies glistening with water droplets and salt stars, dark, tanned skin, taut, sore and hungry, did they all feel this heat, this heat under the eyes, between the legs, so hot that the mass of drifting thoughts no longer made sense?

Who belonged to whom here?

That morning, Gilles had casually wiped a baguette crumb from the corner of Julie's mouth, brushed a strand of her hair aside. The feeling of being assimilated into the body of a family was intensifying: she was no longer Julie, but 'the daughter-in-law'. A function rather than a person.

And she would come to Brittany every summer from now on. For ten years, twenty, thirty – and then?

Would she have a son one day, and find she had turned into a stone woman who looked at her husband when he looked away? She got up and took off her sunglasses; for a few seconds, everything was harsh light and white spume.

She walked towards the sea, the breeze cooling her skin.

Tiny, shimmering particles in the sand. At last: the cool water on her feet – it felt so good.

So good.

Somewhere out there, she saw the orange canoe: Anaëlle was paddling towards Raguénez. Claire, on the board, had her back to the beach.

Perhaps just as well.

Julie took a few more steps into the water, feeling the surf gently sucking the sand from under her feet back into the open sea.

Next to her, a little girl with dainty green water wings was swimming with her father's support. Beads of water gleamed on his tanned shoulders.

Salt stars, Julie thought again, and then she thought of the three sisters of Orion's belt that Claire had pointed out to her, and the fact that the stars are still there even when we don't see them.

'Perhaps that's it,' she murmured, 'all the possibilities are there even if we're not aware of them.'

Was that what Claire had meant?

Julie waded into the water up to her knees, bathed her hands and wrists in it, rubbing its refreshing coolness into her skin.

The water was turquoise close to the shore. She waded in further, and still further, until the waves were lapping around her thighs, then exhaled through pursed lips, her hands resting on the water surface as if to support herself. Another step. And another. Now she was up to her hips in the water and felt no panic, no, but . . .

She still couldn't breathe.

She closed her eyes. She wanted so desperately to be able to breathe more freely: what was it that was stopping her? She wanted to float again, like she had floated when

Claire held her, so safe and yet so free, so boundless, so absolutely present and free from all heaviness.

She turned round slowly, looking back at the beach.

For a long time.

So that's what the world looked like to the sea.

How small we are and how driven, she thought.

The ground was still there.

She could lean back and float like a starfish, the buoyancy, the energy of the waves was bound to carry her. She had managed it before: it would be fine.

She let herself fall backwards.

As she did so a wave lifted her up and she tried to stand again, reaching down frantically with her legs, but there was nothing there, *nothing* beneath her! She felt her chest suddenly constrict and was gripped with horror and alarm.

She flailed against the water with her arms but it wouldn't carry her and she sank down, swallowing water, feeling in vain for the ground: there was nothing there, nothing!

It was like suddenly waking up from one of those nightmares where you step over a precipice and fall from a great height, and your heart hammers against your chest as if trying to escape from the cage of your own surging panic. Then a second wave lifted Julie and took her further from the shore: she was drifting, drifting away on the tide!

'Claire!' she cried, or rather whimpered: the sound that came out was more like a gasp.

She felt herself drowning, and desperately snatched some air through her nose, which was all but blocked with sea water. As she sank, she tried vainly to push upwards with her feet, but there was nothing to kick against. She tried climbing movements, but all to no avail . . .

The world was turning upside down, everything was turning upside down, there was nothing but water, and she needed air! Air! She opened her mouth, but there was only water.

No-I-don't-want-to-die-I-don't-want-to-die-I-don't-want-to-I-don't-want-to-I-don't

Arms grabbing her from behind, forcing her in one direction, with two, three strong yanks, breaking through the surface of the water, air, air! the wave washing into her wide-open mouth, taking her breath away again, salt scouring her chest, acid, please, air!

The body under her back, holding her, the arm under her arms, stability, the world turning back up the right way, being rolled onto a board, wobbling, steadying, solidity at last, the water beneath her, flowing, and Claire's face beside her, above her: Claire.

Claire.

'Claire,' she gasped, sobbing, 'Claire.'

I've made a mistake, Claire.

I knew it, Claire,

the second after.

'Shh,' said Claire, swimming alongside and pushing Julie back to the shore. A few moments later, the board glided onto the beach, the fin digging into the sand with a crunch.

'Can you stand up?' asked Claire.

She helped Julie to her feet and sat her down a few metres up the beach on the hot, dry sand before quickly pulling the board fully ashore. Then she hurried back to Julie and knelt in front of her, grasping her by the shoulders.

'Say ha!' she instructed. 'Go on.'

Julie did as she was told.

'That's it. Ha! And dig your fingers in the sand. Hard. Your toes as well. Look at me. Look at me, Julie.'

Claire took Julie's face in her hands and held her firmly.

'Ha!' Julie panted, quietly at first, then louder and louder until her lungs were full of air and 'ha's.

She looked at Claire, her eyes, her limpid green eyes.

She breathed and concentrated on Claire's eyes, her face.

Her red mouth under the open blue sky and above the ancient land.

Julie silently screamed the words that so urgently needed to be said. She screamed them inwardly, where no one could hear them except herself, in the darkness of her doorless room.

I've made a mistake, Claire.
I knew it, Claire,
the second after.
What shall I do now?
What shall I do?

When Anaëlle came ashore, she sat down next to Claire and Julie under the sunshade. She didn't notice that Julie was clinging with one hand to the sand, and with the other to Claire.

And so the three women sat, until Julie's heart began to beat normally again. At length, Anaëlle remarked: 'It takes big changes to make a big change.'

Later, back at Jeanne's house, neither Claire nor Julie mentioned what had happened in the water.

27

The Bastille Day weekend was behind them; it was their last evening together.

Ludo would return to Paris tomorrow: Carla and the children were at her parents' in Normandy for two weeks, and he looked forward to a respite from sleeping in the laundry room. Anaëlle and Nikita were moving on to Sanary-sur-Mer, and after that? 'Who knows,' Anaëlle had said, 'the next film shoot . . .' Which was as good as saying: the next man.

After the long days on the beach, with all the paddle-boarding, canoeing, swimming races and frisbee games, their bodies were tired of bathing in the sea of people. Instead, they had pushed aside the sofas, dining table and chairs to create a miniature dance floor in the middle of the room. The records Nikita had fetched from the car were of Argentinian tango music, the big orchestras of the '20s, '30s and '40s: Carlos Gardel's 'Volver', Osvaldo Pugliese's 'Patético', Anibal Troilo's 'La Cumparsita', Carlos di Sarli's 'Junto a Tu Corazón', Canaro and Famá's 'El Llorón'.

'Tango . . .' said Nikita, 'tango is a love without a home.' He dropped the needle carefully onto the old vinyl record. 'Tango is the *retour de plage*. It brings the beach back into our lives.'

A piano sprinkled high-pitched pearls of sound into the room, a bandoneon answered with a sharply accented rhythm, the strings soared proudly over the top in a single, long, wistful sigh, and a violin began to tell a story in a dark whisper. 'Bomboncito' by Fulvio Salamanca, sung by Armando Guerrico.

Nikita looked across at Anaëlle and moved towards her. His whole deportment had changed. The Nikita who took nothing too seriously, nothing too personally, always had a ready smile, stepped back from the limelight, a one-summer man, was now resolute, purposeful, commanding, filling the room with his presence.

'Tango brings back the feeling that, for the space of a song, there are only two people in the world,' he said, raising his voice above the plaintive, intimate sequence of the melody. 'It's about filling that emptiness deep within your breast that always hurts even when you don't think about it.'

'Gosh!' said Nico.

Gilles's hand reached instinctively for Claire's, but stopped halfway and returned to rest on his thigh.

The wistful strains alternated with rhythmic sections: it was a music that burst into flower, that gushed and strutted and gasped for air; it created a whole other world, invisible and full of secrets of the soul.

Nikita carried on talking as he danced with Anaëlle: 'Tango is an embrace. An intimacy of great dignity and unconditional transience.'

They had stopped turning; now Nikita was stepping forwards and Anaëlle backwards, with long, flowing leg movements. How could a woman move so gracefully?

'Tango is walking, walking together through space and time. In the most honest embrace we can give each other.

What Argentine tango is not is dominance and submission. It's not about leading and being led. It's about offering and interpreting. The first duty of the leader is to make his or her follower look good.'

And that was clear to see. Something had happened to Claire's sister. She was more upright, proud and at the same time filled with a smiling, inner calm. There was nothing girlish in her demeanour: she was pure woman – a queen.

Not submissive. And yet fearlessly willing to surrender herself.

'Did you say *her* follower?' asked Nicolas, sceptically.

'*Bah oui!* Traditionalists will crucify me for saying so, but there's no reason why a woman can't lead a man. Or two men dance together, for that matter. Or two women.'

The music played. Music that told timeless stories of dirty streets and tender love, of pleading women and imploring men, of knifings, wine-drinking and the realisation of having lost someone, for ever.

'Steps won't make you happy. You can learn all sorts of spectacular step sequences, but the spirit of tango isn't in the figures. It's in the soul.'

Nikita's eyes shone like two stars; he filled the room with energy, gaiety and intensity. It was so easy with him, as if you could never do anything wrong. Once again, Claire wished she could see him become a more permanent companion for Anaëlle: that this one would last. That Nikita would be able to put up with all that such a relationship entailed: the press, whose juicy tales of the mature wildcat on the hunt for fresh meat would go on for years; and the acting fraternity, who would accuse him, the Russian tango instructor, of standing on the shoulders of a

French celebrity. She had no doubt that he was capable of rising above all that.

But Anaëlle? Would she stick it out, this closeness that she could just about accept on the dance floor, for a *tanda*, the space of three or four songs, ten minutes perhaps – but no longer than ten weeks?

Meanwhile, Anaëlle and Nikita were demonstrating what Nikita introduced as 'a technical secret of the tango that's worth mastering'. 'Firstly,' the young Russian explained, 'never have more contact with your partner than with the floor. Each must remain in their own axis at all times. Stability and balance. Even when we let go of each other. Two independent "me's" that become an "us", but neither is supporting the other.'

'Welcome to the marriage guidance council,' muttered Ludo.

Nikita got them all to stand up and balance on the balls of their feet, then on their heels, and then to roll forwards, backwards and sideways through the foot. Ludo lurched slightly against the dresser.

'Alcohol is the axis of evil,' Anaëlle remarked drily.

It struck Claire that Carla was Ludo's axis: how would he walk or stand without her?

'Secondly: the leader must always know where their follower's weight is. On the left or right foot? They must lead clearly and signal to the follower which foot they are on.'

He and Anaëlle shifted their weight exaggeratedly from left to right.

'Thirdly: calm. Inner calm. Every movement has a beginning and an end. Let's try it with a partner,' Nikita instructed.

Nicolas got up and stood doubtfully in front of Julie, shoulders hunched.

'I think I'll give this one a miss,' said Ludo, his eye on the last drop of Bourgogne Aligoté.

'Well then,' murmured Gilles.

He and Claire arranged themselves in the practice hold and shifted together from one foot to the other. It was the first movement of any kind they'd performed together for a long time.

'Nici, Nici, Nici! Your queen is not a packing case. Don't just move your hips from left to right, she won't feel that. Imagine you're treading in deep mud and pushing up out of it again,' said Nikita, stepping into Julie's place and proceeding to lead Nico, who was visibly embarrassed at being so close to another man.

'My friend, you're not a shopping trolley, you're allowed to breathe,' Nikita remarked.

Nico reddened.

'Can you feel that?' murmured Gilles, rocking continuously from left to right.

'Perfectly,' said Claire. And it was true.

Suddenly Gilles set off. Calm and determined. It went well, for three steps. Claire tried to imitate Anaëlle's movements, the backward extension of the leg, but ended up backing into Julie.

'The leader mustn't get his queen into difficulty,' Nikita chided gently. 'Whoever's leading has to know where they're going.'

'Machiavelli was a tango dancer!' called out Ludo, pouring himself a drink.

Claire and Gilles changed places.

'You're good at this,' Gilles said. 'I can feel you perfectly even though you're hardly moving.'

Nikita put another record on. It was a song that cast the listener down into the abyss of their soul. Claire never knew music could be like this, inviting her to dance with her own despair.

'Remember: tango is walking in an embrace.'

Nico rolled his eyes. He was clearly uncomfortable with the whole situation, and with Nikita. He and Julie eyed each other suspiciously, as if each were a trapdoor the other might fall through at any moment. Eventually they gave up, and Anaëlle came over to dance with Julie.

Meanwhile, Claire was leading Gilles, taking care not to look him in the eye, but diagonally over his right shoulder.

'Ah! Claire's got it. She's leading with her spine. That's the initiating impulse.'

'That's not what you told me when we were training for the film,' Anaëlle said. 'You said it came from somewhere quite different.'

'Of course,' Nikita replied. 'I wanted to seduce you.'

'So it's not true?'

'What isn't?' asked Julie.

'Oh yes, it's absolutely true. But that's something a man can only explain to a woman properly in private, although . . .'

'OK, then I'll do it,' said Anaëlle with a malicious smile. 'The initial impetus for a movement comes . . . from here,' she said, folding her hands and placing them over her pubic bone. 'From your glorious, ecstatic, dancing sex organ.'

'Thank you, Anaëlle, for that important reminder. But

I meant the inner impulse, sweetie,' Nikita corrected her gently.

'Did you just call me sweetie?'

'*Oui, madame.* Sweetie. I like that word.'

They eyed each other across the room, a private conflict resolution playing out deep beneath their protective shell.

Nikita clapped his hands, interrupting the moment, and continued: 'The inner movement comes from the root of your being, but it would look strange if you led with the pelvis.' He walked across the room with his hips thrust forward. There was laughter all round, defusing the tension. 'Change partners!'

Anaëlle reached for Nico, Nikita for Gilles, and Julie found herself in Claire's arms.

'Who's leading?' asked Claire.

'You.'

The music changed. 'Milongueo del Ayer'. Guitar, drums, a dark, red music that would have suited the intimacy of a bedroom.

You could tell by listening how it had passed through the strumming fingers of countless thousands of uprooted migrants, the payadas of the South American gauchos, the habaneras of the Cubans, the candombes and canyengues of the Africans, the milongas of the Argentine ports and the tarantellas of the Italians, telling of love and homelessness, a cry for help, seasoned with the melancholy of the button accordion.

The pain and the joy of being alive, at least for that hour, even if it should turn out to be the last.

Claire shifted her weight gently.

She felt her centre. Her loins. It felt warmer there, more present. The warm base of her spine.

But perhaps it was just the summer.

The heat.

The sea.

The wine.

Julie closed her eyes, letting herself be rocked back and forth.

Suddenly Anaëlle was beside them, a silent presence arranging Julie's hand gently under Claire's right shoulder blade, pushing Claire closer to Julie, placing her hand in the middle of Julie's back.

Folding their fingers together.

Was it Julie's heart or her own that Claire could feel beating against her chest?

This sense of familiarity. Recognising your own contours in the other. Embracing yourself.

The sweetness of feeling the other's warmth, wanting to be gentle with her, with her body, that young body that was once your own: gentle, beguiling, tender.

Anaëlle looked at Claire over Julie's shoulders with an expression she hadn't seen in a long time. It was a familiar, discreet look exchanged between them alone. When they had to tell a shared lie. When they shared a secret no one else must know, for the sake of their own survival. Lying to the welfare office, to the school, to shop assistants, about the fact that their family of minors was lurching and stumbling through life alone, with a mother who was growing increasingly oblivious to their existence. Lying in order to stay together. That look was Anaëlle's way of conspiring, of communicating with her half-sister: in those moments she wasn't acting a part, she was Anaëlle, fighting for survival, a cat with broken paws, determined not to be ground down.

Claire led Julie around the floor, and Julie responded instantly but unhurriedly. Claire questioned with her body and Julie answered. Claire heard the beat beneath the layers of music and rhythm, she embraced Julie and Julie embraced her. It was as if they were one body, intertwined in the same steps.

At the end of that dark-red song – an end that came all too soon – the room began to take shape again. The room and everyone in it. Everyone else had stopped dancing and stood watching Claire and Julie. Ludo was frowning, his hand raised to his mouth. Nikita was smiling. Nicolas was watching Claire with a furious look on his face, the look of a son that snarled: *She always has to know better, even at this; will she never stop trying to prove it to me?*

Only in Gilles's expression did Claire see something more searching.

The skin that had grown so warm where their bodies touched began to cool.

Julie opened her eyes. Her gaze was soft and deep. Until, drawing a veil over it, she hurried to join Nicolas and leaned up close to him.

'I think tango's a stupid dance,' he burst out.

'We don't have to do it,' said Julie quietly.

Anaëlle interrupted the next song.

'Right! Shall we go for a last swim?' she asked, looking round the room. 'I'd like to say goodbye to the sea in style.'

Only Claire went with her.

28

The moonlit sea was cool, and they waded in hand in hand up to their hips.

They were silent, until a shooting star streaked across the sky. When they were small, Anaëlle used to tell Claire they were the teardrops of planets.

'We've changed,' Anaëlle observed after a while. 'Are we any better?'

'I don't know,' replied Claire. 'Sometimes I feel we should return to the time when we still knew who we wanted to be.'

'When was that for you, roughly?' asked her sister.

Above the horizon, they could just make out the distant glow of Saturn.

'Eleven,' she said.

'Nine for me,' said Anaëlle. 'I wish I was as brave and confident now as I was at nine.' She squeezed Claire's hand. 'On the count of three.'

After 'two' they dived hand in hand into the water. It was a game they had played since childhood – diving in before the last count. Lies were tools that could save them: lies, silence and disguise.

As they waded back to the shore, Claire felt the waves break more determinedly against her calves than in the previous weeks. It was no longer a gentle, distracted wash. The sea had grown more purposeful. Bigger. It was gathering force.

She looked up at the sky. The stars were clearly visible. The wind was from the northwest. Cool. Strong. A storm was brewing.

Something was coming her way. From out there, from out of the darkness – and it promised to reshape her world.

They sat together in the kitchen, with only the faint light from the extractor hood to see by. Claire opened a couple of beers.

'Are you happy?' Anaëlle asked calmly.

'No,' said Claire.

'Me neither,' said Anaëlle, toying with the label on the bottle.

'Why not just settle for Nikita?' asked Claire. 'I know it sounds tame, but he's a good person. A good man. In so many ways.'

'I know, but I simply enjoy meeting new men,' Anaëlle sighed.

'That doesn't mean you have to sleep with them all.'

Anaëlle smiled, a disarmingly sad smile. 'Until I've slept with a man and left him, it's like I don't really know him. It's only by having sex with someone and losing them that you get to see the real person.'

'Or yourself?'

'Or yourself. We're one hour into your birthday, by the way, *ma poule*,' said Anaëlle.

'And I thought things couldn't get any worse,' said Claire.

They clinked bottles and drank.

'The tango . . . that tells you something about yourself too,' Anaëlle began dreamily, looking at the bottle. 'Without sex. Without being left. When I first started, I thought: no one can lead me. Lead *me*! I mean: seriously tell me how to understand the music? How to understand *myself*?' She snorted. 'But it's not like that. Every good tango dancer knows that it's about finding a shared understanding of the music. And once you've found it . . . you suddenly know you're no longer alone. With that sadness you feel without knowing why. With that lust for life that makes you want to really accomplish something, savour it to the full. Bathe in it. And best of all: no one blames me for being strong and feeling attractive, in a place that no diet can ever reach, a strong and attractive woman.'

Anaëlle looked up. The wind was hammering even more angrily against the house, making the old, exposed beams in the lounge creak.

'You know, it's simply not done to be happy with your body as an actress. It's against the professional etiquette. It's our duty to constantly point out our own shortcomings.'

'Among female academics the body is an object of irony,' said Claire. 'We admit to having one. But we have to be brutal with it otherwise we risk being accused of vanity or cheap sentimentality.'

And yet, she reflected, the body is so many things. Capable of desire. Of seduction. Of life.

'The tango . . .' Anaëlle returned to her theme. 'When you lead, as a woman . . . you felt it too, didn't you?'

'What?'

'Everything. Yourself. The other you.'

Claire was seized with an absurd feeling of shame. Relief and delirium surged through her body.

The other me?

A warm stream of images, Chloé's cool, round tongue piercing playing in her mouth. Julie's back disappearing behind a zip. The moment when Julie emerged naked from the bathroom, and the moment when Claire leaned against the wall listening to her voice.

Anaëlle continued: 'When I was preparing for the role of Leda – do you remember? The Neapolitan girl who lands up in Buenos Aires and survives against the odds by disguising herself as Dante the violinist and playing with a troupe of tango musicians? Based on the novel by Carolina De Robertis?'

Claire nodded. She had been to the cinema three times just to see her big sister in it.

'I trained for it by dressing as a man and hanging out in Paris for a few weeks. Going shopping, to the cinema, to bars, and simply living as Adrian. It's quite easy and yet complicated at the same time. Easy because clothes, posture and hairstyle can turn any woman into a man – in the eyes of others. But the rest of it? You wouldn't believe how much our gestures have adapted to our role as women . . . and how little that role reflects our own personality.' Anaëlle looked up. 'But who am I telling? You know more about body language than old muggins here! You know what I mean though?'

'Yes. The human view of humanity is far from the whole picture. We call that premise-based reasoning. The brain works on assumption rather than analysis, purely to save time. In our world it's known as the cliché generator.'

'Well, it works a treat. But I still had to learn the role of "man" first. As a guy, you don't tilt your head sweetly to one side when you're ordering a beer at the bar. You don't cross your legs discreetly on the bar stool to stop people looking up your skirt. You don't run your hand through your hair when you don't know what to say to someone who's just insulted you for fear of upsetting them. I had to learn to walk and stand like a man. To stop putting on the helpless smile. My back pains disappeared overnight.' Anaëlle drank her beer, this time taking a long swig, then spread her thighs and leaned on the kitchen counter with both elbows. 'I've never been so relaxed as when I was Monsieur Adrian, believe me. Men don't know what they've got – or rather, what we women haven't. Or don't allow ourselves. But what do I know, you're the expert.' She concentrated for a moment, then let out a practised belch. 'Baby, that one was for you.'

Claire had to laugh.

The fridge hummed; a stray fly buzzed around the light of the extractor hood.

'And you know what?' said Anaëlle, switching back to Anaëlle: laughing, mocking, glorious Anaëlle. 'Best of all were the guys who saw me as a rival. First, they would size me up: how strong is this dude? That was a revelation: I wasn't being judged on my looks any more, but on how strong, fast, witty or smart I was. A completely different set of criteria. And this great solidarity once you're accepted. The next thing they want to know is: is this guy a hit with women? That infuriated them. Because I was good at dancing with women. I paid them compliments. I treated them the way they'd always secretly wanted to be treated. Of course, I acted out all the men I never had! And I acted out the Anaëlle who's always been ashamed of being "too much". I no longer felt embarrassed about being strong, having a big mouth and tending to view love as an occupation.' She laughed, loud and uncontrollably;

it sounded like something halfway between a sob and a scream, as if the fact that she had clipped her own wings still gnawed away at her.

Claire thought about how she had felt with Julie in her arms. In the role that demands the very things women so often conceal from themselves and others: strength, initiative, leadership. Sensuality for its own sake. She had wanted to tell Julie how beautiful she was. How glorious. And by that she meant a different kind of beauty than that of her skin, her hair – *oh really? Not just that, Claire, not just that, but can you really articulate it here, in the dim light of the kitchen, over the hum of the fridge with all its mundane contents: the mustard, the butter, the milk?*

It had been a moment of exposure, that trembling in the other's proximity, feeling the breath, the breast-to-breast contact, not threatening, but unsettling in its intensity, its softness, the pain that accompanied it, the feeling of music flowing through you, drawing sparks from the stone of your soul. A few steps, together, the loss of external boundaries, because there is no longer one who pushes and one who yields, but the creation of something new. A centre, something that says: I know. I want.

The scent of hair, the hint of Parisian perfume, the dew on the upper lip, on the temples, between their joined palms.

'And the women?' Claire enquired tentatively.

Anaëlle smiled. Half Adrian, half herself. 'They knew who they were dealing with, of course, or they soon realised on the dance floor, when they noticed I didn't have a roll of coins in my trouser pocket. Eventually I bought myself a red tennis ball, cut it in half and stuck it in my Calvins.' She laughed absently at the memory. 'Did you know that you automatically walk differently, look at things differently, when you're conscious of your sex organ?'

'No,' said Claire, fascinated by her sister's frank intimacy. She wished she could speak as freely about the tide that was raging inside her, the pull, the undertow.

'They still played along with it though. For the hell of it perhaps, I don't know. To get one over on the other guys. Or, who knows ... maybe because they knew I meant exactly what I said. My looks never lied. I saw them as they really were. No illusions, no testosterone-fuelled, five-minute crush. No shame. No fear. They simply weren't afraid, of anything, and that makes me wonder: what is it that we women are afraid of when we meet a man we like? Is it really of him? Or of all the talk in our head? Are we afraid of wanting him so much and then not finding what we're looking for?'

They drank simultaneously. Long sips of ice-cold beer.

'Why don't you ask how far I went as Adrian?'

'Do you want to tell me?'

'Do you want to know?'

Yes, thought Claire.

No, she thought.

'Do you have to be an Adrian to do that?' she asked eventually, in a barely audible whisper.

Anaëlle took her time answering.

Her finger traced the delicate ring of condensation left on the counter by the beer bottle.

'The sounds they made,' she said. 'Their breath. Their sighs. That bird-like quaver, from deep in the throat. Such self-abandon. It was ... it was like falling, plunging into ever-widening arms and eyes and lips. I never managed to let myself fall all the way, to the very bottom. I was afraid. Of the deep. Of the incredible depth of emotional sensibility and surrender, of abandon and bottomless trust. Men fall into pleasure; women can fly. They can float. I fell, and what I saw looking back at me—' She looked at Claire, a raging, damp fire in her violet-blue eyes '—it was me. Adrian-Anaëlle, whatever, neither man nor woman but a universal being, just me. I fell. But I didn't want to lose myself in my own reflection. I couldn't take that plunge. I haven't got the guts. Not me.' She exhaled slowly. 'But you have.'

The fridge stopped humming. Absolute silence; even the wind held its breath.

'At first I thought you were jealous of me,' Anaëlle went on. 'That evening, on the fourteenth. You looked at me when I was talking to Julie as if you wanted to throw me overboard, to the bottom of the ocean. I thought it was the jealousy of a sister who wants what it's too late for her to have: celebrity, lovers, too much drinking time. But then . . . then I remembered. You were looking at me like the men in Paris. The way a man eyes a rival when he touches the woman he wants for himself.'

'Anaëlle . . .'

'That's the first and last time I'm going to talk about this. I'm not brave enough to go any further, and believe me: without your courage back then none of us would have survived. Writing to our grandmother. Throwing away the key. Making sure we had something to eat and didn't just let ourselves go to the dogs. I sometimes wonder what would have happened if you'd used up that courage on yourself instead of wasting it on us.'

Claire stood up and opened the door to the garden.

The wind was getting stronger, gusting around corners; it smelled of wet grass, wet from the fine salt-water mist. And deep beneath it the smell of the distant autumn, a reminder that this day too would soon belong to the past, the summer respite at an end.

'You ought to try it, by the way. Disguising yourself,' said Anaëlle. 'Just to see what kind of man you could be. How about Stéphan? You wouldn't have so much bust to strap down either.'

'Oh, thanks!'

They giggled.

'Another beer, Adrian?' Claire asked in a deep voice.

'You bet, Stéphan,' Anaëlle replied.

Claire planted two bottles of Leffe Blonde on the table between them.

'Give it a go. It might tell you things about yourself that you never knew. Or didn't want to know.'

Claire waited until Anaëlle had gone up to the attic room and closed the door; until the house was completely quiet. She waited in the dark, with the light over the gas stove switched off, the night breeze on her skin, images of red half tennis balls and quavering moans whirling round her head.

She reached for her mobile and downloaded album after album from Songstore. Then she stood in the middle of the improvised *pista* between the sofas, the black, gaping cavity of the fireplace, and the window, through which a windswept moon was peering into the darkness.

She clicked on the first song and it poured out of her phone into the room, a tide of sound rising higher and higher. Claire closed her eyes and raised her arms, as if she were leading a partner. Her right fist pressed to her heart, her left hand in the air.

The tango whispered and called, beckoned and proudly took the floor. 'Bomboncito'.

It was her birthday. She was in the midsummer of her life.

Her autumn was approaching, then it would be winter, life would begin to fade like the light at the end of the day. And eventually she would drop out of the stream of life. Never finished, never arriving.

But in the meantime, Claire?

Who can I become?

Who is the other me?

A universal being?

She danced in the dark, advancing step by step into the room. Alone. Alone and erect.

It wasn't the same, there was no partner to pick up on her impulses, follow them through, answer them.

Julie.

Claire swapped holds, now imagining herself as the follower. Suddenly finding her balance. She didn't need leading, it was all inside her, the leading and the following.

We women can dance alone.

Unlike men.

She followed, leading herself in her imagination, embracing her own body. She swapped places again, going forwards instead of backwards, her arms around herself, and something inside her unfolded, unfurled and grew into something new.

She opened her eyes: a shadow at the foot of the stairs. Its silhouette even more familiar than her own.

How long had he been watching her?

Can you see me, she asked silently, can you see the other me?

She stopped dancing. Opened her arms slowly, took her fist away from her heart, opened the closed fingers of her other hand.

Gilles moved towards her in the dark and her hands opened wider. His fingers slid into hers, his arm around her back. A touch, a warm, contradictory, indefinable sensation.

The shock of looking into his eyes, so close, so naked, unveiled, unsmiling.

The violins, the rebellious desire. Is the tango a man? A woman?

They slipped into the close hold, and she felt a torrent of simultaneous emotions.

To press up close to him never leave don't leave me I want to leave and be free and breathe and hold me and go with me and don't follow me and I don't know where but I want to know I want to know where I can go when I'm the sole leader and follower – of myself.

She pivoted out of his embrace and he caught her, his fingers holding her tight, pulling with an iron force she had never known before.

She resisted. Force and counter-force.

They were enemies recognising each other as equals and giving as good as they got. Now that each knew what the other could take and what they could dish out, they let their force gradually ebb away, sinking slowly.

Towards each other, their bodies up close.

Holding on tight, digging her fingers into his back. Wanting to wound him. Hurt him. Brand him with her anger, the anger she had swallowed, suppressed, rationalised away a thousand times.

Feeling the heat of her own being, this is me, all of this, my loins, my heart, my thoughts, all of it!

So many women I once was and am no more. The child who believes in the overwhelming force of life; the girl who distrusts beauty and follows a woman with sunshine in her eyes, longing to be kissed by her once more; the young woman who turns to stone to make her way in a man's world; a woman whose legs are wrenched apart and her life with them; who becomes a mother and finally grows into the role only to see it vanish; who waits for something to change; who hides in hotels in order to be herself at last, and who has now vanished likewise; who thinks looking away is an act of kindness – all of those women are gone, Gilles, including the one you once so desired, where are those Claires, and who is the *other* me? Who *might* I have been?

She bit his lower lip, they bit each other with an animal passion, his teeth sinking into her mouth, meeting anger with anger. She pressed her hands against his cheeks, he gripped the back of her neck hard.

Rawness, brutality.

Pushing him away, being released, her hand questioning his at the last moment: do you understand?

Swaying with him as he felt for his balance, stepping gingerly. Moving very gently now that they had wounded and been wounded. Brow to brow, breathless, bloody-mouthed.

Two bodies speaking to each other through the increasing pressure of their hands. Through the smell of their bodies, hot, sweaty and violent. Hungry for love, weary, sore, the life returning under their skin.

Forgive me.

Do you forgive me?

What a shame that an 'I love you' doesn't keep its promise. To be good, to remain good, it's impossible.

I know. Do you know too?

And now?

We must say goodbye. Otherwise we'll ossify. We'll deceive each other more and more. For whatever reasons.

But where shall we go?

I don't know.

Hold me tight all the same. Just for a while.

Let us turn and turn and turn until we stop and find that everything is somewhere else.

The song left the room.

Their hands let go first.

Then their bodies separated.

And there they stood, in the hour of the wolf, in the dark, silently eyeing each other, as the wind rattled the shutters.

29

They had no choice but to spend that last night in the same bed. The wind ran its fingers ever more clamorously over the house and roof. The treetops swayed in the garden, making the leaves cast restless shadows on the wall.

'You can go to Juna's if you want,' whispered Claire, as they stood facing each other in his room.

'I haven't been to Juna's for a long time,' Gilles whispered back equally softly. 'And I don't want to either.'

'Why did you want to before?'

They lowered their voices, quiet as the crackle of a stylus, so as not to disturb the others' sleep, not to cause any embarrassment, not to wake the child, the child! Never quarrel in front of the child. That was always Claire's first thought, even now. *Protect the child, from the world and from me –*

'Because I couldn't have you.'

'Have me? In what way?'

'Claire. You have a boundary inside you no one can cross except you.'

'Have you tried?'

He shook his head. 'Not hard enough. And I wanted . . .' He closed his eyes and simply stood there, and when he opened them again his look was sincere. 'I wanted it to matter to you. I wanted to feel that I can reach you. Hurt you. That I can get that close to you. So I'd know if I mean the world to you.' She understood only too well. She hated him for not trying another method, but she understood.

'The world?' she hissed, 'nothing less than that?'

'Yes,' Gilles replied gruffly. 'And I know that's unfair and no one is or should be another person's whole world, no one can be that. I know, Claire! And yet you can't escape that feeling! Our whole goddamn culture, music, literature, art – it all revolves around the existence of that absurd, wonderful, utterly unreasonable feeling. And yes, I wanted to mean the world to you, even if it was just . . . for the space of a song, a damn Miossec song! The space of a look, a kiss!'

She looked at her husband: she had known nothing of this hunger in him. And not because she wasn't familiar with it herself.

No. Claire knew that hunger, oh yes. But it had become a survival strategy, since her first day at school, not to give in to it. To bury it completely behind a phalanx of formulae, facts, phrases, diagrams and analytical videos, and to shift the centre of her desire, her being, to her head, far enough from her heart, far enough from her loins. She had prostituted herself for the sake of education and rationality – but how to tell him that?

'You're jealous of Miossec,' she said.

'Yes! You gave *him* your desire. And you listened to him, his desires, you took him seriously – a complete stranger. And I know it's irrational.'

'It's not true that I didn't care,' she said. 'About the women, I did care!' She had raised her voice too much: was that a creak outside the door? She reined it in, pushed it back underwater, the dark water they were both swimming in. 'I assumed you just wanted to be free. You wanted to do something, experience something, just for yourself.'

'Yes! That too, Claire, that too. But I wasn't sure that you still felt anything for me. As a man. You were never jealous. You always understood, I could tell, and God! I loved you for that, for understanding me! How often in life do you find someone who can put themselves in the other person's shoes? Even when it hurts to do so? You're a bestower of freedom, Claire. But I didn't always want that freedom, especially when it was readily granted. I fantasised about what it would be like if you hadn't been so damned understanding, just for once, but had terrorised me instead with jealousy and scenes and tears and ultimatums . . .'

'The whole gamut of religious convention, in other words. The A to Z of emotional blackmail. A total misunderstanding of human nature.'

'. . . if you say so, yes! An illogical, unfair, naive reaction. Exactly. What most people feel who have neither your goodness nor your education.'

'What part of that is meant to be ironic?'

'None of it, for God's sake! You're good to everyone except yourself. One outburst. That's all I asked. In twenty-two years. One moment when you're overwhelmed by your feelings and say the very same unfair, illogical, naive things. That you're afraid. That you don't want to lose me. That you miss me. But you never needed me enough for that.'

'I want to hit you right now, Gilles.'

He crossed to her side of the bed and stood right in front of her.

His frown melted into an incredulous smile. 'Now? At last?'

'I could have scratched your eyes out,' she said, 'yours and theirs, I could have cut your fingers off!' Her voice shook; it was the truth, the absolute truth. The anger inside her was boundless and shocking. 'And yes, take that! It's true, I never *wanted* to need you! I don't *want* to need anyone! But I wanted *you*. Did that never occur to you amid all your . . . your . . .'

'Go on!'

'Your self-centred histrionics. What's that supposed to mean: I sleep with other women because my wife never shouts at me?'

'Yes. Yes! You've always been able to live without me, that was clear! I didn't know if I could do the same. Without you. And with others instead. Others who need me, who I mean the world to, for quarter of an hour! Juna needed me for one afternoon and then never again, and I didn't need her either.'

'Coward,' she said quietly.

'Yes,' he conceded. 'And you? What about you, Claire?'

How she loved him in that very moment: for saying 'yes' and confessing, to everything, without trying to downplay or justify it. And at the same time for being unafraid to throw the question back at her, accusing her of cowardice instead of courage, fear instead of understanding.

'And?' she queried, more gently. 'What was the outcome of the experiment?'

'That I don't want to mean the world to those other women. I came to understand very well how you feel, how hard it can be to put your own life on hold for someone else's sake. And I knew I wanted to mean the world to you. Precisely because you *don't* need me. Because you let me breathe.'

Claire raised her hand and pushed Gilles's hair out of his eyes, stroking his brow slowly and firmly with her cupped hand, over and over again. 'For a long time, I think I blamed you more than myself for having a child, Gilles. So soon. I would like to have discovered what I could have done instead. What we might have done. Without that constraint. Without the needing or the wanting to be needed.'

'I know. Oh, Claire, I know, and it's not nice being the man who made a woman become less than she wanted to be, than she was capable of being. Who expected her to give up her own life for a child. Who watched her struggle in a world that has never been fully open to women.'

'Why did you never say that to me? So clearly?'

'I was no wiser than you back then, you know. I fear I'm still not, even today. It took me a long time to see the light, a very long time. Nico had already reached puberty by the time I realised how torn you were inside. Not in the same way as me. More damaged. I gained something: you and a child. But you lost something: yourself.'

She bowed her head, feeling the weight of her arms, and small, rapid tears fell onto the floor in front of her.

'Yes,' she said, 'I *have* lost myself, Gilles. I'm not there any more. I'm not there.'

Gilles undressed, held out his hand and whispered: 'Come on. Quick. Let's find you.'

Our last night, thought Claire. In the same room as the first. This is where it all began, and this is where it will all end.

Looking up at the ceiling above her, where the leaf shadows traced restless hands and shapes of their own, she visualised the words THE END printed on the air between them, floating on the breeze above their joined hands. They were just one story, and it was all coming to an end. Afterwards, they would never be spoken of again, and their life would be slammed shut with the same dull thud as a book, leaving them behind, frozen in time. The idea took her breath away.

His fingers stroked hers gently.

'And you?' he asked. 'How many?'

'A few,' Claire replied. 'But never more than once.'

'Even that you were better at. I always stayed too long.'

'Is that what it's about, Gilles? Being better than me?'

'Maybe. An attempt to measure up.'

'That's absurd. It makes no sense.'

'I know. Was it . . .?' He paused, and inhaled deeply.

'You want to know what it was like with them? Or why?'

'What it was like. And why it was like that. What was good about it.'

'Being looked at,' said Claire after a while. 'I showed myself. And I was looked at, with open eyes.'

'That was what you didn't get from me.'

'Yes. I wanted to be looked at. From the outside. And I wanted you to look inside me too, at the other, inner me. Instead of keeping your own version of Claire before your eyes. Like a pair of glasses that obscures everything else. Distorts it.'

'I could leave with Ludo tomorrow . . . I mean today, if you want,' Gilles said eventually, 'or should I stay? It's your birthday.'

'No. It's . . . it's a good birthday present,' Claire replied. She meant it sincerely: it was both sad and welcome, being granted the time to herself that she so longed for.

'Are you in love with someone?' he asked suddenly.

Someone: he didn't say *another man*.

'Perhaps,' she said.

'So it's all over?' he whispered.

She turned to him.

Yes, it was all over.

And suddenly everything was clear.

Having finally plunged over the precipice, she had found a foothold on the way down; just as the moment of separation and freedom was approaching, and with it the uncertainty of an unknown future, she had come to rest on a narrow ledge. She knew that the fall wasn't over yet though, that her descent was only just beginning; from here, she would plunge ever deeper into the abyss, into the 'perhaps'.

But meanwhile, on this rocky shelf, she could pause, pull Gilles's ear to her lips and, inaudibly to all the ears that were listening out tonight, to the eerie, raging, moaning lament of the wind – or was it a woman's cry, a man's gasp? – make him a proposal.

An agreement.

'This is our last night together, the last night as *us*, as the people we were . . .' she began.

Never again did she want to return as the Claire she had become up until this summer, never again did she want this husband back, all the lies, the silence, the secrecy, the self-repression, the ignoring of unsaid words, never again. From now on, from this very second, there would be no going back, everything had to be smashed to pieces – their flat, their car, their beds, their silence – it all had to end.

All this Claire whispered into Gilles's ear and more: her conditions, her proposal – the only possible way out that she could see; nor could she even promise a successful outcome for either of them. He nodded and said 'OK', then he burst into tears like a lost boy, and it was the saddest thing she had ever heard or seen, it broke her heart, but that too was part of the necessary termination process. She took his head in her hands and he hers as her tears too began to flow.

He kissed the tears away from the corners of her mouth. Then he laid her down.

Her desire for him took Claire by surprise, it was an urge that welled up from deep within her core, a raging hunger to expose every wound, every reality, and this time their bites were kisses, though no less brutal, no less relentless, so hard did they press up against each other in their despair – a despair that drove them closer together than in all the preceding years and decades. Pleasure and pain, the greedy man, the destructive woman; he pressed her legs apart with one hand and she held him tight, one arm around his back, one leg around his thighs, his buttocks, muscles taut, biting into his shoulder till he cried out: 'Claire!' It was more frenzy than love, or rather the flip side of love, its silent, ever-present companion, the shadow we choose to overlook, and which knows everything that remains unspoken.

Time burst apart at a loose seam, and they were suddenly together in a place they normally only entered alone. Full of life, pain, loneliness, and grief at being alone there.

Now, thought Claire, *now we can see each other, now we can see each other as we really are.* And it was as if they were strangers, she saw the stranger in him that he had always repressed, always concealed, just as carefully as she had: someone who defied description, but who we all recognise in ourselves when we finally discover them behind a locked door, looking back at us through unfamiliar eyes.

This wasn't lovemaking. It was a mutual conquest.

When Claire came, she bit Gilles once more. He made no sound, and nor did she. *The walls are thin, the skin is thin.*

As they reached climax, Gilles flung his head back in a mixture of pleasure, despair and arousal. Afterwards, he remained inside her, one hand in her hair, the other cupping her breast.

So that was our last night together, Claire thought as they lay there, half in and half upon each other. She wanted to remember everything, this room, the scene of their first and last encounter.

For a long time we have swum against the tide, run up against walls, walls we have built from our own thoughts, our own silence and paralysis, only to return, in our mid-forties, so long after the hopeful days of childhood and youth, to this same place and show each other our true selves. The other me, the other you. It's only now, now that it's all over, that we are finally getting to know each other.

30

Every moment of our lives has its origin in tiny decisions, sometimes made just hours, sometimes years, and often decades ago. Today, too, things would happen and thoughts occur, consciously or unconsciously, and the effects of others would be felt. Those of today might impinge on us as soon as tomorrow, or only years later; they might bring tears or smiles: no one could say.

In the morning, when Gilles announced almost casually at the kitchen table that he was returning to Paris with Ludovic, and invited Nicolas and Julie to come with them, Nico blurted out in horror: 'But it's Maman's birthday!'

Anaëlle gave Claire a lingering hug before climbing into the black Peugeot saloon beside Nikita. They drove off with a flash of the warning lights, then disappeared around a bend and were gone.

Everyone would be leaving today: everyone.

'I'm sorry,' said Ludo, 'about you and Gilles . . . it feels like my bad luck's catching. Do you want to keep my cigarettes?'

Claire nodded, kissed her brother on the forehead and said: 'Stop making everything about you, that would be more useful.'

He got into his car and sat looking at the sea while waiting for Gilles, Nicolas and Julie to join him.

Nico carried the bags from the house. Claire sat on the bench, smoking and watching life take on a new shape, opening up huge gaps, terrible but necessary gaps, taking an axe to her fossilised existence.

'Maman,' said Nicolas, when the two of them were alone outside, 'are you still angry with me?'

'No. If anything, I'm angry with myself.'

'And with Papa?'

'Yes, but not as much as I was.'

She could see the next question written in Nico's face, the question of the horrified child fearing the break-up of his parental home, divorce and estrangement, and wondering what role he might have played in it.

'Nici,' she said softly, 'grow together. Grow to be great, free individuals. If you can be that for each other, then that's perhaps the greatest miracle of all.'

And miracles were things you shouldn't disturb, but discreetly get out of their way when they happen to others.

She opened her arms and her grown-up child knelt before her and yielded to her embrace. She held his head in her hands. How little he knew of life, and how much he already sensed it had in store for him in his turn.

'Will you come home after the summer?' he asked.

'I don't know. Probably not.' She kissed the crown of his head. 'I'll always love you, that has never changed.'

He stood up awkwardly, rubbed his face and looked out at the sea, the rolling sea. There was a fine drizzle on the wind but it was warm at the same time; the elements would collide in a summer storm before the day was out.

'Well then,' said Nicolas.

He looked up as Gilles and Julie appeared at the door.

Claire felt a pang of melancholy. Julie hadn't yet discovered who was swimming beside her when she swam. Would she ever find out? In time?

She shook hands with Julie. 'Take care,' she said, and kicked herself afterwards for her lame words.

But what else could she say with Gilles standing there, earnest and raw and magnanimous and different: a stranger, yet still the same Gilles. How could she say more when her child, the defining element of her life, was standing there too?

Sing! Swim! Explore your potential, even if the terrain of your inner self seems to you like a map with a hundred blank spaces and you would rather stay on the patch of land that you know: go out into the world, alone, beware of wariness, don't let yourself turn to stone!

All this Claire poured, wordlessly, into Julie's eyes.

'I'll try,' Julie replied, and rummaged in her bag for something. A small box with a ribbon round it. 'Many happy returns. I didn't know, otherwise I would have . . .'

Claire opened the box.

She took a long look at the contents. 'Thank you, it's beautiful,' she said, slowly taking out the object inside.

The stone. With its star-shaped fossil.

It's just a pebble, a random, whitish-grey fossil with a rust-red pattern, the remains of a five-legged, star-shaped scutella, a sea urchin, of the kind that's washed up by the million onto beaches the world over, stirred up from unknown depths. Thirteen million years old. From a time when the European mainland was still in its infancy. Of no practical or monetary value whatsoever.

Claire's fossilised heart.

None of the men spoke: no 'Oh, how pretty' or similar. It would have been too banal, too obvious an attempt to gloss over the situation. They weren't having a birthday party with Breton kouign-amann cake and Veuve Clicquot. They were witnessing the end of a shared history, and there were no harmless gestures left to resort to.

Even the fact that they didn't recognise Claire's stone, the stone that symbolised her whole life, was now a mere side issue. She had never mentioned how important it was, never passed it around; it was simply part of her desk paraphernalia, no more noticed by Nicolas and Gilles than her pen, her coffee cup, her tears or her ambition.

'I guess you found the fossil? On the beach?' Claire asked Julie.

And Julie looked at her impassively, without emotion, except for a smile that didn't reach her eyes: they remained serious as she replied: 'Yes. On the beach.'

They didn't need to lie any more – she could have said 'It was at the Langlois, where we met before we were officially introduced' – but they still did: they lied one last time in front of the men.

'Thank you,' said Claire, slipping the stone in her trouser pocket. They embraced clumsily, bending forward from the hip, faces turned aside, hands holding each other's shoulders at a distance, and then it was over.

Gilles nodded to Claire and climbed into the front seat next to Ludo, while Nico and Julie huddled in the back. Claire raised her hand and left it there while the car reversed onto the road, drove off, rounded the bend and disappeared, leaving her standing with one hand still held aloft, the other clasping the stone in her trouser pocket. The stone that Julie had kept all this time.

My life in her hands.

Her old life was back in her pocket again, smooth, hard, without a single rupture, all the days of her existence up to that afternoon at the Langlois. Now it was hers to do whatever she wanted with: the best thing would be to throw it away.

Claire walked along the coast path, leaning into the wind that gusted angrily, interspersed with temporary lulls.

'Time to take stock,' she said. Aloud, and slowly.

Hearing her own voice, with no one else present, made that familiar feeling of solitude and strength, defiance and clarity rise up within her. Like every birthday when she subjected herself to this ritual. Examining her own trajectory in soliloquy under the open sky, stripping what had been, what she had and hadn't done, right down to the bones, in order to find out what held it all together.

Nearly all her birthday mornings since the age of eleven had begun by the sea. Only a few in other places: petrol-station toilets, the waiting room in the paediatric department, at the Institute office with an aching neck, and once in Sanary-sur-Mer, the year when Gilles was drinking heavily and wrestling with himself, oblivious of his wife and son. But most had been by the sea. Something Claire assigned to the heading of things to be grateful for.

Also part of the ritual was remembering with a pang how her mother had always stuck matchsticks in a piece of bread and butter or a dry piece of marble cake and tried with shaking fingers to light them using a lighter with a worn-out flint. The understanding that had grown year by year for that mother, who had been a woman and a girl herself once, and who had lost a part of herself to each new child. In the end, she had had to divide herself into four: three young souls and a residual self. Each child changed a mother's DNA, leaving genetic traces in her blood that masked her own. Each child stole an element of their mother's identity. What was left after that?

Claire no longer resented Leontine's matchstick bread, or her open resentment of her children's existence, that had robbed her of everything that was hers. The compensations they brought were lost on her. Such was human nature.

Claire clambered over the rocks to get closer to the waves. The water was grey-blue, and an electrostatic scent hung in the air. The birds, too, were flying before the impending storm.

Claire bowed her head against the wind-whipped sea spray, and her mouth filled with salt and water as she listed aloud: 'A not-yet-paid-off flat in an unaffordable district of Paris. A profession that has answers en masse, but not to my questions. A marriage that lasted until last night, and was good in many respects. It was good.'

She drew breath. 'A son, a clever son, who has never yet known heartbreak, and who will go his own way, stand on his own two feet. Who doesn't need me, and that's a good thing.'

She made her way down the cliffs onto the beach. The sand was growing steadily wetter and her feet sank in deep; from the west, a wall of rain stretching from the horizon to the sky was approaching. Heavy, angry rain.

'A house without Jeanne. A house without Julie.'

Her heart was pumping, but she needed to do this, to articulate everything she felt.

Refusing to hide the unspeakable was her only chance of survival.

'Healthy,' she gasped, 'forty-five and healthy. But I'm already working on changing that.' She took out Ludo's cigarettes, turned away from the wind and tried to light one, once, twice, five times, until the flame finally caught. The cigarette tasted stale, the nicotine made her head burn.

'And what else?' asked Claire, to which the outer Claire replied: 'Why, that's a lot, more than other people have,' while the second Claire, the inner, hidden Claire, answered scornfully: 'You pathetic woman. You always wanted to *be* someone, always striving never to be loud or angry, never to be the sort of person who is overwhelmed by emotions. Everything cooled down nicely to drinking temperature. Mrs Dial It Down. You never crawled out of a bar late at night, rarely went to the cinema, spent too much time bent over your books and not enough reading novels, or dancing, even though you longed to dance, to drink, to sob your way through cringeworthy romances. You wanted to be a sculptor, turning hardness into softness. But instead you took the softness and cast it in stone. Always working, always achieving, did you think you'd find peace that way? That you had to earn everything: trips to the cinema, cocktails, girlfriends?'

Yes!

What were you thinking? Do you have to achieve in order to finally earn the right to exist?

The wall of rain drew closer, she would never make it back to Jeanne's house before it hit. Not even up to a bus shelter on the road, and there was nothing out here to shield her from the indifferent raging of the elements.

What the hell.

She stubbed out the cigarette and put it in her pocket, then stood up straight and faced into the fast-approaching, rumbling storm, letting the rain pour down on her bare face, her open eyes and mouth, her body.

She would walk tall through the storm.

This was living. Absorbing everything. Neglecting nothing, avoiding nothing, concealing nothing!

Madame Dial It Down?

She stood facing the sea with her feet planted wide, arms braced, fists clenched, and let out an almighty yell. A loud, thunderous roar. She roared at the sea and the sea roared back.

She must absorb it all. The cold, the wet, the pain. The longing, the shadows, the music. The hunger, the thirst, the fear of arousal, she must absorb it all, feel it all! She felt for the stone in her pocket: she would take it and hurl it back to where it came from!

Vertigo marée, the urge to sink without resistance, throwing away yourself and your life, as if you had come from the gorges of the sea and were destined to return there one day.

Claire started walking. She would climb up onto the cliffs, behind the Pointe de Raguénez, by the Plage de Tahiti, and throw it from there, and the sea would swallow it down or hurl it against the rocks until it shattered.

There was nothing romantic about this storm: the sea rolled and crashed onto the sandy beaches, surged into cavities and creeks, and boiled and frothed in gaps between the granite crags. The land huddled under the rain, dull, grey and shrunken, and Claire felt cold. She was utterly alone: there was nothing and nobody out here. She carried on walking.

She climbed the path leading to the landing stage of the Pointe de Raguénez. The island was surrounded by high water; this was where she had found the fossil all that time ago. She slipped and slid down the path and the crumbling stone steps onto the Plage de Tahiti, which was already half-devoured by waves. She would cross the beach and climb back up onto the cliffs again at the far end.

Just then, a shadow emerged from the murky grey, solidifying into a dark, oblong blob as it came towards her and gradually resolving into a figure with legs, arms, a face and dark, wet hair – an apparition under the wide, gaping sky. Claire watched it run, stumble, slow down, hold its sides, then run again for all it was worth.

She recognised it instantly.

31

'Stop,' she had said.

'What?'

'Please, stop.'

'Have you left something behind?' asked Nicolas.

Ludo pulled over; they had just left the coast road and were heading towards Nevez and Pont-Aven to pick up the *voie express*.

Julie got out.

'What's wrong?' Nicolas asked, audibly alarmed.

'I'm not coming with you.'

'What do you mean, you're not coming with us?'

'What I say. I'm staying here.'

Nicolas got out and walked around the car to join her by the roadside. The rain was pelting against the roof; it was running down Julie's neck. Gilles remained strangely silent; he said nothing, and nor did Ludo.

I've made a mistake, Claire.

I knew it, Claire,

the second after.

No, even before that, when she gave form, breath and sound to the mistake, when she made the promise:

Yes.

I said *yes.*

The echo of her '*Oui*, Nicolas' had turned into something nauseous before the warm airstream of the words had even left her throat. The deep shock of having just slipped, having taken that small, wrong step when you weren't looking where you were going.

She had instantly suppressed it, ruthlessly cutting off her own inner monologue and refusing to entertain this inner contradiction: these were the sentiments of a girl who didn't believe herself good enough! Yes, that was what it was all about, and that was why she must hold her tongue. And so she had said yes.

But that wasn't what it was about.

She didn't want to marry. She didn't want to be someone's wife.

She didn't want to belong to anyone, only to Julie – to herself and no one else.

The truth had hit her that moment in the sea, when everything had turned upside down and she no longer knew where the light and the air were.

She had barely recovered from the shock of having narrowly survived her thoughtless escapade, and now here was another: the realisation that the life she had fought for so desperately was one she didn't want to go back to.

'Come on, let's talk in the car.'

'No.'

'Julie, please . . . What is it?'

On the count of three, she thought. On the count of three, Beauchamp, go on. If you wait too long you'll never learn to swim.

'I don't want to get married.'

'Is that all?' Nico breathed a sigh of relief. 'We don't have to! OK? We don't have to. Perhaps my mother was right when she said we should give each other space. Fine,

I get that, I love you, and we don't have to get married. OK?' He looked at her with pleading, uncertain eyes. 'All right, Julie?' he asked in a quieter tone.

Rain, rain, rain.

She wanted to throw back her head and run into the rain, she wanted to see the ocean in the rain.

'You're soaking wet,' she said to Nico hoarsely, 'why don't you get in.'

He looked at her and pressed his lips together.

Come on, Beauchamp, don't make him say it, it's your job, stop letting your life just wash over you.

'I don't want to get married. And I . . .' She closed her eyes, opened them again and shook her head. 'And I don't want to live with you.'

'What?' said Nico. And again: 'What? What's happened?'

'I can't swim,' said Julie.

He shook his head uncomprehendingly. His hair was all wet: it moved her, the way it stuck to his temples, he looked so young, and she felt so old, she was outgrowing herself, acting faster than she could think.

She smoothed Nicolas's hair out of his face; he turned away, evading her touch.

'I sing,' she said. 'I love doing it. I need it. It's the only time I feel free. Did you know that? And I was ashamed to admit it. Even to you.'

He shook his head, his expression changing: he was probably thinking she had lost her mind.

But better that way than . . .

. . . than telling him the third reason. Never. I'm the one he should despise, not her. Not Claire.

'Don't you love me any more?' he asked in a voice that was at once angry and full of a terrible sadness.

'Yes,' said Julie. 'In a way.' She looked aside: did she have to be so brutal? Yes, she did, there was no point leaving him clinging to a vain hope. She had to be ruthless and make him so furious with her that it would be easier for him to let go. 'I love you as a person. Not as a man. Not as the man in my life, not as the face I want to be the last thing I see before I die.'

The pallor beneath his tan, the trauma she sensed in his soul: why had she said that, why? Why had she stopped lying out of kindness and told the truth?

'I don't understand it. I don't know what's happened.'

'Don't take it the wrong way,' said Julie.

'Whose face *do* you want to be the last one you see then, huh?'

His anger was only natural. She deserved his bitter reproaches. For not realising earlier.

'I don't know. But I want to find out. I want to find out, and I want to breathe, do you see? I don't want to be suffocated inside, by myself, by us, by all this!'

'Nicolas,' said his father calmly, 'come on.'

Gilles passed Julie's handbag to her and, fumbling in his jacket, gave her a key, a front door key. 'Shall we drive you?' he asked.

She shook her head. She had to manage the whole way alone. The whole way.

'But I want to see yours,' said Nicolas. 'Your face.'

His cruelly wounded expression. A mixture of hope, desire and hate. 'Not any more, though,' he said, spitting the words out, then immediately retracting them: 'That's not true! It was a lie. I just hope this feeling will pass one day, and it won't be your face any more!' He turned round, slammed Julie's door shut, climbed in on the other side and pulled his door shut with equal force, turning away to avoid looking at her: he mustn't look at her at any cost.

Ludo raised his hands questioningly from the steering wheel: 'Really? You want to leave a woman standing in the rain? Get in, child! You can split up in the warm! What's to become of us – a road movie with three idiots who never managed to understand their wives?'

'Give it a rest, will you?' said Gilles.

Gilles, oh Gilles! Her almost-accomplice, her almost-admirer, the man she had heard crying Claire's name last night. He had sized her up, nodded, stood by her, covered for her. And covered for his wife by leaving Julie there just as she wanted, so that she was free to go, far and fast. It was Gilles, too, whose eyes met hers now through the rain-blurred window. She saw his recognition, his understanding, his inner standing aside. A faint, sad smile, acquiescence: she read it all in his face, and the fact that he understood, that he too had long been on a journey, and was no stranger to improbability.

That's how much he loves Claire, she reflected.

Once Ludo had driven off at speed, through the puddles, spraying dirt and tears, Julie turned and ran, her idiotic handbag swinging back and forth under her arm, until she found a sign to the GR 34 and the Plage de Tahiti. She wanted to get to the sea: to her.

She emptied the bag into the first rubbish bin she came to. All she needed was her phone, passport, purse and the precious key, and that could go in her jacket and trouser pockets. What else: did she really need any of the stuff that was in her bag? Lip balm, lipstick, cover stick, comb, Tic Tacs, any of it?

She dumped the handbag next to the bin.

At last.

Now she could breathe. She breathed the air deep down into her body and felt everything stretch and widen, her lungs, her back, her belly.

She carried on running. Into a village, past granite houses, blue-painted wooden gates, hydrangeas glistening with raindrops, past the windows of kitchens where people sat around talking or in silence, waiting for the rain to pass. She ran till she had a stitch in her side, forcing her to slow down, then she began to sing, breathlessly now, but she would have breath enough one day – it was already beginning. Yes, it was already beginning.

She reached the headland; she was no longer cold, just cool and clammy. She clambered down over the wet, slippery stones to the beach. There was the solitary beach shower, indifferent and superfluous in the rain. The sand was damp and firm.

She wanted to walk back by the sea, knowing that that was where Claire would be, somewhere by the sea, on the boundary between solidity and fluidity, the rock whose face was shaped by the ocean, she would be there, at the beginning of the world.

Julie recognised her from a long way off, from her posture, her chin held high. She was too breathless to shout.

Neither of them stopped, but kept moving towards each

other as the sea crept closer; perhaps it would beat them to it and swallow up the last bit of beach, jumping up at the rocks like a frenzied, barking dog, all water and teeth.

The legs of her trousers were soaked from the surf.

The sea inched closer. It was coming for her.

Or she for it.

And then she was face to face with Claire, her rain-soaked face.

'What are you doing here?' Claire exclaimed, and then, more gently: 'What are you doing here?' She looked up at the cliffs, her eyes searching.

'They've gone,' said Julie, 'all of them.' She clenched her fists. 'I don't want to marry your son.'

What had she expected?

That Claire would fling her arms around her?

Certainly not that she would recoil, clapping her hand to her mouth, as she did now.

'What?' cried Julie.

'You can't do that.'

'Yes, I can. I just did.'

'That's not what I meant to—' murmured Claire.

'What have you got to do with it?'

'Well, isn't it to do with me? Do you mean to say you've been running through the rain merely to tell me it has nothing to do with me?'

They stood facing each other, the surf washing around their calves, sucking the ground from under their feet.

'I would only marry him to be able to stay close to his mother. Close to you, Claire. Should I do that? Tell me! If that's what you want, for him, to make yourself feel better, I'll do it, I'll marry him.'

'Let's go back. I'll drive you to the station.'

'No,' said Julie.

'No?'

'No! Not unless you tell me I'm wrong. That I should go away. But I'll come back. I'll marry Nicolas sooner than you think, and then I'll be there as often as possible, to see you, and nothing you can do will stop me, absolutely nothing. But you'll always know I never married him for his own sake.'

'That's a strange way of telling someone you like them.'

'Like? *Like?* As you might say: with due fucking respect, you fail to recognise the seriousness of the situation!' Julie closed her eyes. She knew why Claire was being like this. She had to be. Nicolas was her son, and it was her whole life that she would be destroying if she gave in, if she gave in now; but there was no other way of . . . well, what? conquering? breaking? this rock of a woman.

She looked Claire straight in the eye. 'I love you, Claire. I can breathe easier because you're in the world. Don't you know that?'

The wet, beautiful face before her changed. It began to glow, the look in her eyes deepened and darkened, and at the end of the darkness was a laughing, crying light.

'Yes,' said Claire. 'Yes, I know.'

They stood looking at each other as the rain subsided and strips of blue began to break up the grey sky.

'It's impossible, Julie.'

'I know. It's impossible. And yet here we are.'

The sea crashed onto the shore, the waves ceaselessly chasing each other.

Julie had never known that you could find yourself in

the very same moment that you lost yourself. She had been lost.

And here, right here, she was finding herself.

It was Claire who made the first move. Who touched Julie's hands, ran her hands up Julie's arms, took her by the shoulders. Paused. Looked into her eyes.

And then moved closer.

Her kiss was cool at first, salty, until her lips grew warm. Julie felt a surge of shock go through her, then, with a hunger that welled up from unknown depths, she enclosed Claire's mouth in hers. Claire returned her fierceness, taking her face in her slender, strong hands.

Softness. Passion.

Strangeness.

The darkness and the light.

Now the world wasn't just slipping out of kilter, it was turning completely upside down, it was turning, opening, a crack that widened into a gateway.

Julie would never go back, because this was it, this was Life – a much bigger space than she had ever dreamed, with much more despair, much more vitality.

It was this woman, and beyond: an unknown, wild freedom.

That was where her future lay.

32

The summer returned that same night. It stretched out, and would linger for several weeks until it had exhausted all its heat, till Brittany began to empty, till the mornings smelled increasingly of autumn coolness and sparkling dew on hard-baked grass, and the nights fell more swiftly.

Claire lay in bed on her side, naked and alone, her skin wet from the shower; she and Julie had been swimming, and the ends of her hair tasted of salt. Her star-shaped fossil lay on the bedside table.

She lay reflecting, on this summer and those to come, on the truths they were exploring together.

They had all the time in the world.

They had only this time.

Julie entered the room, her bare feet padding damply on the floor; she held the towel in her hand, not around her naked body, smiling, at once shy and proud. Dropping the towel to the floor, she slipped in beside Claire.

The soft swish of the pillow cover.

Their faces touching.

Warm. Wet. Close.

Eyes calmly exploring.

The sun warmed their bodies and neither made a sound as they traced paths along each other's skin with their fingertips, looking intently at each other.

One at the end of her journey.

One just starting out.

The playful caress of their lips.

No room left for fear, thought Claire, there's no room left between us for panic, not even for a drop of sweat. Only for the peace that followed the shock of discovering that this was it, that what they were doing right now was the right thing, and that there was no name for it.

No category.

The closeness of this woman. Her warmth. Her surrender, her soaring, her floating, her movements, the different pitches of her sighs, her stillness. The experience of being on the other side, of losing yourself in it and finding yourself in the other's surrender. And the fall, the plunging descent that transformed into flight.

The way uncertainty alternated with pleasure in both of them.

When they took to the air again.

They were doing everything for the first time, they were beginners and yet so familiar, so infinitely familiar with each other's contours, the topography of the female body, its need for tenderness and resoluteness, release and intoxication, firmness and fluidity.

The days followed one another, merging into one long rhythmic tide.

Julie and Claire swam.

They explored each other. Ventured further, became more familiar with each other's bodies, their glowing, sun- and sea-weathered bodies, gilded with salty sweat. Their smell filling the room. The mingling of similar elements.

They slept, hand in hand and exhausted.

They ate, sometimes ceremoniously, picnicking on white tablecloths spread over the big stone in the garden, in the Silent Centre of the World, sometimes straight from the fridge, kicking aside the crumbs and swigging ice-cold beer from the bottle in the afternoon.

In their conversations, by the fire or in the garden, during the night, or sitting on the rocks by the water with a bottle of wine, they talked only of things that concerned the two of them. They didn't talk about men, either those they knew or those they didn't.

They said nothing about the thing their caresses were built upon: others' pain. Gilles's pain. Nicolas's. And when they saw it in each other's eyes, they held each other tight. They made no attempt to gloss over it.

There was no right to desire. There was no absolution for a heart inflamed with longing.

People hurt each other in order to become the person they were capable of being in this, their one and only life. It was a truth that couldn't be sugar-coated.

They talked about books, women, Anaëlle, swimming and dancing. About singing, their bodies, the image of women in our time and other times, in other countries, and about the women they saw on the beach who sat passively waiting, their bodies poised, with no one answering their silent calls, a caricature of the free woman; they talked about how they had been the same, how they had persistently shied away from that freedom – a lonely, demanding freedom that had to be conquered anew each day.

They talked about the films they saw at the cinema: *Wonder Woman*, which they'd watched hand in hand in Concarneau, and others in Lorient or Quimper. Often they didn't talk at all, but sat watching the sky slipping into its evening attire, and counting its colours.

They found a beginners' tango course in Pleuven and Lorient and learned to dance the Argentine tango with each other; they took it in turns to lead and follow, although Claire was slightly better at leading, while Julie preferred dancing the *ochos*, sliding her foot up Claire's leg, her eyes glinting mischievously like two shiny cherries.

And they went in the sea.

After three weeks – nearly mid-August – Julie could swim, and she ventured out beyond the rocks, past the Elephant, the Sloth and the Rabbit, further and further each time. Once, when they were back on dry land, Julie said: 'You've never said it.'

'That I love you?' asked Claire.

It was the first time she had consciously used the familiar *tu*.

And she kissed Julie. Right there, under the sunshade.

'Yes, I have,' replied Claire. 'Like this,' she said, closing her mouth over Julie's. 'And this,' she added, stroking Julie's face, her defiant, soft face, whose features were now fully defined, revealing the whole woman. 'And this,' taking Julie's hand and placing it over her heart, that was beating very slowly and very hard.

All this right there on the beach, at the boundary between solidity and fluidity.

'But we won't stay together, will we?'

Claire took her time answering.

She tried herself and Julie on for size in her mind, putting their bodies and faces together into an everyday routine:

the fully fledged woman and the fledgling. She foresaw the traps they would set each other. She, the know-all, the mother: she would lecture and nag. And Julie: she should be wary of getting stuck with someone too early, whether man or woman; of becoming part of their life and moving into their plans and projects as if into an occupied house where she had to find her own little corner. She needed the whole space of her own personality, without constraints.

And you, Claire? Don't you need that too – the whole space?

There would be no holidays together. No evenings in front of the TV. No perusing of property ads and no joint visits to the hairdresser.

Claire shook her head. 'No. We are just the beginning.'

Julie looked down and swallowed. 'I knew it. In fact that's how I want it to be. It's just that there are times when I can't bear it, when the beginning isn't enough, and the very fact of knowing it's only the beginning is cruel and . . .'

'You need to live, Julie! You've only just begun. Don't stop now. Don't stop at me. One day you'll land at someone else's door, only to move on and land up somewhere new. Again and again.'

Julie looked up in surprise. 'Did I ever tell you your sermonising really is hard to take?'

'Hardly ever. Only about half a dozen times.'

Julie laughed, throwing sand at Claire. Then, catching her eye, she grew serious.

'What are we? I mean, as opposed to them?' She gestured with her chin towards the families. The groups of girls. The men and children in the water.

Claire could tell from Julie's expression, her eyebrows,

the play of her cheek muscles, that she saw the women around them as scandalised onlookers, attacking the two of them with a thousand glances ranging from contempt to panic.

For her part, Claire saw people who were far more interested in themselves than in others, and whose indifference might contain at least a spark of tolerance. More than that: wasn't that another Claire and Julie over there? A couple who had grown old gracefully together, sitting in their striped folding chairs enjoying the warmth of the sun on their wrinkled faces? Weren't those two young girlfriends over there, touching each other with tenderness and respect and without shame, in their gestures and looks, their way of caring and listening – even if they would never cross the line into floating and falling? Didn't togetherness and love have as many forms of expression as there were couples looking and smiling at each other?

We see the world through the prism of our fears, Claire mused. And she remembered that Julie hated being lectured. At last, smiling at the vehemence of her impatient lover, she answered her question: 'What are we? We are Julie and Claire.'

'No, I meant . . .'

'I know what you mean. But if we start thinking like that we end up putting ourselves in a box. A narrow, neat little box. Labelled lesbian, bisexual, queer, fake gay, perverted, frustrated and so on and so forth. I can tell you that others do that. Of course. But only some others. Is that what you wanted to hear? It's not the true picture though.'

'And what is the true picture?'

'You are Julie. I am Claire. The whole world is full of Claires and Julies. Some have already met—' She looked over at the women in the folding chairs '—and many will never find each other in the way we have. We are in cities all over the world, we are everywhere. We are two people. That's all.' Claire took out the sunscreen and, gently taking hold of Julie's foot and pulling her leg onto her lap, she began to spray the apricot-scented lotion onto her skin. 'You're far too careless of the sun when you're by the sea, Mademoiselle Julie.'

'And you have a sunscreen fetish, Madame le Professeur.'

'Alas, one that started all too late – or did you think the three dozen moles on my skin have always been there?'

'Sixty-four,' murmured Julie. 'And two of them flirt with me when you're not looking.'

Julie leaned back while Claire massaged the lotion into her calves.

'Anaëlle once said we are "universal beings". I like that more and more, even though it came from my sister.'

'Your sister's very beautiful.'

'The trouble is, she knows it . . .'

Claire concentrated on the fullness of Julie's calf muscles, the soft, gently curving flesh that yielded under her fingers, shaped like the smooth belly of a salmon.

'Sleep with me,' said Julie all of a sudden, sitting up and grasping Claire's wrist.

Claire's heart, fluttering like a bird in her breast, fluttering and finally taking wing.

The silence, triggered by a sudden surge of desire. Claire took Julie's hand and pulled her to her feet. They walked back across the meadow to the house, to Jeanne's house, where they took off each other's swimsuits and tasted four kinds of salt.

Claire and Julie never spoke again about the After.

And only about the Before up to the moment when they first set eyes on each other. That Before ended with the door that closed behind Claire at the Langlois and flowed seamlessly into the Now.

Julie lay with her hand between Claire's legs, her head on Claire's shoulder. Claire stroked Julie's hair, over and over.

'What did you think when you saw me?'

'I heard you first. And I thought . . . I thought, there's so much trapped within that voice. So much turmoil under that breath. A giantess. And yet: beneath the fear, there is fearlessness. That's what I thought. And then the door opened, and there you were. Folded back neatly into your little box.'

'You too. You were in the room upstairs, and I was cleaning in the one below. I heard you, Claire, your laughter, your cries. What you said to him. What you demanded. I heard a woman who makes love like she's dancing, like a warrior. And then there you were. With your pressed skirt, your clean, expensive shoes, your groomed hair, all back under full control. You'd melted and then hardened again. Into a stone.'

'And you found it, the stone.'

'I didn't know it was yours. I only knew I wanted to keep it.'

'It's been my companion for thirty-four years. Whenever I was in danger of melting, I held on tight to it. My fossilised life. It was once the beginning of the world. It still is.'

Claire picked up the stone from the bedside table.

Then she placed her past life in Julie's hand, closing her fingers over it.

'Now I'll always know where I am,' she whispered.

Julie gently disengaged herself from Claire's arms, knelt at the foot of the bed, straightened her back, and placed both hands loosely in her lap, holding the stone. She closed her eyes and took a few deep, light breaths. With her eyes still closed, she began to sing.

'Je m'en vais bien avant l'heure'

Her husky rich dark voice and Miossec's song, written for his older brother, turned the song of someone who is leaving while everything is still good, before he betrays and disappoints the one left behind, into an anticipatory farewell to Claire. As Julie sang, Claire watched how her breaths changed the shape of her ribcage, belly and back from the inside. How much strength and energy she released when she sang! It was as if she were breathing into invisible wings that spread wide, filling the whole room, wings of music, power and beauty. *I'm leaving because we've seen each other fly, I'm leaving before we can land, I'm leaving because our love was so strong.* She sang both their lives. Two rivers that had converged and would soon have to separate again of their own accord before they were forced to, before love had to bow to the demands of everyday life, the demands of decency.

She will leave, thought Claire, she will leave while we're

both still free to go wherever we want. At the end of the song, Julie opened her eyes. Those dark eyes, those shiny nail heads in a door that was now wide open.

They smiled at one another, knowing that neither of them would be broken, no: they felt the power, the strength, it was the very source of their mutual attraction; they were made of the same element, they believed in each other's ability to do anything they chose. They were quite ruthless in everything they did and said to each other, sparing each other nothing.

But afterwards they kissed as tenderly as if their lips were made of thin, fine glass.

Only once did Claire break out of their time capsule. She picked up the phone.

Gilles answered immediately. They talked about the necessary things: Gaumont had finally made him an offer for a new soundtrack to a series; Nicolas had moved to Strasbourg. If they wanted, they could start to reorganise the building blocks of their life. Here, you take that, I need this, let's leave this behind. They soon came to an agreement.

'And Nicolas?' she asked afterwards.

'He doesn't understand. Not yet.'

'Does he know . . .?'

'No.'

Gilles was silent. Then he said: 'I know there mustn't be any more lies between you and me. I'm going to stick to that, only too gladly. But . . . I think he oughtn't to know. Agreed?'

Claire looked out at Julie, lying in the garden reading;

she was working her way voraciously and indiscriminately through Claire's library.

'That his fiancée has left him for his mother? That his mother of all people has robbed him of his future?'

There was a hum on the line. Claire heard the muted noise of Paris, the car horns, the murmured voices: it all seemed so far away.

'No,' said Gilles. 'You haven't robbed him of anything. Ever. I was there. I would tell you. It was Julie who decided. For herself. It wouldn't have changed anything if you hadn't . . .'

'Even if I hadn't kissed her?'

The line hummed; there was a long silence. Then Gilles replied quietly: 'When we do things like that, it's usually because of something that started before. Long before. I know that, Claire. When I . . .' He hesitated. Inhaled. 'The first time I kissed another woman, I'd already gone a long way down that road without admitting it to myself. It didn't happen out of the blue. And that's . . . that's how it is with you. With Julie. You were both already well on the way. Until one day you happened to meet.'

'You're my best friend,' said Claire. 'I never knew how well you understand.'

'Nor did I,' he said. 'And I've learnt something fundamental, too. Something I hope our son will fully understand one day. And not wait till he's as old as his father to learn it.'

The sounds of Paris grew louder: Gilles must have gone over to the window. He shut it, and there was silence. Then he continued: 'The worst thing isn't being left by a woman. The worst thing is knowing that a woman has held herself back for your sake. And that's what Julie would have done. She would have held herself back for him.'

'But wouldn't it help him?' Claire asked quietly. 'To be . . . angry with me?'

'Does anything help a broken heart?'

She gave a faint laugh. 'No, nothing. Absolutely nothing. Only time, alcohol and one day someone else who's very gentle and very good to you.'

Julie had got up and was walking through the garden. She was naked apart from a pair of white briefs, and moved as if no one was looking. She was singing, practising a repertoire: there were a number of jazz-singing academies in France, and in Switzerland and Germany too; the application process would start after the *rentrée*.

'Who's that singing? Sounds amazing.'

'Julie.'

'My God. My God, Claire.'

'Yes. I know.'

They listened together to Julie's singing.

Claire didn't ask: How are you? Gilles didn't ask: And you? It wasn't the right time; it wasn't the right year.

'Are we still on?' Gilles enquired. 'With our agreement?'

'Yes,' Claire replied. He couldn't see it on the phone, but she was smiling.

'So this is our last phone call then.'

'Yes,' she said again, and then: 'Gilles?'

'Yes?'

'Thank you for being you. And thank you for Nicolas. For our child. And . . . do what you want to do. What you need to do. And if we end up having to abandon our agreement, then . . .'

'I love you,' he interrupted, 'I've never stopped loving you. Thank you for never expecting me to be perfect.'

Claire pressed the red off button, lingered a moment with the phone in her hand, then held it to her cheek and kissed it.

Julie was singing 'Feeling Good'.

She came towards Claire, still singing, then knelt in front of her, looked into her eyes and sang to her.

Claire knew their time was up when, after a long hour alone in the water one day, Julie waded back to the shore where Claire was keeping watch. She knew it when Julie said breathlessly, arms akimbo, her wet hair clinging to her cheeks, her chest rising and falling under the red swimsuit: 'I know now who it is that's swimming beside me. You asked me that, right at the beginning. Who's always there, by my side.'

Claire thought of Jeanne. Had she felt the same sadness, the same happiness, the same closeness that Claire felt now, as if she were entering Julie's soul and looking around it like a great illuminated hall?

'It's me,' said Julie. 'I'm the one swimming beside me. I am my own mistress. My friend. My rock. I'm the one holding me up. I'm the one who's always there.'

18 August, Claire noted: from now on, this will be Julie's day in my life. You've finally found yourself, Julie.

From now on, you won't need me any more. Or anyone. You're free to live out your own desires and your own identity.

Julie sat down next to Claire on the rocks, seemingly impervious to the rough crust of barnacles.

Claire contemplated Julie: nineteen, a singer with wide, invisible wings. The woman who had been the biggest rupture in her life. Her profile, on which the wind, the sun and the sea salt had left its mark – the eternal elements honing the contours of the land.

And I search for myself, too, in her face. Myself, our time together, whether any of it has left its mark on her, changed her.

It's absurd to want to have contributed to the softness of her lower lip, or the wider inward sweep of her gaze, or the glow in the depths of her eyes, that warm glow that now finally speaks so openly of her strength, the warm current that flows from her, and which, when it touches you, reminds you who you once could have been.

Julie turned to Claire. 'Shall we swim?' she asked.

33

Summer, a year later. She asks for a room with a terrace, and a view across to the islands in the Gulf of Morbihan. A cat rubs up against her legs, a small, slender tabby with big eyes above its small chin.

'Lili, stop it,' the *maître* scolds. It's meant to sound stern, but his voice is gentle. 'For one night?' he asks.

'Maybe. Maybe not,' she says.

He studies the twelve heavy brass key fobs hanging up behind the narrow counter, then looks back at her face, as if making sure.

She knows her face has changed. Into her own, her true face.

He takes the third key from the left, weighing it in his hand.

'It's a large room,' he says. 'Would you like a table for this evening?'

The restaurant is small and popular; the glass panel of the door is covered in red Michelin stickers, the oldest dating back to 2003. The pale, sun-bleached planks of the terrace creak when anyone walks over them, and the metal lanterns with their big white candles jangle softly. The tables under the blue awning have blue tablecloths, there are sand-coloured cushions on the large wicker chairs, and the purple bougainvillea is in bloom. White boats and sparkling beads of July light are dancing on the sunny blue water, the rigging is singing in the breeze, the water lapping against the harbour wall directly below the terrace.

The water is laughing, she thinks.

This is a good place to wait.

A good place to begin.

Arradon.

She chose it because she has never been here before. And because it sounds like somewhere she would like to remember. Later. Afterwards.

She nods, yes, she would like a table.

'For two?'

'Maybe, maybe not,' she says again, and the *maître* says *pas de souci*, no worries. He is Breton, and moves like a man who has spent many years on boats: a slight backward lean, his feet planted firmly on the ground.

She climbs the steep, winding stairs, her footsteps muffled by the red carpet. The room awaits her with a balcony looking out onto water and sky, and a bed like an island.

She showers in the bathroom with its shiny dark-blue tiles; the soap smells of milk and salt. She can hear voices from the kitchen below and the rear entrance: a man singing, a woman laughing, someone shouting: 'Lili! Get down off that sideboard, you little Breton devil!'

She lies, wet and naked, on the smooth white sheets, and through the wide-open French door she hears the laughing waves, the cries of the children out on the red-and-white sailing-school boats, she hears her heart beating, and the wind strokes her skin, gentle as a perfume.

A ray of sunlight falls directly onto the hand resting on her left thigh; she looks at the light and thinks: that's my hand. That's me. I am alive. I am here.

Anything is possible.

Hearing a knock at the door, she smiles.

He brings a bunch of roses, white and red. It's her birthday, and the year, the year of magical thinking, action and discovery, is over.

Scented roses from an unfamiliar man. A stranger.

He looks at the naked woman before him, and he too sees a woman he doesn't recognise. Who lives by the sea and has begun to weld metal sculptures, sprouting blisters on her fingers and developing new, smooth muscles at the back of her neck. Who studies the biology of the deep ocean, dances the tango, and is fond of her son's new girlfriend (a lawyer who doesn't believe in marriage). A woman who feels proud and attractive and has loved another woman. Who has kissed and desired a woman, kindled the flames of her own desire, and forgiven herself. Who still accompanies that woman from afar, and often hears her favourite songs, on the radio, in kiosks and bars or in the car, and thinks of her. One day she will look up and see her on a stage: look up from the darkness at the woman in the light.

The stranger looks at her as if she is completely new to him – and she is.

'I'll be straight with you from the start,' she says, addressing him as *vous* and unable to resist a smile, a laugh, as she takes his face tentatively in her hands. But he is here. He came. And that means he has agreed to her conditions.

'I don't want to get used to you. I don't want to hold back. I want to devour and be devoured, and you must keep your eyes open, lift me up and dive down deep. Never stop desiring me and showing me that you do, let us never get used to each other and never judge each other. And: I won't always be the person I am today.'

'How beautiful you are,' he says, using *vous* likewise. He gets up and undresses in front of her; he looks at her and she remains lying as she is, arms beside her head, one knee drawn up. He caresses her with his eyes, every part of her, and she feels wanted, she is fully present, and he can see her.

A year ago, during the last night of their marriage, she had told her husband what had gone wrong for her. That she had ossified beside him and held herself back, and that she wanted to change her side of their marriage: she would develop her full potential, blossom and grow into the whole person she had so doggedly repressed, and she would spare him all reproaches. When the year was up, she would give him what he needed from her: direct, raw emotion. Including rage. Including jealousy. And desire, impatience and chaos too. Never again would she keep anything from him.

The other side of the bargain was his: he must articulate the words of desire, the words of love, retrieve them from the cold ashes of their marriage. He shouldn't just need Claire, but want her. And he should be free, free of her, her money, her arranging and organising. Treat her as if he doesn't know her, doesn't know (or only thinks he knows!) how she will react to things, what her habits are and her flaws, doesn't know that she bore and raised a child, that she was once the queen of self-control, the *glaçon*. As of today, he is to forget all that and begin to explore her. What she wants from him is nothing less than the unflinching desire to see her, as she really is.

As he stands there looking at her, he too is a different person. She can tell that, over this past year, he too has found someone he had long lost.

Himself.

Now he too is naked, and Claire whispers to him: 'Come, I want *us*.' And she opens her arms, free at last.

Acknowledgements

It's cold right now in Berlin, the November light is powdery, and the air smells of winter. By the time you read these lines, I'll be speaking to you from the past, and taking you back even further in time, back to the blazing hot Breton summer of 2016.

And to the afternoon when it all began.

From my desk in Trévignon I can look out over the Atlantic, the coastline of Beg Meil and Benodet and a small Breton fjord, a so-called *aber*.

In the summer, the sea recedes and a peninsula rises out of the *aber*: a patch of beach, nestled against tussocks moulded by the wind and peppered with purple globe thistles. A hidden, sheltered spot.

And that's where they hang out. Every summer.

Young people exclusively, hovering on the cusp of adulthood. They come from Paris, Lyon, Orléans or Besançon. None are older than twenty-two. It's their beach. Their place. Whenever I looked up from writing my last novel (*The Book of Dreams*) to see these green young women and men and their shy, inexperienced and sometimes clumsy attempts at flirting, I was struck by their air of melancholy: they were waiting. Their bodies glowed, they glowed, as they looked forward full of hope to the hours rolling towards them as slowly and steadily as the breaking waves. They were waiting for something – or some*one* – to happen to them. Waiting impatiently – in their last summer of absolute freedom, freedom from all the decisions they would later have to make – for it to begin: LIFE! The destiny reserved for them alone.

These youngsters haven't yet walled and caged themselves in with commitments, jobs and family responsibilities; life lies before them like the open sea, with its lure of infinity. They long to plunge in and start swimming.

Only they don't know where to. Or who with. And whether it will ever happen.

I looked away. I looked back again. It nagged at me. Got under my skin. Ached. Stirred up memories. And what about me? I asked myself. Did I wait like them? Or did I surge ahead, plunging headlong into life as into the sea? Where have I washed up? Have I become the person I hoped to be at eighteen or nineteen? Have I experienced the passion I longed for back then? Am I in the right place, is this really my life?

The summer was on its way out, the sun was weakening, sinking lower in the sky. The other novel was finished. The questions remained. The summer heat had lodged itself inside me. I wanted to write, so urgently, about the journey to womanhood, about femininity, sexuality, desire and the changing nature of love, marriage, the soul. The body. Dreams. I wanted to write about going with the flow, about turning to stone, about the secrets we women keep, sometimes even from ourselves.

And that's how the story of Claire and Julie was born. Claire, the mature woman, and Julie, the evolving woman.

I had to set *One Night in Paris* on these Breton shores, under this starry sky, amid this scent of heat, salt and summer grass.

They say every book changes its author.

If, through writing, we succeed in gaining a better understanding of ourselves and our view of the world – which is often different from the one we had at thirty or twenty – we may ultimately, in the silent, innermost centre of ourselves where words are few, discover another layer we never knew was there: a self that has no name, that sees the world with new eyes and is inspired to write about it.

And that's why my first thank you goes to the two women I have explored in writing: Claire and Julie.

They gave me courage to go on. To go on living and writing again and again about the hidden, wistful, light and dark sides of a woman's nature; I don't want to turn to stone, I want to dance; I don't want to divide life into categories. I want to be free.

As with my earlier novels, *The Little French Bistro*, *The Little Paris Bookshop* and *The Book of Dreams*, I owe a debt of thanks to my husband, the writer Jens Johannes Kramer. We talked at length about the ending, about Gilles, his pain and his decency, even though he too inhabits a room in his life apart from others. We went to Paris together, where I was able to do some background research at the universities and the Institute of Palaeontology, gather impressions and wander the streets in search of authentic restaurants, routes and colours.

We also had endless discussions of my eighteen draft openings – yes, I actually spent four months just writing openings, ranging from half a page to forty-five, and rejected every single one – until I finally wrote the first three chapters as they are now, in one day, under a fig tree in Sanary-sur-Mer.

The fig tree belongs to a small villa in the Portissol district of Sanary, a holiday home rented out by the delightful Juliette Huard – and I would like to say *merci* to her too: Les Oponces was a third home to me, and us, and it was where I finally found my way to Claire and her secrets.

During the core writing process between 12 June and 9 September 2017, I was supported by two readers – my sister, the author and tour guide Catrin George, and the history professor Carlos Collado Seidel. It was remarkable how often both were moved by the same passages, even though neither of them know each other or are particularly alike. The letters they wrote me after each 100-page instalment invisibly strengthened and tautened the threads of the novel.

You can't tell by reading a book how fast or slow, enjoyable or agonising the writing process was. Passages that can be read in five minutes or half an hour, or descriptions where you – perhaps, hopefully? – think: yes, that's just what it feels like! – all this took many nights of reflection and revision. And before that, years of living through those emotions, processing them and, finally, understanding them. I couldn't have written in my early thirties what I write now.

For the days and nights of writing I often retreated to a house in the village of Trémorvézen, La Clarté ('Clarity'), which I rented from Véronique Guittard – *merci* and *kenavo, ma copine!*

Thanks also go to Linus Giese; some will know Linus under his former name, Mara Giese. Linus wrote an essay about himself in 2017 in which he relates how he wanted to be a girl – but not the things that are supposed to define girls, such as clothes, decorative cosmetics, good manners and self-denial. That essay stirred up something in me: something that finds expression in Julie's memories of her childhood, before she became aware of the distinctions made by society. That loss of one's own inner freedom is a strong motif of Julie's character.

Talking about my developing characters is an act of intimacy. I am glad to know people who I can have such intimate conversations with: the wonderful Hamburg-based writer Petra Oelker, my publisher, Doris Janhsen, Oliver Wenzlaff, and my agent Anja Keil.

A key moment of the novel is the tango scene. Nikita, the Russian tango teacher, is real – although not currently the lover of a French actress, I hasten to add . . . I myself have been attending tango lessons with Nikita Gerdt in Berlin since early 2016, and the Argentine tango has introduced me to a whole new, safe, refreshing and sensual form of proximity, expression and femininity – whether as follower or leader. Should you be interested in private lessons, either individually or as a couple or group, you can find Nikita's contact details on his website www.nikitagerdt.com.

*

A manuscript is not a finished novel, let alone a book. Julie and Claire's story only became a novel once my editor, Julia Cremer, had posed some highly perceptive questions, my in-house copy-editor, Carolin Graehl, walked the emotional tightrope with me, and my favourite proofreader, Gisela Klemt, straightened out crooked metaphors and double-checked street names, route descriptions and French vocabulary.

The novel only became a book once Bettina Halstrick, Elena Hoenig and the agency ZERO had tracked down and adapted the cover image, the producer Julia Heiserholt put meaning into readable form, and the printer CPI books GmbH carefully bound and laminated it.

Sales reps such as Delia Peters, Katrin Englberger and Matthias Kuhlemann spread the novel far and wide – what would all those books do without you, the people who spend the all-too-limited hours of the freelancer pitching them to booksellers so that they know exactly: Frau Ilsebeck will love that one, this one can go on the summer display, I can work with that one . . .

It is these local book experts who are the ultimate, essential mediators and custodians of literary diversity and freedom. And if it wasn't for local booksellers, I wouldn't be able to thank you too, the reader, because your letters and your imagination, that effectively bring this story and the women and men in it to life, and your mental conversations – all this is what literature is fundamentally about. The fact that each reader's own resonance chamber produces a completely different book, a different world, a different variation. The same words, yet completely different images and emotions.

*

Making art means creating variations of the (supposedly) sole possible reality. Variations of love, hate, morality and decisions; every book, film, poem or song tells of differences and distinctions, of individual emotions and peculiarities. And that's why art is part of the survival kit we need in these times – because it reminds us that the defining quality of humanity is diversity, not sameness, and that no country or culture is above any other.

       Nina George, Berlin, November 2017

My grateful thanks go to Sharon Howe for the sensitive translation, to Madeleine Woodfield for the lucid editing, and to Hilary Teeman for the enthusiasm she brought to the project. My heartfelt praise also goes to my agents, Anja Keil and Cecile Barendsma, for making the stories I have to tell accessible to the wider world.

       Nina George, Trévignon, November 2024